PRAISE FOR T. KINGFISHER

"Dive in... if you are looking to be charmed and delighted."

LOCUS

"...[A] knack for creating colorful, instantly memorable characters, and inhuman creatures capable of inspiring awe and wonder."

NPR BOOKS

"The writing. It is superb. T. Kingfisher, where have you been all my life?"

THE BOOK SMUGGLERS

"...you walk away going 'Damn, that was good but there's a new layer of trauma living inside me.'"

KB SPANGLER, DIGITAL DIVIDE

A Wizard's Guide to Defensive Baking

A Wizard's Guide to Defensive Baking

T. Kingfisher

Ebook by Red Wombat Studio

Print edition by Argyll Productions

Dallas, Texas

www.argyllproductions.com

Print ISBN 978-1-61450-524-2

eBook ISBN 978-1-61450-525-9

First Edition Paperback July 2020

ONE

There was a dead girl in my aunt's bakery.

I let out an undignified yelp and backed up a step, then another, until I ran into the bakery door. We keep the door open most of the time because the big ovens get swelteringly hot otherwise, but it was four in the morning and nothing was warmed up yet.

I could tell right away that she was dead. I haven't seen a lot of dead bodies in my life—I'm only fourteen, and baking's not exactly a high-mortality profession—but the red stuff oozing out from under her head definitely wasn't raspberry filling. And she was lying at an awkward angle that nobody would choose to sleep in, even assuming they'd break into a bakery to take a nap in the first place.

My stomach made an awful clenching, like somebody had grabbed it and squeezed hard, and I clapped both hands over my mouth to keep from getting sick. There was already enough of a mess to clean up without adding my secondhand breakfast to it.

The worst thing I've ever seen in the kitchen was the occasional rat—don't judge us, you can't keep rats out in this city, and we're as clean an establishment as you'll ever find—and the zombie frog that crawled out of the canals. Poor thing had been downstream of the cathedral, and sometimes they dump the holy water a little recklessly, and you get a plague of undead frogs and newts and whatnot. (The crawfish are the worst. You can get the frogs with a broom, but you have to call a priest in for a zombie crawfish.)

But I would have preferred any number of zombie frogs to a corpse.

I have to get Aunt Tabitha. She'll know what to do. Not that Aunt Tabitha had bodies in her bakery on a regular basis, but she's one of those competent people who always know what to do. If a herd of ravenous centaurs descended on the city and went galloping through the streets, devouring small children and cats, Aunt Tabitha would calmly go about setting up barricades and manning crossbows as if she did it twice a week.

Unfortunately, to get to the hallway that led to the stairs up to Aunt Tabitha's bedroom, I would have to walk the length of the kitchen, and that meant walking past the corpse. Stepping over it, in fact.

Okay. Okay. Feet, are you with me? Knees? Can we do this?

The feet and knees reported their willingness. The stomach was not so happy with this plan. I wrapped one hand around my waist and clamped the other firmly over my mouth in case it decided to rebel.

Okay. Okay, here we go...

I inched into the kitchen. I spent six days a week here,

sometimes seven, running back and forth across the tile, flinging dough onto counters and pans into ovens. I crossed the kitchen floor hundreds of times a day, without even thinking about it. Now it seemed to be about a mile long, an unfamiliar and hostile landscape.

I had a dilemma. I didn't want to look at the body, but if I didn't, I might step on it—on her—and that just didn't bear thinking about.

No help for it. I looked down.

The dead girl's legs were splayed across the floor. She was wearing grimy boots with mismatched socks. That seemed very sad. I mean, it was sad that she was dead anyway—probably, unless she'd been a horrible person—but dying with mismatched socks seemed especially sad somehow.

I imagined her throwing the socks on, never thinking that a few hours later, an apprentice baker and half-baked wizard of dough would be tiptoeing past her and thinking about the condition of her footwear.

There was probably a moral lesson there somewhere, but I'm not a priest. I thought about becoming one once, but they don't really like wizards, even minor wizards whose only talents are making bread rise and keeping the pastry dough from sticking together. Right about the time I gave up on hopes of joining the priesthood, Aunt Tabitha had taken me on in the bakery, and the siren song of flour and shortening pretty much sealed my fate.

I wondered what had sealed this poor girl's fate. Her hair was mostly over her face, so it was hard to tell how old she was —and I wasn't looking very closely—but I got the feeling she was young, maybe not much older than me. How did she wind up dead in our bakery? Somebody who was cold or hungry might conceivably creep into the bakery—it's warm, even at night, since we bank the big stoves but we don't put them out, and there's always food around, even just the day-old stuff in the case. But that didn't explain why she was *dead*.

I could see one of her eyes. It was open. I looked away again.

Maybe she slipped and hit her head. Aunt Tabitha always swears I'll break my neck one of these days, the way I race around the kitchen like a flour-crazed greyhound, but it seems weird that you'd break into a bakery and then run around inside it.

Maybe she was murdered, whispered a traitorous little voice in my brain.

Shut up, shut up! That's just stupid! I told it. People hold murders in back alleys and things, not in my aunt's kitchen. And it'd be stupid to leave a body in a bakery. The whole city is built on canals, there are fifty bridges to a street, and the basements flood every spring. Who'd dump a body in a bakery when you could dump it in a perfectly good canal not twenty feet from the door?

I held my breath and stepped over the dead girl's ankles.

Nothing happened. I wasn't expecting anything to happen, but I was still relieved.

I looked straight ahead, took two more careful steps, then broke into a run. I knocked the door open with my shoulder and tore up the stairs, yelling *"Aunt Tabithaaaaa! Come quick!"*

It was four in the morning, but bakers are used to getting up at four in the morning, and the only reason that Aunt Tabitha was sleeping until the decadent hour of six-thirty was because her niece had finally been trusted to open the bakery in the last few months. (That's me, in case you aren't following along.) She'd been nervous about letting me take over, and I'd been really proud that nothing had gone wrong when I was opening.

This made me feel twice as guilty that a dead body had turned up on my watch, even though it wasn't my fault. I mean, it's not like *I* had killed her.

Don't be stupid, nobody *killed her. She just slipped. Probably.*

"Aunt Tabithaaaa!"

"Gracious, Mona..." muttered my aunt from behind the door. "Is the building on fire?"

"No, Aunt Tabitha, I have discovered a dead body in our kitchen!" was what I meant to say. What came out was something more along the lines of "Aunt Body! There's a Tabitha—the kitchen—dead, she's dead—I—come quick—she's *dead!*"

The door at the top of the stairs was flung open, and my aunt emerged, shouldering into her housedress. Her housedress is large and pink and has winged croissants embroidered across it. It's quite hideous. Aunt Tabitha herself is large and pink but doesn't have winged croissants flying across her except when wearing the housedress.

"Dead?" She narrowed her eyes down at me. "Who's dead?"

"The body in the kitchen!"

"In *my* kitchen!?" Aunt Tabitha came barreling down the stairs at top speed, and not wanting to be trampled, I retreated in front of her. She brushed me aside, not unkindly, and went sideways through the door to the bakery. I followed, poking my head timidly around the doorframe and waiting for the explosion.

"Huh." Aunt Tabitha put a fist on each generous hip. "That's a dead body, all right. Lord save us. *Huh.*"

There was a long silence, while I stared at her back and she stared at the dead girl and the dead girl stared at the ceiling.

"Err... Aunt Tabitha... what should we do?" I finally asked.

Aunt Tabitha shook herself. "Well. I'll go wake your uncle up and send him around to the constables. You start lighting the fires and put a tray of sweet buns on."

"*Sweet buns?* We're going to *bake?*"

"We're a bakery, girl!" my aunt snapped. "Besides, never knew a copper who didn't love a sweet bun, and we'll be swarming with 'em before long. Better put on two trays, there's a dear."

"Err..." I drew myself together. "Should I start the rest of the baking then?"

My aunt frowned and tugged at her lower lip. "N-o-o-o... no, I don't think so. They'll be in and out and making a mess of things for a few hours at least. We'll just have to open late, I suppose."

She turned and stalked heavily away to roust my uncle.

I was left alone with the dead girl and the ovens.

I could get to one of the ovens easily enough, and I poked up the fire underneath and threw another log on. There's a trick to keeping the ovens heated evenly, and it's the first thing you learn. If you have spots that are too hot or too cool, your bread gets fallen spots and comes out looking lumpy and sort of squashed in places.

I couldn't reach the other oven without stepping over her. After a moment's thought, I threw one of our dishtowels over her face. It was easier somehow if I couldn't see that one eye staring upward at nothing. I fired up the other oven.

Sweet buns are easy. I could make sweet buns in my sleep, and occasionally, at four in the morning, I pretty much do. I threw the dry ingredients together in a bowl and started whisking them together. I gazed up at the rafters so that I didn't have any chance of seeing the body. There was a brief shine of eyes as a mouse looked down at me, then scurried across the rafters on his way back to his mousehole. (Having mice is actually a good thing, since it means we don't have rats any more. Rats think mice are yummy.)

There were eggs on the counter and a big crockery jar of shortening in the corner. I cracked the eggs and separated out the yolks—perfectly, I might add—and dumped all the ingredients into a bigger bowl and started beating.

I heard the front door open and close, as Uncle Albert went out to get the constable. Aunt Tabitha was bustling around the front of the shop, probably getting ready to turn the first wave of customers away.

I wondered how many constables we'd get. A couple, right, for a murder? Murders are important. Would the body wagon come? Well, it'd have to, wouldn't it? We couldn't very well just set the body out with the garbage. The wagon would come, and then all the neighbors would think my uncle had died—nobody'd think Tabitha had died, of course, she was a force of nature—and they'd come around gossiping, and they'd find out there had been a murder—

Wait, when did I decide it was a murder? She just slipped, right?

I discovered that between not-looking at the dead girl and wondering about the constables that I'd been kneading the sweet bun dough for much too long. You don't want to knead them too much, or it makes them tough. I stuck a floury hand in the dough and suggested that maybe it didn't want to be tough. There was a sort of fizziness around my fingers and the dough went a little stickier. Dough is very amicable to persuasion if you know how to ask it right. Sometimes I forget that other people can't do it.

I separated out a dozen evenly sized lumps of raw dough and set them on the wooden baking paddle, then shoved them into the oven with strict orders that they didn't want to burn. They wouldn't. Not burning is one of the few magics I'm really good at. Once, when I was having a really awful day, I did it too hard, and half the bread wouldn't bake at all.

That was the sweet buns done. I wiped my hands on my apron and dipped a cup of flour out of one of the bins. There was one other task that had to be done, no matter what, whether there was one body in the kitchen or a dozen.

The steps down to the basement are slippery, because everybody's basements leak. It's amazing we still have basements. My father, who was a builder before he died, used to say that it was because there was another city down there, and people just kept on building upwards as the canals rose, so the basement floors were really the roofs and ceilings of old houses.

In the darkest, warmest corner of the basement, a bucket bubbled slowly. Every now and then one of the bubbles would pop, and exhale a damp, yeasty aroma.

"C'mon, Bob..." I said, using the sugary tones you'd use to approach an unpredictable animal. "C'mon. I've got some nice flour for you..."

Bob popped several bubbles, which is his version of an enthusiastic greeting.

Bob is my sourdough starter. He's the first big magic I ever really did, and I didn't know what I was doing, so I overdid it.

A sourdough starter is kind of a gloppy mess of all the yeast and weird little growing things that you need to make bread rise. The taste of the bread can change a lot depending on the starter. Most of them live for a couple of weeks, but in the right hands, they can stay alive for years. There's one in Constantine that's supposed to be over a century old.

When I first started working in my aunt's bakery, I was just ten, and really scared that I'd screw something up. My magic tended to do weird things to recipes sometimes. So I was put in charge of tending her sourdough starter, which she'd been using since she started the bakery, and which was really important, because Aunt Tabitha's bread was famous.

And... I don't know if I gave it too much flour or too much water or not enough of either, but it dried up and nearly died. When I found that out, I was so scared that I stuck both hands into it (and it was pretty icky, let me tell you) and *ordered* it not to die. *Live!* I told it. *C'mon, don't die on me, live! Grow! Eat! Don't dry up!*

Well, I was ten, and I was really scared, and sometimes being scared does weird things to the magic. Supercharges it, for one thing. The starter didn't die, and it grew. A *lot.* It foamed out of the jar and over my hands and I started yelling for Aunt Tabitha, but by the time she got there, the starter had reached the sack of flour I'd been using to feed it and ate the whole thing. I started crying but Aunt Tabitha just put her hands on her hips and said, "It's still alive, it'll be fine," and scraped it into a much bigger jar and that was the beginning of Bob.

I'm not actually sure if we could kill him any more. One

time the city froze so hard that nobody could go anywhere, and Aunt Tabitha was stuck across town for three days and I couldn't get down the block, and nobody fed Bob. I expected to come back and find him frozen or starved or something.

Instead, the bucket had moved across the basement, and there were the remains of a couple of rats scattered around. He hadn't eaten the bones. That was how we figured out that Bob could feed himself. I'm still not sure how he moves—like a slime-mold maybe. I'm not going to pick the bucket up and find out. I doubt there's a bottom on it any more, but I don't want to risk annoying Bob.

He likes me best, maybe because I feed him the most often. He tolerates Aunt Tabitha. My uncle won't go into the basement any more, he claims Bob actually hissed at him once. It would have been a belching sort of hiss, I imagine.

I dumped the flour in on top of Bob, and he glubbed happily in his bucket and extended a sort of mushy tentacle. I pulled it off, and the starter settled back and began digesting the flour. He doesn't seem to mind me taking bits to make bread, and it's still the best sourdough in town.

We just don't tell anybody about the eating-rats thing.

TWO

Constable Alphonse was tall and broad and red-faced. He came into the kitchen, stopped, and said, sounding surprised "There's a dead body in here!"

"That's what I *told* you," said Uncle Albert behind him, sounding aggrieved.

"Well, yes, but..." The Constable trailed off, but still made it abundantly clear that he'd expected a hysterical member of the public to be getting upset about nothing, not that there would be a genuine dead body in a respectable bakery.

Aunt Tabitha took charge. "It's a dead body all right. Mona found it this morning when she came in. Have a sweet bun."

Constable Alphonse took a sweet bun, chewed it thoughtfully, and decided to go for a second opinion.

Constable Montgomery was also tall, also broad, but instead of being red-faced was rather sallow. He ate three sweet buns, confirmed that yes, indeed, it was a dead body, and then he and Alphonse stood in the kitchen in silence until Aunt

Tabitha testily suggested that maybe they should call for the body-wagon.

"We'll need the coroner," said Montgomery, and helped himself to another sweet bun.

"The coroner, yep," agreed Alphonse.

They went out.

"Better put in another tray of sweet buns," said Aunt Tabitha heavily. "And a pot of tea, I think. Looks like we'll be all morning about this."

The coroner, when he arrived, was a short man, bald and slabby, like a half-melted candle. He ate most of a tray of sweet buns by himself, but I didn't get to hear what he said, because once they started moving the body, Aunt Tabitha shooed me out to the front of the store to take care of customers.

Most of the customers are regulars (with their regular orders) and while they were disappointed that their muffins and bread and scones weren't available, they were more worried that something was wrong. I repeated over and over again that everything was fine, somebody'd just broken into the kitchen and the police were looking at it, but nothing seemed to have been stolen, and we hoped to be open for business later today.

"Nobody's safe anymore," said old Miss McGrammar (one lemon scone, no icing) with a sniff. She rapped her cane against the counter for emphasis. "Imagine, someone breaking into a bakery! We'll all be murdered in our beds soon and no mistake!"

"Some of us sooner than others," muttered Master Elwidge the carpenter, (two cinnamon rolls, one loaf of cheese bread) winking at me.

"Hmmph!" Miss McGrammar shook her cane at him. "You

can laugh! Little Sidney, the boy of Mrs. Weatherfort who does the washing, he went missing just last week, and have they seen hide nor hair of him since?"

"No?" I ventured.

"They have not!" She smacked her cane down like a judge's gavel.

"Probably ran away to sea," offered Brutus the chandler (one of whatever looks good today, m'dear, and a loaf of the day-old for the pigeons if you have it).

"Run away to *sea?*" asked Miss McGrammar, scandalized. Elwidge put a hand over his mouth to stifle a smile. "Sidney? Nothing doing! He was a good boy, he was!"

"Even good boys will be boys," said Brutus mildly, rubbing his forearms. He had several faded tattoos, and I suspect he was speaking from personal experience.

"Sidney Weatherfort wouldn't run away to sea," piped up the tiny Widow Holloway (one blackberry muffin, two ginger cookies, and thank you so *much*, dear Mona, you're getting to look more like your poor dear mother every day, you know...) "He was a magicker, and you know how superstitious sailors are about taking on wizard-folk. They think the winds will fail if you're carrying wizard-folk aboard."

"A magicker?" Elwidge looked surprised. "I didn't know that."

"He was a mender," said the Widow Holloway. "Little things. He fixed my glasses for me once when the lens cracked, and I thought I'd have to send away to Constantine to have a new one ground." She smiled at me. "Small things, though. Nothing like as good as our Mona, here."

I flushed. As wizards go, I'm pretty much the bottom of the barrel. Even Master Elwidge, who's got just enough magic to take knots out of wooden boards, is better than me. Dough and pastries are about all I can do. The great wizards, the magi that serve the Duchess, they can throw fireballs around or rip mountains out of the earth, heal the dying, turn lead into gold.

Me, I can turn flour and yeast into tasty bread, on a good day. And occasionally make carnivorous sourdough starters.

Still, they were all looking at me expectantly, and I didn't have any food for them, so I felt like I ought to do something. I reached into the case and pulled out one of the day-old gingerbread men. It's early spring, and much too late to still be carrying gingerbread men, but we're the one bakery that stocks a few all year 'round, just for this purpose.

I set the gingerbread man up on the counter and focused my attention on it. *Live. Move. Up, up, up!*

The cookie woke up. It stretched its arms and pushed itself up onto its gingerbread feet. Then it bowed to the Widow Holloway, and to Miss McGrammar, threw a salute to Elwidge and Brutus, and walked along the counter until it came to a clear space.

Dance, I ordered it.

The gingerbread man began to dance a very respectable hornpipe. Don't ask me where the cookies get the dances they do—this batch had been doing hornpipes. The last batch did waltzes, and the one before that had performed a decidedly lewd little number that had even made Aunt Tabitha blush. A little too much spice in those, I think. We had to add a lot of vanilla to settle them down.

I don't know how I learned to make cookies dance. Apparently I used to do it when I was very, very young. Aunt Tabitha still loves to tell the story of the time I was three and threw a tantrum in the bakery, and the entire case of gingerbread men came alive, even the ones that were still in the oven. Those started hammering on the door to be let out, and the already-baked ones ran through the store, giggling like little maniacs. "They got into the mouseholes," she always says, "and it took us months to see the end of the little devils! That's when I knew our Mona was meant to be a baker." (Depending on how much she's gotten into the kitchen sherry at that point, I get either an affectionate glance or a floury pat on the back. During rum-cake season, there is hugging.)

Being a wizard is almost all like that—you don't know what you can do until you actually do it, and then sometimes you aren't sure what you just did. There aren't teachers who can help you, either. Everybody's different, and there's usually only a couple dozen magic folk in any given city anyway. A few hundred if it's a really big city. Maybe in the army the war-wizards get special training, but down here, it's all trial and error and a lot of wasted bread dough.

Anyway, the cookies. For me, it works best with cookies that are mostly people or animal shaped. Something to do with sympathetic magic, the parish priest said (six loaves of plain bread and—oh, all right, one berry scone, but don't tell the abbot!) And it has to be something made of dough. The puppeteers who put on the Punch and Judy shows in the park can make wooden puppets dance, but I could focus on wood until I got a splitting headache and it'd just lie there. Dough is all I can do. It's not a very useful skill.

Still, it's occasionally handy. If I can't get something at the back of a shelf, I can usually get a gingerbread man to climb up there and push it forward until I can grab it. We bake up a new batch once a week. Aunt Tabitha says that if nothing else, it's good advertising.

I've heard—well, overheard, I wasn't *supposed* to hear it—that there's some people who won't come into the bakery now that I'm here. I don't know if dancing gingerbread bothers them, or if it's the notion of a magicker baking their bread. I think Aunt Tabitha lost a couple of regulars when I started working, but she's never said anything about it.

I figure if they'll let a little thing like that bother them, they deserve to miss out on the best sourdough in the city.

The gingerbread man finished his hornpipe and bowed to his audience, who applauded. Even Miss McGrammar unbent enough to smile, and she's one of those people who watches magic-folk like they're about to run mad or explode into a shower of frogs. The cookie blew a kiss to the Widow Holloway, who giggled as if she were a much younger woman, and then marched back to his bin.

Thank you, I told it. *That's enough for now.* It saluted me—this batch was rather military, now that I think of it, maybe we went heavy on the cardamom—and went back to being an ordinary cookie.

"Very nice," said Master Elwidge.

"It's not much," I said, embarrassed.

"Better than I can do," he said, and winked at me. I know he's another magicker, but I've never seen him do anything but straighten bent wood. Still, that's got to be more useful than making cookies dance.

When everyone had been shooed out of the shop—which took a while, in the case of Miss McGrammar—I went back into the kitchen, just in time to be accused of murder.

THREE

"Wh-what?"

There was a new man in the bakery, and he didn't look like he was interested in tea or sweet buns. He was wearing dark purple robes past his ankles, and the hems weren't dusty at all. The street sweepers do a good job, once the snow's melted, but not *that* good. He definitely hadn't walked here.

"This is Inquisitor Oberon, Mona," said Aunt Tabitha, in the very careful voice she uses for customers that are being difficult. I looked at her, and she made a very tiny shake of her head. A warning, obviously, but against what?

"You, girl," said Inquisitor Oberon, folding his arms. "You claim to have found the body, do you not?"

"Uh..." That was a sneaky sort of question. "I found the body this morning when I came to work, yes."

"At *four in the morning*?" He looked at me over his glasses. They had tiny, fussy metal frames, the sort of glasses that a bird of prey would wear if its eyesight was starting to go.

"I'm a baker," I said. "I always come to work at four in the morning..." My voice sounded weak and scared, which was no good at all. I sounded like I was apologizing for the hours that bakers keep.

"That's true, Your Lordship," rumbled Constable Alphonse, also sounding apologetic for having the temerity to confirm my story.

From the *Your Lordship,* I knew that Inquisitor Oberon worked for the Duchess (if he'd been a member of the priesthood, he would have been *Your Holiness*, or *Your Worship*) but what a servant of the royal house was doing in our bakery—I mean, even if it *was* a murder, unless the victim was somebody really important, there was no reason for the royals to be involved. And if she was that important, why was she in our bakery, and why was she wearing mismatched socks?

"You're a *wizard,* are you not?" Oberon growled.

"I... sort of... I guess..." I looked helplessly at Aunt Tabitha. "I mean, I can make bread rise..."

"She's a fine baker," put in Aunt Tabitha firmly, as if this put to rest any question of guilt or innocence.

"There is a taint of magic around this girl's death," said Inquisitor Oberon, with such authority that it didn't occur to any of us until much later to ask how he knew, or what exactly that *meant.* "She was murdered here, in a bakery known to employ a wizard. A wizard who *conveniently* was the one to find the body."

The way he said "conveniently" made it sound like I'd been found standing over the body with a bloody baguette.

"But—" I started laughing. I couldn't help it. This was too stupid. "I don't even know who she is! Why would I want to kill her?"

"A question that we will aim to answer," said Inquisitor Oberon, pushing his glasses back up and straightening his shoulders. "Coroner, remove the body. Constables, bring the girl to the palace."

I stopped laughing. This didn't seem funny anymore. The horrible clenching in my stomach was coming back again.

"The palace?" asked Constable Montgomery—not questioning, I could tell, but simply surprised. You didn't bring prisoners to the palace. You took them to jail.

Inquisitor Oberon sniffed, exactly like Miss McGrammar does when we run out of lemon scones. "Her Grace, the Duchess, is concerned with what she perceives as the *rash* of murders by wizards. She insists on overseeing these cases herself. Constables, if you please!"

"But..." I said.

"Now wait just a minute—" Aunt Tabitha said.

"Oh, dear..." Uncle Alfred said.

And despite what any of us said, I found myself pushed into a coach, and driven away to the palace.

The coach was dark wood and drawn by two large grey horses with platter-sized shoes and great soft drifts of hair around their hooves. They were very pretty horses. I can't say the same about the coach. It had so many curlicues and carvings and finials and gargoyles and cherubs that it looked like a mahogany wedding cake. (We do wedding cakes occasionally. I hate them. It's all tiny fiddly work, and while I can magic the dough so the icing goes on smoothly, it gives me a headache. Icing is not nearly as friendly as dough.)

Since I was—apparently—a dangerous criminal, one of the constables rode in the coach with us, possibly to protect Inquisitor Oberon. I guess he might have thought he needed protection from a fourteen-year-old girl because I was a magicker. People get uneasy about that sort of thing. You can't testify in court if you're a magicker unless you're holding a piece of iron, because iron is supposed to counteract magic, even though it doesn't do anything of the sort. I use an iron skillet all the time. It's just an old superstition.

Frankly, an iron skillet would be a lot more dangerous than my magic at the moment. I could at least hit Oberon with it.

To give credit where credit is due, Constable Alphonse looked awfully embarrassed by the whole thing.

I sat miserably on the bench seat, with the Inquisitor opposite me, watching me like a constipated vulture, and the constable squeezed in next to me on the bench. It would have made more sense for me to sit next to the Inquisitor, since we were both smaller than Constable Alphonse, but somehow that didn't seem like an option.

I stared at my hands. There was flour on them. There was flour on my trousers, too, and sprinkled over the tops of my boots. There was flour on the constable's boots as well.

No flour had adhered to the hem of the Inquisitor's robes. The robes apparently did not *do* flour.

This was not the worst day of my life—the day when I was seven and I'd found out that both my parents had died of the Cold Fever had been the worst—but this was definitely in the running for second-worst.

The coach rattled through the streets, every bump transmitted up the wheels and directly to our bones. For all the carvings, the carriage wasn't very well sprung. There was probably a moral lesson in that, too, but I wasn't in the mood. I folded my hands together.

We rumbled past the big clocktower. The clock's been stopped forever. (It's a landmark, it doesn't have to be functional.) Still, it couldn't have been much past seven in the morning. Three hours. It had been a long three hours.

If I were back in the bakery, I'd be almost done with the early baking, and I'd be starting on the second round: the delicate pastries; the tarts that require little individual crusts; mixing up all the stuff that needs to be chilled or settled overnight, so they'd be ready for tomorrow. The bread sponges would have to be set out to trap the wild yeast. With none of that done, Aunt Tabitha would have to work all day, and she'd still be short of bread tomorrow.

"Will this take long?" I asked plaintively.

"That will depend on your guilt or innocence," said the Inquisitor, in a voice that was not reassuring. I stared out the window and wondered what the Duchess was going to do to me.

Everybody calls our land a kingdom, but that's just a holdover from the old days, hundreds of years ago. There's just a bunch of cities now, each with their own little government and their own army and their own laws—"nation-states" if you want to use fancy words like the priest. Some of them have kings, but they only control the city and the land around it.

Our city is called Riverbraid, because of the canals. We don't have a king. We had a bunch of dukes and a couple of earls, and I think there was a prince at some point in there. For the last thirty years or so, the person in charge is the Duchess.

The palace of the Duchess is built on a hill overlooking the city, or at least it looks like a hill. Actually it's the remains of the former half-dozen palaces, which sank like everything else in the city, except for one which burned down. Because it's higher, the streets slope up, and the buildings are more expensive because their basements don't flood every spring. There are stories that underneath the palaces are old catacombs that used to be old dungeons, full of the ghosts of prisoners who were forgotten when the old buildings were walled up. There are also stories that there are still people under there, who live by eating rats, but nobody really believes them. Much.

I really hoped that I wouldn't have a chance to find out for myself.

FOUR

We arrived in the courtyard of the palace, which had high stone walls and pale stone cobbles the color of the grey horses' coats. Inquisitor Oberon leapt out before the coach had come entirely to a halt.

"Bring the prisoner," I heard him say, as the door swung behind him.

It took me a minute to realize that by "prisoner" he meant *me*. Probably that was pretty slow of me, but it had been a really awful morning, and some part of my brain, the bit that had been laughing hysterically earlier, still couldn't get over how completely impossible this all was. Me, a prisoner? I baked *bread*. The worst thing I'd ever done in my life—the absolute and complete worst—was the time I was ten and snuck out with Tommy the butcher's son and we stole a jug of sacrificial wine from the chapel down the street and drank it. I got sick as a dog. Tommy threw up. My headache the next day was so bad that it felt like divine retribution, but really, that isn't the sort of thing that gets you dragged up before the Duchess.

I'd never even seen the Duchess close up. When she goes out for parades, there's always a crowd and lots of guards around her.

Bring the prisoner.

How had this even *happened?*

Who was the dead girl in the bakery?

A large hand opened the door. It was attached to a guard, who was wearing shiny armor and looking very military. He reached the other hand inside the coach and made a beckoning gesture then clicked his tongue, as if I were a dog.

I looked at Constable Alphonse. He looked as bewildered and uncomfortable as I felt.

There was another, slightly more impatient tongue click.

I held out an arm, and was grabbed, not unkindly but very firmly, and lifted out of the carriage.

Inquisitor Oberon was tossing out orders on the other side of the courtyard. Most of them went by without making any sense. I caught the last one though—"Take the girl to a waiting room. She will be judged at the afternoon audience."

I disliked "judged" only slightly less than I disliked "prisoner."

Come to think of it, I wasn't all that keen on "girl" either, when it was delivered in that tone of voice. Aunt Tabitha is allowed to call me "girl." Weird men in robes who think I've murdered someone aren't.

The guard in the shiny armor took me through a pair of doors set in the wall of the carriage yard. It seemed very dark after the brightness outside, and the hand on my arm was hurrying me along, so all I saw was a blur of doors and corridors with shiny tile floors that clattered under my boots. The guard's feet didn't clatter. Maybe they wore soft-soled shoes so they wouldn't scuff the tile, or maybe they took lessons in how to walk without sounding like they were wearing horseshoes.

"Prisoner for the afternoon audience," said the guard holding my arm.

There was that word again.

I blinked a few times. My eyes had adjusted enough to see two more guards standing on either side of a small door. The door was bright blue. The guards were not bright blue, although the one on the right looked awfully grumpy.

The guard on the left opened the door. The hand on my arm turned into a hand between my shoulder blades, which propelled me firmly into the room.

It was a small, nondescript room, with a chair and a door opposite the one I'd come through. No windows. There was a small table, and two wall sconces that provided light. And that was all.

The door behind me started to close.

"Hey!" I said, startled into protest. "Hey, wait—what do I *do?*"

"You wait," said the grumpy guard.

"Someone will come for you," said the less-grumpy guard.

The door closed. I heard a loud clacking as it was locked from the other side.

It probably says something about the difference between royalty and commoners that they have waiting rooms that lock from the outside.

Still. This could be worse, I told myself, looking around the featureless room. *It's not the dungeon. There's a chair. And light. And no bars or rats or anything.*

The chair wasn't very comfortable—there was straw coming out of the seat, and it made sitting rather poky—but at least it was a seat. They didn't give you seats in prison, did they?

And sure, the doors are locked, but it's okay, it's not like you have to pee or anything.

As soon as I thought it, I realized I'd made a mistake. You can't think that sort of thing without immediately having to go.

Uh-oh.

Well, it's not like I'd had a chance to go, during all the confusion, and then there was the carriage ride, which had not been exactly easy on the ol' bladder, and I'd had two cups of black tea this morning, and what goes in must come out, after all.

A quick search of the room proved that there was no chamber pot. Neither were there ornamental vases, potted plants, or even a window to hang one's posterior from.

Oh, dear.

I tried to ignore it. I counted the tiles on the floor—forty-six, if you counted each of the half-tiles on the far wall as one—and the rafters on the ceiling—eight, and then I counted them all again, just in case I'd missed one. I hadn't.

Nobody came to get me. I counted everything again, from the other direction. Extra rafters did not spontaneously leap into existence.

Those two cups of tea were really starting to make themselves known.

I wiggled in my chair. It poked me.

At least in the dungeon, they gave you a chamber pot, right?

Or you just went in the corner. I eyed the corners of the room speculatively.

Nah, somebody'd notice. They already suspect you of murder, let's not add public urination to the list.

It was amazing. Terror cannot actually stand up to a full bladder. I was about to be hauled up on murder charges, and all I could think about was *oh god I have to go so baaaaad...*

I got up and pounded on the door.

"Hey! *Hey!*"

No response.

"HEY! I have to pee! Unlock the door!" I rattled the handle futilely.

There was a clattering in the lock, and the door opened an inch. A dark eye peered down at me. "What's all this racket?"

"I have to pee!" I begged the guard. *"Please!"*

"Not my problem," said the guard, starting to close the door.

"Hey!"

"Oh, come on, Jorges," said another voice. "She's just a kid. Take her to the privy already."

"You take her," said Jorges irritably, apparently to the other guard. "I'm eating breakfast. I didn't get a chance before work."

"Fine..." A creak of leather, and the second guard pushed the door open. Jorges stomped back to his post on the far side.

The new guard smiled in a friendly fashion—I'd guess he had kids my age or something—and gestured in front of him. "Come on, m'girl, there's a privy down this way."

"Thank you," I said with heartfelt and genuine gratitude, and hurried out into the hall.

He led the way. As we passed the surly Jorges, I glanced down at his lunch, which was black bread and cheese.

You're feeling really dry, I suggested to the bread. *Really stale. Hard as a rock.* Usually I have to be touching something in order to make it do anything really impressive, but for just going stale, as long as I can see it, I can work with it. It *wants* to go stale. Bread is very accommodating that way.

Then I scurried into the hall after my benefactor.

The privy was a privy. There's a limit to what you can do with privies, even in a castle. Oh, there was a very nicely sanded seat, it was as nice as one could make it, but still, it's basically a board with a hole in it.

I don't think I've ever been so grateful for a board with a hole in it in my life.

On the way back, Jorges the guard was coughing and working his mouth, looking disgruntled. Apparently his bread and cheese hadn't agreed with him.

I had very little time to savor my victory, however, because barely a minute after my guard had ushered me back into the waiting room, Inquisitor Oberon came back for me.

"Up," he said, gesturing with one hand. Again, people treating me like I was a dog. I had an urge to snarl and go for his ankles, but I couldn't see that it would improve the situation, however satisfying it might be.

"What's happening?" I demanded, not getting up from my chair.

He made the hand gesture again, and his eyebrows drew together.

I didn't quite have the nerve to disobey. I got up. "What's happening? Where are you taking me?"

I could actually see him weigh the annoyance of telling me against the annoyance of listening to me ask questions. "You have an audience to be sentenced for your crime," he said finally.

"But I haven't done anything!"

"Such is for the judges to decide." He beckoned again, and I got the impression that I had reached the end of his patience.

What could I do? I went.

FIVE

I expected the audience chamber to be huge, full of echoes and intimidation. I hadn't ever seen one, but it stood to reason that it would be like that, something built to the scale of the vast courtyard, or the sanctuary of the great cathedral. Something like that.

It wasn't. It was a bare room, and it was at a scale I could understand. Big, but no bigger than, say, the common room at the tavern down the street. There were tapestries on the walls, and they were beautiful, but it was a utilitarian sort of beauty.

A ratty little man, dressed in a less dramatic shade of purple than the Inquisitor, sat behind a desk in the center of the room. Behind him, at the far end of the room, sat a large table and behind it, in a large padded chair that was definitely a chair and not a throne, sat a middle-aged woman that I recognized from past parades.

The Duchess was about Aunt Tabitha's age and had much the same build, except that she was a good six inches shorter.

Our ruler wasn't a warrior queen or a teenage princess or anything like that. We're not that kind of city. She was just a woman, rather pudgy, with tired eyes and deep lines carved into her face.

It's a funny thing, though, even having seen her in parades before, even seeing her now without the veil and thinking that she looked like a normal person, like somebody who might come into the shop and buy muffins... even that was no preparation for being in the same room with her. My knees felt like melting ice, and my ears were ringing for no apparent reason.

"We are hearing a case involving an occurrence at a bakery on Gladarat Street." said the little man in purple, in extremely bored tones. "Inquisitor Oberon, presenting report."

There were several other people at the table. I'm embarrassed to say that I didn't see most of them. I had a vague impression of bodies, and some guards behind the Duchess's chair, but the only other presence in the room that I really *saw* was a man in saffron broadcloth sitting next to the Duchess.

I knew immediately who it was. Lord Ethan, the Golden General. The wizard who led Her Grace's armies into battle.

Lord Ethan.

He was *famous*.

He had singlehandedly won the battle of Wightbarn and they say when the Carex mercenaries were raiding the outlying farms a few years ago, he captured their leader and hung him upside down over a cliff-edge in a fist made of clouds.

You may think that I'm being ridiculous, mooning over how famous a man is when I'm being accused of murder, but—well —it was *Lord Ethan*. The closest we had to a living legend, like one of the heroes in the old stories who slew monsters. He had a chiseled jaw and wavy hair the color of melted butter and dark eyes like cinnamon and broad shoulders and—look, I'm not doing this well at all, he sounds like a pastry when I do it. He looked heroic, let's leave it at that. He looked like he should wear gleaming armor and carry a sword that sang.

More than that, he looked *nice*. His lips were quirked up in a smile, as he leaned to the Duchess and murmured something into her ear.

I wished he'd speak to me. It didn't matter what. "I'd like to buy a dozen blueberry scones," would have been just as good as "Follow me! We'll save the kingdom together!" Better, in fact, because I at least knew what to do when somebody bought blueberry scones.

It occurred to me that the Inquisitor was talking. He had probably been talking for some time, but I'd been woolgathering about Lord Ethan and scones. However, he'd just uttered the word "murder" which is a remarkably good word for focusing one's mind.

"This girl was found with the body," the Inquisitor continued, sounding bored.

"I *found* the body," I burst out. "I wasn't found *with* the body!"

The man in purple gave me an annoyed glance that said very clearly that I was holding up the process. If I would just hurry up and be guilty, they could get this over with. By refusing to cooperate, I was wasting everyone's time.

That made me angry. It might just be work to them, but it was my *life* to me! I buried my hands in my apron and clenched them into fists.

"*Found* the body," said the Inquisitor with a sigh. "Very well. Obviously suspicion in this case is sufficient—"

"Excuse me," said a woman's voice.

The Duchess was speaking.

The Inquisitor looked startled. Did she not usually speak during these procedures? Was everything conducted between the two men in purple, and the Duchess just sat there?

I'm fourteen. Politics aren't my strong suit. Still, that didn't seem right at all.

"Tell me, child," said the Duchess kindly, "do your parents know where you are?"

"My parents are dead, ma'am—" *No, not ma'am, you're talking to the Duchess, not a customer!* "—err. Your Grace."

"Do you have no family to live with, child?"

"Oh, no! Err, I mean, yes, I do—I work for my Aunt Tabitha at the bakery, ma'a—er, Your Grace—" I actually lived in my own little room over the top of the glassblower's shop, six doors down, because the bakery didn't have any spare rooms and nobody thought it was a good idea to sleep in the basement with Bob. I spent seven days a week at the bakery anyway, so it was nice to have someplace else to go, and the room over the glass kilns was nice and warm, if you didn't mind the occasional shattering sounds. And Aunt Tabitha was good friends with the glassblower's wife, and she brought me soup whenever I got sick.

All of this seemed entirely too complicated to explain to the Duchess. Fortunately she didn't seem interested in asking any follow-up questions.

She turned and consulted in a low voice with Lord Ethan.

The Inquisitor's hand came down on my shoulder and squeezed so hard I jumped. I wondered if I dared to worm away. Would he hurt me in the presence of the Duchess? Would I look like a mistreated girl, or a troublemaker?

I clenched my fingers tighter in my apron and gritted my teeth.

"Tell me, child," said the Duchess, "are you a wizard?"

"No, Your Grace. I mean—not a real wizard—not like—" The Inquisitor's fingers dug brutally into my shoulder. I tore my eyes way from Lord Ethan and looked hopelessly at the Duchess.

She smiled a little. I hadn't expected that. It gave me the courage to go on.

"I can magic bread, Your Grace. Make dough rise, or keep the muffins from burning, or make sure they come out of the pan clean. Just bread, though. I can't do anything but bread. Well, icing, sometimes, a little, but it's harder—"

I was babbling. I stopped. Lord Ethan leaned over and murmured in the Duchess's ear again.

"Could your magic kill someone?" asked the Duchess. Her voice was quiet, but stern. "You must forgive me for asking, child, but you must understand that those of us who have no magic do not always understand how it works for those of you who do."

"No!" I took a step forward involuntarily, and the Inquisitor had to release me or get dragged forward. I don't think either of us had expected that. I could feel him glaring at the back of my neck, but at least he wasn't squeezing the blood out of my shoulder any more. "I mean, no, Your Grace. I don't—I mean, it's *bread.* How do you kill someone with *bread?*"

Lord Ethan laughed and covered his mouth with his hand. I hoped that meant he agreed with me.

The ratty man in purple rolled his eyes.

"It is not the purpose of this inquiry—" began the Inquisitor.

"I think," said the Duchess, in a carrying voice, "that in your—hmm—*understandable* zeal, Oberon, to get to the bottom of this rash of murders, you have mistaken an innocent bystander for one of the wrongdoers. Please release the girl with our apologies."

There was an exhalation of breath behind me, almost a huff, and then the Inquisitor stepped forward and bowed smoothly to the Duchess.

"As Your Grace commands. My sincerest apologies for my error, and for taking Your Grace's valuable time."

She was letting me go. The Duchess was letting me go. She knew I was innocent, or Lord Ethan had told her...

I pried my fingers out of my apron and tried to make a curtsey, realized too late that I was wearing trousers, and settled for an awkward bow. When I straightened, the Duchess was looking down at her papers, and seem to have forgotten that I existed. I stole a glance at Lord Ethan and met his eyes.

He smiled at me. Really honestly smiled. The Golden General, smiling at a bakery girl.

My insides melted like butter.

"Fine," said the Inquisitor, over my head. He did not sound as if it were fine. He sounded nettled, in fact. It was surprising to recognize an emotion that shallow in his voice.

He hadn't spoken in the entire trip from the audience chamber to the outer hallway, and I had been too busy alternating between relief—I was free! They were letting me go!—and elation—the Golden General *noticed* me!—to say anything either.

What happened next *wasn't* that surprising, I suppose, although it surprised the heck out of me.

I got mad.

"What? *Fine*? That's it?"

He looked at me, really looked at me, instead of over me or through me or at some spot on the back of the inside of my skull, for the first time since we'd reached the palace. "Did you expect something else, child?"

One of the guards made a stifled noise.

It occurred to me that I was talking back to an Inquisitor, a man who had just had me dragged up in front of the Duchess, who could probably order me thrown in the dungeon for contempt of—I don't know, inquisitors or something—and the mad went away and left the rest of me holding the bag.

"You could at least apologize," I mumbled.

The Inquisitor's eyebrows went up. He leaned forward, and for an instant I could see something dark and hot at the bottom of his eyes, like coals glowing in a dark oven.

The mad bit came back enough to lean forward in response, despite the fact that the rest of me was trying to cower away.

"This is not over, little witch," he growled.

And then it *was* over, because the Inquisitor seemed to realize that standing toe to toe with a baker girl was beneath his dignity, and he turned on his heel and stalked away.

A guard grabbed my shoulder, shaking his head. My shoulder was beginning to get awfully tired of this treatment. I was going to have finger marks on that arm for days. "You don't know just how lucky you are, magicker," he said ruefully, hurrying me down the hall.

The mad part of me did not want to let go of the matter

quite yet and didn't really like being called 'magicker' in that tone of voice. "But—"

He opened the door and pushed me through it.

"But—"

"You're free to go," said the guard. "I suggest you *do* go. Now."

And shut the door.

I stood there and stared at it for a while.

I was at one end of the long courtyard we'd entered that morning. There were no carriages in the yard now, and all the guards were pointedly not looking at me.

I was a good three hours' walk from home, assuming I could find the right canal and follow it all the way home.

How dare they drag me all the way up here, find me innocent, and then not give me a ride back home?

I thought about bursting into tears. The mad feeling had receded, and what it left was a hot itchy feeling behind my eyes.

Then there was a soft hiss and a familiar splattering, and I looked down at an increasing number of little grey splotches all over the pavement.

It had started to rain.

I had to walk home, for hours, through an unfamiliar part of the city, in the rain.

I began, rather absurdly, to laugh. This was ridiculous. Nobody could have luck this bad, could they?

At least they found you innocent, whispered the little voice in the back of my head. *That's pretty good luck, right there.*

I stopped laughing.

Nothing to do with luck, I thought grumpily, folding my arms across my chest and stalking across the courtyard and towards the distant carriageway. *I was innocent. They didn't have a choice.*

Are you sure about that?

This was too much, particularly on top of the rain. Of course they had to find me innocent. That the Inquisitor might have the ability to find me guilty of a murder I hadn't committed wasn't something I wanted to think about.

The rain started to come down with increasing enthusiasm.

I paused at one side of the gateway. I was going to get soaked. I was already fairly soggy, and the rain was just getting warmed up.

I looked back at the guards. They were donning oilcloth slickers. It didn't look like any of them were going to come over and offer me a carriage ride home.

I was hungry and tired and mad and far from home. The baking wasn't going to get done until I got home. If the baking didn't get done... well, it'd be bad.

I wasn't going to get any closer to home unless I started walking.

So, I gritted my teeth, and started.

SIX

The rain had stopped.

It turned out that my estimate of three hours to get home had been conservative. It took closer to six. It doesn't take anything like six hours to walk across our city, so you can guess that I got turned around a lot. I followed a street that looked familiar for nearly forty-five minutes, expecting it to turn into the roadway for the Birdbridge canal, which I could follow home. Then it hit a wall, literally ran smack into the side of a church that I didn't recognize. The angel over the doorway was eight feet tall and had a stone blindfold over her face. She looked as if she were weeping. The carving under her feet read, "Our Lady of Sorrowful Angels."

I thought about going in to ask for directions, but I wasn't in the mood to talk to any more strangers today, so I just turned around and went back. That was probably pretty dumb, but I'd had a really lousy day, and even the Lady of Sorrowful Angels probably wouldn't want anything to do with me.

Anyway, I found the right street eventually and made it to the Birdbridge, which is covered in carvings of kingfishers and oystercatchers, the edges of their wings melting away under wet green moss. Then from the Birdbridge canal, through the Tailor District, where everyone was inside or under tarps, trying to keep their wares dry, and up to Market Street, which crosses all the big canals. You can take Market pretty much anywhere, even to Aunt Tabitha's bakery, but it's a roundabout sort of way.

On the other hand, if your nerves are good—or if you're in no mood for delays—you can take a short cut from one end of Market, through the crooked alley called the Rat's Elbow, and you come out less than a block from the bakery. Rat's Elbow wasn't really all that bad, but it had a number of offshoots, and most of those led into the Rat's Nest, which really *is* all that bad. Beer is cheap and blood is cheaper in there, or so they say.

I don't know how much blood costs out here, come to think of it—we don't use it much in baking—but presumably it's even cheaper in the Rat's Nest. (We do use beer to make the dark ale bread. It costs six pennies a keg from the tavern down the street, and Aunt Tabitha says that's highway robbery, but she's never suggested buying beer in the Rat's Nest.)

By the time I made it to the Rat's Elbow, the rain had slowed to a tentative drizzle. The sun wasn't exactly shining, but there were some bright patches of cloud. I could see them reflected in the puddles down the middle of the cobblestones.

The problem with the Rat's Elbow, even leaving aside the name and the proximity to the Rat's Nest, is that the street settled badly on one side, so the road slopes sharply from the north side down to the south. The settling made the houses on the south all lean in over the road. Various generations of owners have propped up the leaning walls with wooden beams, usually wedged right up against the street, so now it's impossible to get a carriage through and half the road is always in the shadow of the leaning buildings. Plus there's a real drainage problem. Even though the rain had been stopped for a little bit, the right side of the Rat's Elbow looked like a lake, with murky water swirling around (and occasionally over) the front steps of the leaning buildings.

People watched me from the wet front steps. There were people on the porches and in the dark, unshuttered windows. They weren't doing anything threatening. They were playing cards and talking, and a dead-faced woman was pinning up laundry to a clothesline, standing knee deep in brown water. Nobody said anything to me, and they didn't exactly stare, but they knew I was there, and I knew that they knew, and they knew that I knew that they knew, all in a creepy, crackling tangle of mutual awareness.

It occurred to me that it was much easier to scoot through the Rat's Elbow when Aunt Tabitha was expecting me back any minute and would raise holy hell if I didn't arrive. But she had no idea where I was, and if she was going to start looking for me, she'd start back at the palace. Nobody knew where I was, except for the people in Rat's Elbow.

They probably wouldn't do anything to me. They were poor, obviously—if you were rich, you wouldn't live in Rat's Elbow—but just because you were poor didn't mean you were bad. I mean, poverty didn't mean that you were going to, to take an example *completely* and *totally* at random, hit a bedraggled young woman over the head and go through her pockets to see if she had any money. It was just that it also didn't mean that you *weren't*.

That one woman is doing laundry. Do bad people do laundry?

It's not like I have anything worth stealing...

But do they know that?

I walked a little faster.

I could hear them talking quietly, and some kids had come out and were playing, but they got quieter when I walked by, and then it took a minute for the noise to start up again behind me.

I wish Aunt Tabitha were here.

I wish Uncle Alfred were here.

I even sort of wish Bob the sourdough starter was here. I don't think anybody'd mess with Bob. Not twice, anyway.

There was a clattering noise behind me. The skin on the back of my neck crawled, but I was not going to look around, no I wasn't, definitely not—

"Hey, bread girl!"

I turned around.

Two empty eye-sockets, dark as sorrow, hung a little above my head. The skeletal face swept down into long, smooth bones that framed a cavernous nasal passage stuffed with twigs. An empty jaw opened and closed with a hollow clacking.

I stared into the face of a dead horse and nearly fainted with relief.

SEVEN

Knackering Molly was, to put it bluntly, insane.

She wasn't stupid, though. There was a sharp, glittering intelligence inside the insanity that had learned early on that it was much easier to get away with being insane if you were also useful and had a little bit of money, and if people were just a little bit scared of you.

Molly was, like me, a very minor wizard, but her talent was even weirder. She could make dead horses walk.

This may not sound like a very good talent, but if you live in a large city with narrow streets, it's actually quite handy. Horses are useful animals, but they die like everybody else, and when they're dead, they're about a thousand pounds of meat and bone that you have to dispose of before it starts to stink. The knackermen who run the big rendering yards at the edge of town will pay money for the dead horse, but they also charge money to come take it away, and they have to roll a cart in, and the cart takes up space and disrupts traffic and blocks people's doorways. Then the people loading the horse onto the cart want to get paid, and sometimes they have to start butchering the horse right there if they can't carry it out and it's just a horrible business with blood and nastiness everywhere, and the neighbors get very put out.

Or you can go get Knackering Molly, and for sixpence, she'll put her hand on the horse's head, and it will stand up and walk to the knackers under its own power. It's still pretty horrible to watch, but it's a lot less trouble.

Anyway, you can spot Molly pretty easily. She rides around the city on Nag. Nag's been dead longer than I've been alive, and he's mostly bones now, so she pads him with rags and straw and old flour sacks. He looks like a magpie nest with hooves.

People are sometimes a little nervous about us magic-folk. I mean, we're born this way, and nobody knows quite why—my parents weren't magic at all, and nobody else in the family is either—but if you start complaining about magickers, there's always a chance that the person you're talking to knows one or is married to one or has one in the family and they'll get annoyed about it. And it's not like everyone advertises their ability. Presumably some people have talents so obscure that they never get to use them. There's a fairytale about a girl who could talk to tornadoes, which would be pretty impressive, but we haven't had a tornado in Riverbraid in a hundred years, so how often does it really come up?

We're lucky here, though. Our city's really nice about magickers. Other than holding bits of iron in court, they don't treat you differently. Some cities don't allow magickers to live there, or make them register with the government. Delta City has the Spell Quarter, which is a kind of ghetto like the Rat's Nest, only just for wizards.

None of that happens here in Riverbraid. If you're going to be a magicker, this is the place to live.

If you're a wizard who can do big scary impressive things, you usually wind up in the army or working for the Duchess. Nobody really wants to live next to someone who can summon lightning out of the sky. The rest of us, who do little small not-very-impressive things, usually go out of our way to act harmless and useful so that people don't start making signs to ward off bad luck when we walk around.

Knackering Molly doesn't care about any of that. If people make signs against bad luck when Nag trots by, she figures it's good advertising.

Molly's the only other magicker, other than Master Elwidge, that I talk to regularly. There's a girl at the farmer's market and we nod to each other, but that's as far as it goes. I think most magic-folk don't want to talk about it, and maybe they think that making gingerbread dance is a little too flamboyant... although nobody's as flamboyant as Knackering Molly.

"Hi, Molly." I patted Nag's nose. The bones are so old that they're not icky any more, just dry and smooth. (The rags are still pretty icky.) There's not very much to Nag, but Molly told me once that he liked having his nose petted, so I try.

"What're you doin' in the Elbow, duck?" asked Molly, nudging Nag into a walk beside me.

"Trying to get home," I said wearily. Nag's hooves went *clonk-clonk-clonk* on the pavement. (Regular horse hooves go *clop*. Don't ask me why Nag's went *clonk*.)

She peered down at me, her lined face drawing even more lines as she frowned. "If you don't mind me saying so, love, you look like the ass end of a seagull."

Which was pretty insulting, if you think about it, but

perversely, it made me feel better. When you feel absolutely wretched, it's consoling to know that you look just as awful as you feel.

"Your uncle's not dead, is he now? Saw the body wagon at your aunt's place."

"No, my uncle's fine." I kept walking. People weren't staring now. Apparently a girl walking through the Elbow was unusual, but a girl with a madwoman riding a dead horse was perfectly acceptable. There was probably a moral lesson in there somewhere, but I had given up on moral lessons for today. "There was a dead girl in the bakery."

"Huh," said Knackering Molly. "Who killed 'er?"

"They thought I did it," I said gloomily.

"Did you?"

"No!"

"Well, then." She sat back. "You're a good girl, you'd probably have a good reason. I ain't judging. But if you didn't do it, who did?"

"I don't know." My shoes squelched. Nag went through a puddle and splashed water up the side of my trousers. "They sent a man out from the palace. He said something about her death being magic."

"Magic?" Molly threaded her hands into Nag's rags. "No good comes of poking around in death magic."

Says the woman riding the dead horse, I thought, but didn't say it. "I don't know. I had nothing to do with it. I went up to the palace and saw the Duchess..."

It occurred to me as I was saying it that it should have been very exciting, seeing the duchess, even with everything else. She'd actually spoken to me. She'd been distant and busy, but she'd kept me from getting thrown in jail. I wasn't excited, though. I was just bone tired, and maybe still a little mad.

Molly didn't say that it should have been exciting. She only said "Huh!" again. And then, after a minute, "There's a thing, anyway. Huh."

"She told them to let me go. Well... I mean... she talked to a wizard, and I guess *he* told her—"

"Wizards!" Knackering Molly leaned over Nag's withers and spat on the ground.

"*We're* wizards," I said mildly.

"Not like real wizards, duck. We're just little people, you and me." She slapped Nag's skeletal shoulder. "The big wizards, well, now. The *gov'mint* wizards. You stay clear of them, bread girl. They're no good for nobody, and worse for people like us."

They say some wizards came around once, when Molly was young, to ask her if she could make dead people walk, probably thinking that if she could make dead soldiers get up and fight, she'd be worth a lot to the right people. She doesn't talk about that. Miss McGrammar said that she couldn't do it, but I heard Brutus the chandler say once that he thought she *had* been able to do it, and that's why she came back crazy. Even if she just made the cavalry horses get up and charge again, they would have shoved her out on a battlefield to do it, and how awful would that be?

I wanted to ask him more about it, but all he'd say was that she hadn't been any crazier than anybody else before the wizards took her away.

She hates the government now. She mutters about that a lot, but then again, she also mutters that the fleas are the ghosts of ancient philosophers and they're trying to suck out the truth from her ankles.

This doesn't stop her from driving a very hard bargain when you want a horse moved, though. People have tried to take advantage of her because they think she's not right in the head. It doesn't end well for them.

"Lord Ethan's okay," I said, remembering that golden glittering presence in the audience chamber, and the way he'd smiled at me. "I mean, I think he told her I couldn't have done it."

"Feh." Molly was unconvinced. "Waves in parades, maybe, but he's a war wizard, right enough. Maybe he did you a good turn now, but he'll kill you if you get in his way, not outta meanness like some of 'em, but just like a bug." She rooted in her bird's-nest hair for a minute and pulled out some small wiggly thing. "Like a *bug*." Her thumbnail came down and cracked it.

"At least he's not mean," I said faintly. Lord Ethan could call storms out of the sky to slam the enemy flat. The songs the minstrels sing on street corners said he could control the lightning. But I still couldn't imagine him crushing somebody like a bug.

"Mean 'r not, you're still dead, bread girl." She straightened up. "And here we are, almost home."

"Oh... oh." I looked around, surprised. We'd emerged from the Rat's Elbow onto the street, and I hadn't even noticed. "Oh. *Thank* you."

Knackering Molly shrugged. "Rat's Elbow's not as bad as some places, but y' gotta walk careful. Never hurts to have a friend with you, even if it's just ol' Nag." She leaned down over the dead horse's neck and gestured. "Come here, bread girl."

Somewhat reluctantly, I came. I was grateful for her escort, but she was still insane, and more importantly, she stank to high heaven. Most of it was unwashed woman and unwashed cloth, but there was a distinct reek of the knackeryards clinging to her too.

"Word of advice," she hissed, leaning close in. I tried not to flinch, expecting her breath to stink as bad as the rest of her, but it was unexpectedly sweet, like mint. "Walk careful, bread girl. Little people like us, we're not safe these days. Watch your back."

"Wh-what?"

Her eyes stabbed into mine. "Look out for the Spring Green Man."

I blinked.

The who?

Molly leaned back and put her heels into Nag, and he turned as neatly as a parade mount and clattered back into Rat's Elbow. It didn't occur to me until after she'd gone that I should run after her, maybe ask her what she'd heard, or who the Spring Green Man was supposed to be, or even what that *meant.*

But I was only a block from the bakery, and it had been a long, long, *long* day. Chasing a madwoman on a dead horse into the bad part of town just didn't seem worth the effort right now, particularly since her Spring Green Man was probably just another figment of her imagination, like the truth-sucking fleas.

Still, the name made me uneasy somehow, in a way that the fleas never did.

"Stupid," I muttered to myself, folding my arms tight and hurrying toward the bakery. "Stupid name. Stupid Inquisitor. Stupid long day."

EIGHT

When I walked in the door, Aunt Tabitha made all the proper noises and sat me down with a mug of hot tea and made me tell the story three times, and then snapped at Uncle Albert to stop pestering me about it, couldn't he see I was exhausted (the only thing he'd said all afternoon was "Good heavens!") and sent me home.

The girl was gone out of the bakery, anyway. Presumably the body wagon had come and taken her. I didn't ask.

I did ask if Aunt Tabitha wanted me to set the bread out to rise overnight, but she said that she'd been running the bakery for twenty years and she could manage just this once, and that I should get some sleep.

So I went back to my room. The rain had come back in spurts and spatters, and the cobblestones gleamed wetly. They were lighting the streetlights already, but the lamplighter hadn't gotten this far yet, so the street was dark and gloomy. That didn't matter. It was only six doors down, barely a block. I could have walked it blindfolded.

You'd think after a day like that I would have been jumpy and paranoid, but I wasn't. I wasn't thinking about anything. I was just watching my feet go one in front of the other.

And then somebody grabbed me from out of the dark.

"Where is she?" a voice snarled in my ear, and I was wrenched off the street and into the shadows of the alleyway.

Sweet lady of angels, is this day never *going to end?*

I should probably have been scared. No, I should *definitely* have been scared.

Mostly, though, I was just too tired. I wanted to go home. I wanted to go back to my warm little room over the glassblower's shop, and lie down in the bed and pull the quilt over my head and go to sleep and wake up stupidly early and go make cinnamon rolls and apple pull-aparts and gingerbread men.

"Where's *who?*"

"Tibbie!" said the voice in my ear, sounding frustrated and also surprisingly high-pitched. "What did you do with her?"

"Who's Tibbie?" I tried wiggling. There was an arm around my neck, and it was making it hard to breathe, but my attacker seemed to be shorter than I was and wasn't getting a very good angle. "Let me go!"

"Not until you tell me where Tibbie is!"

"I don't know who that is!" I grabbed for the arm around my neck.

"Stop it! I'm warning you!" The voice was definitely shrill, and I was slapped against the side of the building. Bricks scraped at my hands.

"Let me *go!*"

I got my fingers around the arm, bent forward as far as I could, and pulled. It wouldn't have worked in most cases, but I had two things going for me.

One, I was a baker, and you don't punch dough every day for two years without developing some pretty hefty forearms. I may not be very big, but I'll bet you a tray of cinnamon buns that I can out-arm wrestle any girl my age.

Two, my attacker was a ten-year-old boy.

I wrenched away, turned and faced him. He wasn't big. My neck was probably about the highest he could reach. He was wiry, but he looked skinny and underfed, like a stray dog. His eyes were way too big for his face, and the grime on his face was marred by tear tracks.

"Where is she?" he demanded again, sounding furious and miserable. He bounced on the balls of his feet, apparently not sure if he should launch himself at me again or run away.

"Where's *who?*"

"Tibbie!" he said, practically yelling. "My sister!"

"Why do you think I *know?*"

"She was in your bakery!"

I closed my mouth with a snap.

Uh-oh.

I leaned against the wall next to him. The mad was gone. I was just... so... *tired.*

"Tell me what happened," I said finally, pinching the bridge of my nose. "When did she go into the bakery?"

"Last night," said the boy, snuffling and wiping his nose on the back of his hand. "She went in last night, but she didn't come out again. What did you do with her?"

That was a question I wasn't willing to answer just yet. "Why did she go into the bakery?"

"It was cold. We were hungry. There's good food in there, sometimes." He glared at me, daring me to say anything. "We go in back sometimes, take a few buns. Not *stuff.* We don't nick *stuff.*"

"Um. Thank you." The parish priest would probably argue that stealing was stealing, whether it was day-old buns or Aunt Tabitha's good knives, but the priest wasn't here. I could understand the difference just fine. Food was one thing. Good knives were hard to replace. I wondered how long they'd been breaking into the bakery, and how none of us had noticed.

"We didn't touch nothin'," he said, as if reading my mind. "We're careful. If we nick stuff, you'd put up locks 'n guards 'n whatever, and then we couldn't get buns whenever we want 'em."

There was a certain logic to this. I decided to let it go. "So Tibbie went in? About when was this?"

"I dunno. After midnight. I was gonna go in too, but she said no, she'd do it quick. She was sneaking, you know?"

"Then what happened?"

The boy shrugged. "Then the other man showed up."

"Wait—what other man?"

"You know. Your uncle or whoever. The one in the yellow-greeny outfit."

The notion of Uncle Alfred wandering around after midnight, going into the bakery by the back door was odd. The notion of him wearing anything but baker's whites or threadbare black was ridiculous. Uncle Alfred had strictly monochromatic tastes, probably because of Aunt Tabitha and her housedresses.

Look out for the Spring Green Man, Molly had said.

"That couldn't have been my uncle. Who was it?"

"How should I know? It's your bakery!"

I pinched the bridge of my nose. "So this man went into the bakery?"

"Yeah." The boy snuffled again and stared up into the gloomy eaves above us.

"And then what happened?"

"And then he came out. And then you went in a while later. And then there was a whole ruckus and I couldn't get close enough to see what was happening and then they came and took you away."

I remembered that bit. I sighed.

"Um—I—look. They took a dead body out of the bakery. It must have been your sister. I'm sorry."

There was probably a better way to tell him the news, but I was just so horribly tired.

He stared at me for a moment, then snorted, which was not the response I was expecting. "Don't be stupid."

Be patient, I told myself. *Be kind. He just lost his sister. He's in shock.*

"She's not dead. You're *stupid.*"

I am not as good a person as I should be. I kind of wanted to slap him.

"I'm sorry," I said instead.

"You're wrong," he said. He turned away, and I expected him to stomp off, but he turned back suddenly. "Show me."

"Show you what?"

"The bakery. Show me. She must still be in there, or maybe she slipped out again. Maybe she left me a sign."

"Okay." I shoved my hands in my pockets. I wanted to go to bed. I really, *really* wanted to go to bed. "Now?"

"No. When it's real dark. I don't want to be explaining to a lot of grown-ups. They'll be stupid about it, too."

"Okay." I pointed up the stairs. "I live up there. Come get me when it's late enough for you, and I'll show you."

He nodded once, sharply, and then pelted out of the alley as if there were zombie crawfish after him.

NINE

I was asleep as soon as my head hit the pillow, and approximately five seconds later, someone was shaking me awake.

"Hzzzhhh?" I opened my eyes.

It was the boy again. When he saw I was awake, he stepped back and folded his arms. "Come on. It's nearly midnight."

"It is? Really?" I sat up and squinted at the window. Sure enough, it was deep dark outside. I'd slept for hours. It didn't feel like it at all. My head was pounding. I was also starving, although I had a distinct memory of having wolfed down a couple of cold cinnamon rolls before I fell into bed.

I *also* had a distinct memory of locking the door.

"How did you get in here?"

He looked at me, and then at the door and then back at me, with the sort of pure disdain that only someone under the age of twelve can manage. "I knocked first," he said. "You didn't answer."

Any doubts I'd had about him breaking into the bakery were gone. Aunt Tabitha had bought a *very* sturdy lock for my door, since I was living alone. I wondered how long it had taken him to jimmy it.

"Fine." I swung my feet onto the floor. "You hungry?"

He shrugged, which I took as a yes. "There's some buns on the table." I got up and dug through my clothes chest, looking for a sweater.

By the time I'd found one and pulled it over my head, there was one bun left. The kid, whatever his name was, had gone through them, apparently without chewing. Or breathing.

He'd also left me one, even though he was obviously starving.

"What's your name?" I asked, tearing into the last roll.

He eyed me suspiciously. Suspicion and disdain appeared to be his only two expressions. No, wait. I'd seen anger when he first attacked me. Three expressions.

"Look, you don't have to tell me your real name if you don't want to, I just want something to call you other than 'Hey, you.' I'm Mona."

"Spindle," he said finally.

I doubted that his mother had named him that. Still, he was as thin as a spindle, and nearly as sharp. I decided to go with it. "Okay, Spindle." I brushed crumbs off my front. "Let's go."

Opening the bakery at midnight felt like we were breaking into it, even though I worked there and would normally be doing the exact same thing in about four hours. I shut the door nervously and leaned against the big oven. The banked warmth was a relief from the chill outside.

"She was on the floor, here," I said, pointing to a spot in the middle of the floor. "I think Aunt Tabitha probably cleaned it, though." (I was trying to be tactful. Aunt Tabitha had definitely mopped up, because there wasn't a giant bloodstain on the floor anymore.)

Spindle examined the kitchen with an almost professional detachment. He examined the counters and the floor and even the ceiling. I was almost sorry that we'd cleaned up, because he was doing a much more thorough job than the constables had.

Finally, he went down on his knees on the floor, peering under the tables. My stomach quivered. He was kneeling right where his sister's blood had pooled all over the floor. I wanted to tell him to move, but...

"Um," I said, with no real idea how to continue.

"There's something under here," he interrupted.

"There is?" I crouched down next to him. I had to put a hand down to steady myself, right where the girl's head had been.

Look, you have to stop this. You're going to be working here for years, maybe the rest of your life if you inherit the bakery, and if you do this every time you walk across the floor...

I forcibly shoved away the memory and leaned down.

Sure enough, there was something under there, some bit of metal winking in the lantern light.

"It might be some silverware," I said.

"It's not," Spindle said. "It's something else. I don't know if I can reach it." He wedged his arm under the table, up to the shoulder. "Almost... should be... no." He pulled back, frowning and dusting flour off his clothes. "Can we move the table?"

"I've got a better idea." I cracked open the door to the front and slipped through. There should still be a gingerbread man left from the last batch... yup.

It was starting to get stale, which made it harder to animate, and my headache came roaring back full force, but I gritted my teeth and stared down and thought, *Live*.

The gingerbread man stood up on my palm, stretching. I set him down on the floor. "There's something under the table," I told it. "Will you get it out for me?"

The gingerbread man saluted, ducked his head—it was a tight fit, even for a cookie—and walked under the table.

Spindle's eyebrows had vanished under his hair. "You're a wizard," he said.

His tone wasn't accusing, merely surprised. It was my turn to shrug. "Only with dough," I said. "It's not very useful."

He nodded. "Tibbie's a wizard."

"Really?"

"She sneaks," he said, making a wiggling hand gesture that could have meant anything. "You know."

I didn't know, but presumably she had some kind of magical talent for hiding. "Do you mean that she turns invisible or something?"

"Just about," said Spindle proudly. "Me, I got no magic. I gotta just stay low and quiet, but she can hide in a cat's shadow, almost."

Hmm. That was interesting. Not a huge wizarding talent, maybe, but a pretty good one compared to bread.

Knackering Molly's words came back to me. *Little people like us, we're not safe.*

Had she meant little wizards? Minor magical talents? She warned me about the Spring Green Man, too, and here Spindle had seen somebody in yellow-green trap his sister in my bakery, and then there was a dead wizard girl.

A rash of wizard murders, the Inquisitor had said. I'd assumed he meant murders by wizards, but maybe that's just what he was hoping people would think.

"There's something going on," I said, hugging myself. "Somebody's killing wizards. The Inquisitor said it, and Knackering Molly. They must have gotten your sister."

Spindle scowled. "Somebody's killing wizard-folks all right —word's all over the street—but they didn't get Tibbie, *because Tibbie's not dead.*"

I didn't have anything to say to that.

The gingerbread man emerged from under the table, pushing the metal object. It was some kind of bracelet, a half-moon of silver joined by a chain. The chain was broken and clinked as Spindle picked it up.

In the pale light of the lantern, his face turned the color of old cheese.

"Tibbie's bracelet," he said. "It was our mum's."

"I'm sorry," I said.

He turned and ran out of the bakery.

I called his name, but he wasn't a dog, and he didn't come back. I stood there in the doorway for a while, the gingerbread man on my shoulder, staring out into the dark streets, and the splash of yellow radiance the street-light left across the stones.

I'd known it was Tibbie. It was better Spindle knew it, too. It was better to know than not to know. *Not* knowing was terrible.

Something patted my cheek. I looked down and saw the gingerbread man on my shoulder. He was steadying himself with a hank of hair in one hand, and with the other he reached up and caught the tears I hadn't known I was crying.

TEN

I didn't see Spindle for a couple of days after that. I was busy in the bakery. Not that Aunt Tabitha wouldn't have let me take the time off, but I didn't want to. Baking was normal. If I was baking, then everything else was normal, too, and even if somebody was killing wizards, it was happening somewhere else, on the other side of the counter.

This was maybe not as rational as it could have been, but it *felt* right. I was safe at the bakery. When I walked home at night, the block to the glassblower, with the water gurgling from the gutters into the canal, *then* I wasn't safe. I hunched myself into my jacket and felt like things were following me in the shadows.

I didn't run home. Running would have let whatever was in the shadows chase me.

This wasn't rational either—this was a slightly more grown-up version of monsters hiding under the bed—but I couldn't shake the feeling. So I stayed in the bakery as much as possible, and I hurried home at a fast walk that didn't quite break into a run. And I got up very very early and came into the bakery again, so that when Aunt Tabitha came downstairs, I was already wrist deep in dough.

I worried about Spindle though, in the moments when I wasn't too busy to think. Not that there was any shortage of things to worry about. The news that spring was all bad. Lord Ethan and the army marched out not two days after I'd seen him. Carex mercenaries raiding again, I think. The customers had different ideas. Miss McGrammar just called them "the enemy." Brutus the chandler said it was Mannequa, the next province over, hiring the Carex to attack us. The priest waited until the chandler had left with his scones and told me that was nonsense, nobody hired the Carex for anything anymore, unless you were paying them to go away.

Carex mercenaries are sort of like the boogeyman in our city, and in most of the city-states in the kingdom, probably. Your mom tells you that if you misbehave, the Carex will get you. The problem is that they're actually real, and once you grow up and hear all the stories, they're a lot worse than the boogeyman.

A long time ago, supposedly, they had their own homeland, and then two of the city-states went to war—Edom, I think, and St. Salizburg, or maybe it was Delta City—and one of the cities hired the Carex to fight for them. When the war was over, the Carex decided they liked it here and didn't leave like they were supposed to. Apparently, their homeland is all ice and mountains and things trying to kill you, so you can see why they'd want to stick around our kingdom, which has lots of farmland and rivers and high-quality baked goods.

Don't get me wrong: generally we like foreigners in our

kingdom. We like anybody as long as they have money and buy scones. Some of the big port cities are crammed with people from all over the world, and they don't make them live in their own quarter, the way they do magickers. The man who sells Aunt Tabitha cinnamon is from someplace that nobody else can pronounce quite right and has tattoos all over his skin, even on the little webs in between his fingers.

But the Carex eat all the farm animals, even the horses and dogs and sometimes the people, and then they burn the farms for fun. They are not interested in being neighbors. They just take over towns and eat all the food and kill all the people, and then use it as a base to launch raids on other towns. Whenever that happens, the nearest cities send out the army and burn them out, and the Carex run back to the hills for a couple of seasons, then come out meaner and hungrier than ever.

It was probably just my imagination that the city seemed colder without the Golden General in it. I felt less safe without the war wizards around. You didn't want to need them, and they had scary powers in their own right, like calling lightning and throwing fireballs, but you liked to know they were there, just in case.

One thing I didn't worry about was what the army would do when they found the Carex. The army would win, no question. We have magic, and the Carex don't. Carex hate magickers. If one of their kids turns up with a talent, they expose him. For the longest time I didn't know what that meant, but it turns out that they just leave him on a hillside and let wild animals eat him. This is the sort of thing that makes you glad to live in a civilized city.

The regulars all had their own opinions, but one I didn't

hear was Master Elwidge's. He hadn't come into the bakery in days. I was getting a little worried about him.

I went to the farmer's market one morning, and something happened that worried me even more.

There's a girl at the farmer's market who's a magicker like me. (I think she's a lot better, honestly.) She's a juggler, but when she juggles oranges, they turn blue or green or seem to catch fire. Her dad sells fruit, and every now and then, she'll take out a few oranges and start juggling and people come over to watch. In late summer, she'll turn rutabagas into doves.

Her name's Lena. She's older than me and lives outside of town, and we don't talk very much, so I was surprised when Lena saw me across the crowd and came over. She wasn't juggling oranges today.

"You're Mona, aren't you?" she said. "From the bakery."

"Yes?" I said.

She nodded once, sharply, then looked around, as if afraid that someone might be listening. She pulled me toward the edge of the market, against one of the brick walls. "Are you leaving?" she said.

"Um... I have to buy some strawberries for my aunt..."

Lena shook her head. "The city. Are you leaving the city?"

"*Why* would I leave the city?" I asked, baffled.

"*You* know," she said, waving a hand all around us, as if to take in the entire city.

"No?" I was starting to feel like I'd come in on this conversation halfway through. "What do I know?"

Lena blew air through her bangs, making them flip up. "Haven't you been hearing? The disappearances? The..." she looked around again, "...the *magickers?*"

"Knackering Molly said something," I said cautiously. "But—"

"We're getting out," said Lena. "Dad and me. We're leaving tonight. There's something going on in this city. It's not healthy for magickers anymore. We're going to Dad's cousin in Edom." She looked me over appraisingly. "We're taking the wainwright's boy, too, the one who turns rocks into cheese. You should come with us, too."

"What? No." I took a step back, as if she might try to kidnap me. "My aunt and uncle are here. And the bakery." I took another step back. "I mean—it can't be *that* bad!"

Could it?

I tried to think of all the magickers I knew. There weren't many. Lena, Molly, Elwidge... there was the girl who sang on the street corner and birds came down and sang with her—no, she'd been gone since last winter, hadn't she? There had been a man with a hurdy-gurdy on that street corner for months now.

Still, even if Lena was right... I was fourteen years old. Leave the bakery? That was just nuts.

Lena narrowed her eyes. I took another step back. She didn't have any rutabagas on her, but I wasn't sure what she could do with a strawberry. I needed those strawberries for tarts. If they turned into doves, it was going to be a real problem.

I thought she might yell at me, but she shook her head and said, "Good luck, then. I hope you're right."

She hurried back to the fruit stand.

On the way home with my strawberries, I took Peony Street, which takes you past the shop where Master Elwidge the carpenter works.

The door was closed. There were no lights in the window. It looked like an empty shop, not just a closed one.

I went home as fast as I could, feeling yet again like there was something watching me in the shadows.

I didn't tell Aunt Tabitha about the conversation. Probably she'd say that Lena was being ridiculous, but what if she didn't? And if she took it seriously then I'd have to take it seriously and that meant that I wasn't safe behind the bakery counter after all.

These were depressing thoughts.

I threw myself into work at the bakery, but there was only so much I could do. When the pans had gone in the oven and it wasn't time for anything else to come out, when I had to wait ten minutes before I started the icing for the cinnamon buns, when there weren't any customers, then I had a few minutes, and then the thoughts would start again.

I'd steal downstairs and feed Bob, or if he had already been fed, I'd lean my forehead against the cool stone wall and let the thoughts bubble and ferment like yeast at the bottom of my mind.

Sometimes Bob would put out a mushy tentacle of dough and touch me on the shoulder. I think he knew I was worried. Occasionally he'd even drag his bucket closer to where I was sitting and brooding.

It wasn't exactly *thinking*, if that makes any sense. I wasn't looking at the thoughts. I just knew they were there, roiling around underneath.

Problem was that, like yeast, the thoughts were growing. Pretty soon they'd overflow the edges of my skull, and I wouldn't be able to ignore them any longer.

For the moment, though, I could sort of squash them down,

like dough into a pan, and think about something else. I settled for worrying about Spindle.

I left day-old bakery goods out for him on the stoop a couple of times. They were gone in the morning, although it could have been dogs or raccoons, or even some other street kid. That was fine. Dogs and raccoons and street kids all have to eat, and the day-olds don't do anybody any good in the case.

Five or six days after my trip to the palace, I went down to the Rookshade Bridge with a half loaf of stale bread. Rookshade is a good bridge for feeding ducks because it's low to the water, and the railing has wide enough gaps that you can dangle your feet through and throw bits of bread down to the ducks.

It was a nice afternoon. It wasn't raining for once—we'd had a very damp spring—and Aunt Tabitha had told me to get out of the bakery and go take a break, before she hit me over the head and *forced* me to relax. I walked down the road by the side of the canal, avoiding the carriages and the wheeled carts selling hot buns (nothing so good as *our* buns) with a gingerbread man sitting on my shoulder.

He was the same one from the night Spindle and I had found his sister's bracelet, and he was so stale by now that you'd probably break your teeth if you tried to bite him. I didn't expect him to be walking around still, but I'd been pretty upset that night looking for Tibbie—it had been a really awful day—and when I was upset, my magic worked a lot better or harder or something. I should probably have figured that out with Bob, the unkillable sourdough starter, but it was still a surprise. At any rate, the gingerbread man showed no signs of stopping.

That was fine by me. I kept him sitting on the bedpost at night, watching the door. He was supposed to wake me up if anybody tried to get in. I don't know how well that would really work, but I felt a little better because of it.

Aunt Tabitha hadn't said anything, even when the cookie started displaying a little more initiative than was usual in baked goods. Twice he had brought me the salt without even asking, and I could tell him to put strawberry halves on top of the muffins and he would do the entire tray.

I had been tempted occasionally to try baking a life-size gingerbread man to help out in the kitchen. Fortunately, the ovens weren't big enough for anything like that, and I was becoming glad of it. My little gingerbread familiar was fairly benign, but what if I was upset or nervous and wound up creating some kind of berserk gingerbread golem?

It didn't seem likely that I *could* do that, but... well... best not to find out.

Besides, between Lena and Knackering Molly warning me, I was starting to think that it was best not to call attention to my magic. A person-sized hunk of gingerbread wasn't very subtle. And lately, when I'd made cookies dance, there'd been an edge to the laughter.

We threw out three batches of old gingerbread men. Hardly anybody was willing to buy them. It's maybe not so odd that gingerbread doesn't sell in midsummer, but one or two customers left without buying *anything*.

And Miss McGrammar... well.

"Have you seen the broadsheets yet?" she snapped, when everybody else had left the shop.

"The what?" I put the cookie back in the bakery case.

"You'll see," she said, sniffing. She sounded maliciously pleased about something. "All *you* people'll see soon enough."

She hadn't explained and she hadn't come back since. Nobody missed her, but it was still strange.

On the bright side, she was the only reason we baked lemon scones every day. I started making blackberry tarts instead, and those were much better.

I trudged up to the railing of the Rookshade Bridge, and saw Spindle already sitting there, staring moodily down into the water. I'd caught a glimpse of him once or twice, but this time he didn't run off as soon as he saw me. The ducks had gathered under him, expecting to be fed, and the fact he wasn't throwing anything down was inciting some angry quacking.

I sat down next to him. The gingerbread man steadied himself by holding onto the rim of my ear.

Spindle didn't say anything. Neither did I.

I pulled some stale bread out of my pocket and began tossing bits down to the ducks. I handed Spindle half the loaf. He took the slices wordlessly and put them in his pockets.

Well, so much for that idea. I finished tossing bits down to the ducks and dusted off my hands.

"You doing okay?" I asked.

He shrugged. It was a stupid question. Tibbie was dead. It would never be okay that she was dead. My parents had been dead for years now, ever since the Cold Fever, and it still wasn't okay and it would never be okay, but I guess that's just how it goes.

These are heavy things for a fourteen-year-old baker to have to think.

We sat there in silence while the ducks nosed around the water for any bits they had missed. A cart rolled by behind us with a crunch of wheels and clop of hooves. The gingerbread man peered out from under my hair.

Spindle glanced over at me, looked at the cookie, but didn't comment.

"We haven't heard anything back about the investigation yet," I said finally. "Truth is... I don't know if there even *is* an investigation. They wanted me to be guilty, and when I wasn't... I don't know if anybody's doing anything."

"Nobody ever does anything," said Spindle quietly. "Not for people like us."

I wanted to say something encouraging. I wanted to promise him that the guards would find the killer. I wanted to be strong and hopeful and determined.

It was hard to believe any of that when I thought about Tibbie and her mismatched socks.

"I'm sorry," I said instead, and flicked a pebble into the dark water of the canal. A duck grabbed for it, saw that it wasn't edible and let out a loud quack of annoyance.

"She had to cut 'er hair real short one winter," said Spindle. He wasn't looking at me, and I was afraid to say anything, for fear that he'd stop. "Tibbie, I mean. She couldn't sneak if there was too much light. Lamplighter came around the corner with a lantern just when she was comin' out the second-story window, and there was a constable on the corner, and he got a look at 'er. They went looking for a girl with real long hair, so she had to cut it. I lifted like a dozen hats for 'er, and she wore 'em, but she was never happy 'til she grew it back out again."

He wiped his nose on the collar of his shirt. "I told 'er to be careful," he said, watching the ducks squabble in the water below. "I told 'er. We been hearing about the magickers, you know, how they're turning up dead. Somebody got Willy Thumbs last week, and he wasn't half the magicker she was. She said she'd be careful, but it didn't matter."

He didn't say anything else. I couldn't think of anything to say. I didn't know any of these people, and yet, after hearing Lena talk about leaving the city...

After a while I got up and dusted myself off. "If you need anything..."

Spindle looked up at me with dark eyes. His face was pale and smudged, like an unwashed ghost.

"Be careful," he said.

ELEVEN

Four in the morning again. I woke up to the water-clock chiming and pulled the blankets up to my chin.

A minute or two later, the big bells tolled the hour, a distant sound that you might not hear if you weren't awake and listening for it. I got up.

The gingerbread man sitting sentry on my bedpost gave me a small salute as I stood up. I bundled myself into my clothes, let the gingerbread man climb to his usual perch on my shoulder, and let myself out of the building.

The streets were quiet. They often weren't quiet at midnight, but they were quiet now. Everyone walking at this hour had somewhere to be, and they walked rapidly, with their heads down and their breath frosting in the air. The same way I walked, except most of them didn't have an animate cookie riding on their coat.

I got to the bakery and unlocked the door. The day-olds were gone from the step again. I started up the ovens and was crouched down, reaching under the counter to get the dough that had been left to rise overnight, when the door opened behind me. The noise was so unexpected that I jumped and banged my head on the underside of the table. I staggered back a step, rubbing the top of my skull, and I suspect that saved my life.

The knife that had been about to go into my ribs whooshed through the air instead.

I stared at the blade stupidly, and then the hand holding it, which was coming out of a pale yellow-green sleeve, and my eyes traveled up the sleeve to the shoulder and the face, and I looked into the eyes of the Spring Green Man.

His eyes were almost the same color as his clothes, an unnaturally light green, the pupils dilated in a pale, seamed face. There was a weird smell coming off him too, something heavy and spicy, like incense. It made it hard to breathe and harder to think.

"Ex-excuse me...?" I said stupidly, as if I'd caught him manhandling the baguettes or trying to open the bakery case. Not trying to stab me. Trying to stab me probably deserved something other than "excuse me" but my mind didn't seem to be working.

My body, however, was working just fine. My body realized that I was standing in the kitchen with a murderer and before I'd quite worked out what I was supposed to do next, my body took over, spun me around, and sent me at high speed down the stairs into the basement.

It was dark. I hadn't taken a light. It was black as pitch, and even though I walked through this room at least three times a day, suddenly I couldn't remember where anything was. I tripped over a pile of baking pans and knocked them down with a clatter.

The Spring Green Man laughed at me from the top of the stairs.

His voice wasn't deep, it was thin and sharp like his knife. "Do you think you can hide from me in the dark?"

That *was* exactly what I was thinking, although I didn't seem to be doing it well. I tried to disentangle myself from the baking pans and kicked one instead. The clang seemed to go up my entire spine.

My mind seemed to be working again, but it wasn't doing much except gibbering.

Oh god oh god oh god he's got a knife oh god

"I can smell you," said the Spring Green Man, taking a step down the stairs. The boards creaked. "I can smell your magic, little bread wizard."

I got away from the traitorous baking pans and scurried deeper into the basement, hands held out in front of me to feel my way.

"I would have gotten you eventually," said the voice from the stairs. Another step, another creak. "I'll get you *all* eventually. But that little thief brat ran in here and I couldn't drag her back out without a guard seeing and that... moved you up the list, so to speak." Another step.

A list? There was a list? How many people were on the list?

I found the edge of the big drying rack where we keep the onions and garlic and felt my way around the end. The scent of garlic helped clear the weirdly heavy smell of incense out of my lungs. Unfortunately, being more clear-headed only meant that I was more clear on being in a basement with a murderer standing in the only doorway.

"You should feel privileged. You aren't nearly powerful enough to warrant being eliminated so soon."

Another step down. *Creak*. How many steps were there? Gods and saints, I spent most of my life going up and down those stairs, how did I not know how many stairs there were?

"If that idiot Oberon had taken care of you like he was supposed to, I probably wouldn't be bothering with you at all. You're almost nothing." *Creak. Creak.* "But no, he makes a mess and *I* have to clean it up..." *Creak.*

Oberon?

Inquisitor Oberon?

I sure hadn't liked him, but what did he have to do with the Spring Green Man?

Creak.

I had an idea. It wasn't a good idea, and it was probably going to get me killed, but the only other idea I had was to wait until he was fully in the cellar, and try to sneak past him, and that wasn't much better. I slid along the wall, hopefully far enough, and crouched down. I felt around me, hoping I'd been right, hoping I'd got far enough back—

There!

Creak. "You can't hide, little bread wizard. I don't need light to find you."

Then he giggled.

I'll be honest with you, I wet myself a little when he giggled. That was a sound that signaled not just a murderer, like some of the thugs in the Rat's Nest, but someone who enjoyed killing people. That giggle went straight into the pit of my stomach and played the xylophone on my ribcage. It was completely dark, but there were bright slashes behind my eyes, and my heart wasn't so much pounding as *drumming*, like a woodpecker on a drainpipe.

I think I came close to fainting, and if I had, there wouldn't be much more to read than this. But I didn't. Instead, I wet myself, which was getting off lightly. I wasn't even embarrassed. If there's a killer coming after you with a knife, embarrassment doesn't even register.

There wasn't another creak. Instead, I heard the scuffing of footsteps over stone. He was at the bottom of the stairs and moving into the cellar.

I put one hand over my mouth, because my own breathing sounded incredibly loud, and hunched myself into the smallest ball I could. I had one weapon, and only one chance to use it.

The gingerbread man gripped the edge of my ear and shifted slightly on my shoulder.

"You're over there in the corner," crooned the Spring Green Man, walking slowly toward me. "I can smell it. Little fool, how did *you* manage to outwit Oberon?"

Please, I thought, a desperate and incoherent prayer. For some reason, the only person I could think of to pray to was the statue on the front of the church I had passed walking home from the palace, Our Lady of Sorrowful Angels. I didn't want to be an angel, sorrowful or otherwise. *Please, oh please...*

The footsteps were right on top of me. I held my breath and clenched my fingers.

"Got you!" crowed the Spring Green Man, as he took a last step forward, and I flung the bucket with Bob the sourdough starter over him.

The man screamed. It was shock at first, and then it was pain, because Bob was *mad*. I'd pumped as much of my panic and terror into the dough as I could.

Attack is not a command I've ever given to bread before, but if those rats last winter were any indication, Bob knew exactly what to do.

The Spring Green Man screamed again, and I heard flailing and a crash as he staggered into something. There were globs of sourdough on my clothes. I didn't wait around to see what had happened. I took off for the steps, somehow avoided the baking pans, and shot up the stairs like a rabbit.

"Mona! This way!" hissed a voice from the door.

"Spindle!"

"Come on!" He beckoned furiously. "The Spring Green Man is after you! He came in here!"

"I know!" I raced to the door. "And I think he might be working with Oberon! We have to get Aunt Tabitha—"

"Do you want him to kill *her* too?"

It was like being slapped. I sucked in a lungful of frosty air so hard it hurt.

"But—"

"Come on! There's no *time!*"

He turned and ran. I wavered for a second, no more, heard the basement stairs creaking, and took off after him.

We pounded through the streets, skidding on the frost-slicked cobbles. I kept my eyes fixed on the back of Spindle's jacket. I didn't dare look around. If I looked around, I might lose him—Spindle took a route as twisty as a baked pretzel—but more importantly, I might look behind me and see the face of my pursuer.

It was probably stupid of me, in a morning full of stupidities, but I kept worrying about whether Bob had survived. On the run for my life and fretting over a sourdough starter. It could only happen to me. I realize that a lot of people wouldn't even consider Bob to be alive, as such, but I'd grown attached to that blob.

We ran for at least three blocks, and I couldn't keep it up. "Slow—down—wait—please—" There was a stitch in my side so painful I wondered if I hadn't been stabbed after all.

Spindle twisted his head around, looking annoyed. "What? Already?"

"Please!"

He slowed to a fast walk. "Gonna get us killed..."

I shook my head, clutching at my side. Did it matter if we ran? The Spring Green Man had said he could smell my magic. Did that mean he could track me like some kind of evil bloodhound?

I managed to glance around this time, before we plunged into yet another alleyway. We were off Rat's Elbow and going in deeper. I didn't even protest. While somebody in there might *decide* to kill me, somebody out here had already *tried*.

It *was* scary in the Rat's Nest, though. The buildings weren't just run-down, they were falling apart. Some of them were burned out, and some of them had collapsed completely. Even the ones that were just piles of rubble showed signs of life, though. There was a clothesline running from a hole in a pile of rock to a pillar. Somebody was actually living in the rubble.

There was a dead dog in the middle of the street. It was only barely light enough to see it, and I might have missed it, but Spindle detoured around it. It had been a big dog.

It was too much, in a morning that had already been too much. I threw up.

After a couple of seconds, I felt somebody pull my hair back. When I looked up, shaky and sweating, it was Spindle.

"Th-thanks..." I mumbled, wiping at my mouth. He shrugged.

I felt a little better. Not much. I felt cold, mostly—I hadn't grabbed my jacket on the way out of the bakery, and the wet patch on my pants was *freezing*.

People weren't staring at me here the way they had in the Rat's Elbow. There weren't many people out, but there was a little cluster at the mouth of every alley, and when I looked up, there were people crouched on the edges of the buildings, too.

They were watching the street. Not just us, although we were the biggest and most obvious things on the street at the moment, particularly given the vomiting, but they were watching everything. I realized that they were guards of some sort.

No, not guards. They were *sentries*. These were people who were watching to see what was coming into the Rat's Nest, and if they saw anything, they would go and alert *more* people. Given where we were, I did not want to know what those other people would look like, or what kind of weapons they might be carrying.

"Where are we going?" I asked, trying to keep up with Spindle.

He had slowed to a brisk walk. "Away. Nobody comes in here who doesn't belong here."

I didn't belong in here, but it didn't seem like the right time to say so.

Fortunately, somebody else said it for me.

"Mona? Spindle? What're you doin' in here?"

The voice was familiar, as was the *clunk-clunk-clunk* on the stones. I looked up gratefully into the dead face of Nag, and the bird's-nest tangle of Knackering Molly.

"This is no place for you, girl—or you either, Spindle, even if you think you're tough."

Spindle jerked his head and rolled his eyes. I put a hand on Nag's shoulder and tried to think of something to say, and couldn't come up with anything for a minute.

"I—I—"

Molly tilted her head and looked down at me. "Girl? You okay?"

"Somebody just tried to kill me," I whispered, feeling tears squeeze out of the sides of my eyes. A single painful sob escaped, and I stuffed the side of my hand into my mouth, because the Rat's Nest did not seem like a good place to cry at all.

Molly's mad eyes softened. She rooted around in the nest on Nag's back and dropped a blanket across my shoulders. It was old and tattered and didn't smell very good, but neither did I right at the moment. And it was warm, which was the important thing.

"Come on," she said. "Grab onto Nag's tail, and let's get you someplace a little safer, and you can tell Molly all about it."

She nudged Nag forward. The skeletal tail twitched in front of me, bones wrapped in old ribbons, with bits of stiff horsehair sticking out around the edges. Not the most appealing handhold, but I grabbed on. It felt like holding a bag full of twigs.

The gingerbread man climbed right up Nag's tail and sat on one of the horse's hip bones. He kicked his heels as if to say, "Giddyup!"

Spindle muttered something under his breath, but he followed behind us anyway. We let the dead horse lead us into the twists and turns of the alleys of the Rat's Nest.

TWELVE

Knackering Molly listened to my whole story, and she didn't ask any embarrassing questions, like why I thought attacking somebody with a sourdough starter would work, or why I started crying when I talked about Bob. What if he was *dead?* Really dead this time? What if he'd died saving me?

I mean, you may think it's strange crying over a bucket of yeasty sludge—I know Spindle probably thought I was crazy—but it wasn't just any sludge, it was *Bob.* He made amazing bread, and he liked me, insomuch as sludge likes anybody.

Molly understood, though. When you spend most of your time with a dead horse, you learn to respect other people's weird pets.

By the time I'd gotten to the end of the story my nose was dripping. Molly dug a handkerchief out of her pocket and handed it to me. It was dry. Bits of it were unpleasantly crunchy, but I couldn't afford to be picky.

"Thags," I mumbled, blowing my nose. "Sorry."

"It's all right, girl, you've had a shock and no mistake."

Spindle snorted. He was leaning in a corner with his hands shoved into his pockets and a sour expression. I could tell he thought I was being a baby. That made me pretty mad. I'd bet nobody had tried to stab *him* today. I wiped my eyes and sniffed furiously.

We were at Knackering Molly's home, or at least one of her homes. She called it a squat, which sounded vaguely rude. It was half a house on the edge of the Rat's Nest that had fallen over, so one side looked almost normal and the other side was a crazy-quilt of collapsed beams. There were old crates and ragged bits of rug on the floor, and she'd hung burlap sacks over the windows to block them out.

It probably wasn't very structurally sound, but since there was a whole horse skeleton stomping around the room and the rest of the ceiling hadn't fallen in yet, I decided not to worry about it.

I had much bigger things to worry about, like what to do next and how not to be murdered.

"Okay. Okay." I took a deep breath and scrubbed at my face. I didn't want to cry any more. Crying wouldn't help. "What do we do now? We should find the constables or somebody, right?"

Spindle made a rude sound. "Fat lot of help they'll be. Wouldn't be surprised if they sent him after you."

"Oh, come on!" I rolled my eyes. "You're telling me you think the constables are conspiring to set assassins on bakers?"

That Inquisitor Oberon was a bad apple was obvious. The Spring Green Man had said as much. But thinking that people like Constable Alphonse and Constable Montgomery were in league with Inquisitors and assassins was ridiculous. They were people. They ate pastries. Alphonse's sister lived on the next street over and came in every market-day to buy a scone. They didn't even make signs to ward off bad luck when they thought I wasn't looking.

"Somebody did it," said Spindle stubbornly, dropping his chin onto his chest and glaring at me. "Guards never care about people like us, as long as we don't make trouble. They're trying to wipe magickers out now so *you* don't make trouble. They started with Tibbie, and now they're goin' for you."

I appealed to Knackering Molly. "Molly, this is nuts. You don't think the constables are behind this, do you?"

"Not the constables, no..." said Molly slowly. "They're following orders is all. Somebody's giving those orders, though. I was hearing rumors about the Spring Green Man on the street before you ever turned up in the Rat's Elbow, girl. I need to ask some questions, maybe call in a few favors..." She stood up. "You kids stay here awhile. Not sure how long I'll be gone."

"Wh-what? You're leaving?"

She swung herself up on Nag, who clomped across the creaky floorboards and out the door. Spindle hurried to yank the burlap curtain aside. "Got questions to ask, baker girl!" she shot over her shoulder—and was gone.

The *clunk-clunk-clunk* of Nag's hooves faded into the darkness. It was almost morning, and I could just see the edge of light over the tops of the houses, but it hadn't gotten down to street level yet.

She'd left. Just like that. I mean, sure, she was a little nuts—okay, she rode a dead horse, she was a *lot* nuts—but she was a grown-up and it seemed like she knew what she was doing. I certainly trusted her judgment a lot more than I trusted Spindle's. And if you were a grown-up, you didn't just leave two kids alone in a house with a madman on the prowl trying to kill them, did you?

Apparently, Molly did.

I probably would have stood in the doorway with my mouth hanging open for the next five minutes, but Spindle dropped the sacking back down and I had to step back.

I couldn't help it. I started sniffling again.

It wasn't real crying, I wasn't sobbing or anything, but there were some tears and my chest ached the way it does when you know that a good hard sob is just waiting to get out. I wouldn't let it out. Not with Spindle standing there, looking at me like I was pathetic.

I didn't see what he had to be so smug about. He'd cried after we found Tibbie's bracelet, and I hadn't been mean to him about it or anything.

He let out an annoyed sigh and flopped down in the corner of the room.

This struck me as horribly unfair. Sure, he saved my life and now he was stuck in this shack with me, instead of out doing... whatever he did... but what did he have to be annoyed about? Nobody was trying to kill *him*.

"Sorry this is bothering you," I snapped. "I wouldn't have gotten attacked if I'd known it would be so *inconvenient* for you."

He flushed and mumbled something. I sat down, because there wasn't anything else to do, and we sat in the room in an irritable crackling silence.

I wondered how long it would take Knackering Molly to find out what she wanted to know, or whether the Spring Green Man would find us first.

It was definitely getting light out. The edges of the burlap sacking over the windows went from black to grey to a kind of watery tan. Aunt Tabitha would be getting up soon, and she'd wonder where I was. And the bakery was a mess, and Bob was scattered all over the cellar. She'd probably be worried sick.

She might not even be able to make cinnamon rolls and sticky buns and gingerbread cookies and set the bread out...

My stomach growled.

You wouldn't think that you could be hungry after someone tried to kill you. You'd be wrong.

"I still got that bread you gave me yesterday," said Spindle.

It was probably a peace offering, but I wasn't in the mood to accept it, and anyway, I'd have to magic it a lot softer before I could gnaw through bread that stale. I just didn't have the energy now. "No thanks."

"It's all I got," said Spindle. "Unless you wanna eat that cookie riding around on your shoulder, it's all we're gonna get."

"No!" I put a hand over the gingerbread man protectively. "Nobody eats him! And anyway, he's really stale." The cookie tweaked my ear indignantly at that.

"Might change your mind soon," said Spindle, smirking. "You don't get to be so picky when you're on the lam."

The cookie made a rude gesture at him. My stomach growled again for emphasis.

"I'm *not* on the lam," I said. My chest felt hot and tight, as if the tears had got squeezed until they cracked open. I was angry, nearly as angry as I had been at Inquisitor Oberon. I felt like *I* might split open, right down the middle of my sternum. "*I* haven't done anything wrong! Having somebody try to kill you doesn't make you a criminal!"

Spindle snorted. "Sure. Take that to the constables and see how far you get."

It was the last straw.

"Maybe I will!" I scrambled to my feet. The gingerbread man shifted hastily to hang on.

"What? Mona, no!"

"I *will* go to the constables! You're just paranoid and think 'cos you're a street rat, everybody's like you!" Which wasn't fair and I felt guilty immediately, but the angry squeezing in my chest wouldn't let me stop. I stomped to the burlap curtain and wrenched it aside.

Spindle balled his hands into fists. "Knackering Molly told us to stay here!"

"And then she left us alone! With no food and no explanations, nothing!" I did feel a little guilty about leaving, but mostly I just felt mad. Why shouldn't I go to the constables? I'd never committed a crime in my life, not unless you count filching cookies from the case, and I'd baked those cookies in the first place, so that didn't really count. It was no wonder people like Spindle and Knackering Molly were paranoid, but I was a respectable citizen. The constables were there to protect *me*.

I stalked into the street.

"Mona, don't be stupid!" Spindle tried to get in front of me, but I shouldered past him. "You're gonna be in big trouble!"

We were on the edge of the Rat's Nest. I should have been scared, but the anger was still doing all the talking. If I'd been thinking clearly, I probably would have tried to find the safest way out, but instead I just picked the direction I thought was right and plowed forward, ignoring the scampering of sentries and the puzzled faces watching me.

"Mona!"

The alleyway took a couple of zig-zag turns—if I'd had the

sense to be scared, I wouldn't have made at least two of those, which were prime ambush spots, and probably only the fact that I so clearly had nothing worth stealing kept me from getting mugged right there—then spilled out onto Varley Street. I stomped onto the sidewalk. Spindle halted at the mouth of the alley and made a grab for the back of my jacket but missed.

Varley is a broad avenue running along the canal. It's usually full of street musicians, because the sidewalks are wider than usual, but it was still so early that hardly anybody was about yet. I could hear someone tuning their fiddle a little way away, a few cautious notes, then a halt, then a few more random notes, splattered like drops of rain against the stones.

But I wasn't looking for a street musician. I was looking for a constable, and there one was, leaning against a lamp post across the street, about half a block up the road.

I broke into a run.

"Here now, what's the trouble?" asked the constable, startled, as I raced up to him.

"You have to help me!" I was panting. He wasn't one of the men who patrolled our neighborhood, but he was wearing the uniform, and he had a broad, kind face. "Please!"

"Of course I will, m'dear," he said promptly. "What's wrong?"

"Somebody tried to kill me!" I waved my hands. "It was the Spring Green Man—he was wearing green—I was in the bakery and he had a knife—"

"Tried to *kill* you?" His eyebrows rose sharply. "Spring Green... mercy me!" He put an arm around my shoulders. "Here now, it's all right, m'dear. I'm sure there's been some sort of misunderstanding. Just come with me and we'll get this all sorted out."

I felt the knot in my stomach loosen. This was exactly what I wanted. Some responsible grown-up to get it all sorted out, so I could go back to my normal life and make cinnamon rolls.

"It'll be fine now, Mona," said the constable. "Never you worry."

He turned, still with the arm around my shoulders, so I had to turn with him. He cupped his free hand to his mouth. "Hallooo!" he called, and down the road, a few blocks over, another constable answered "Hallooo!"

How had he known my name?

He was holding me awfully tightly, and I squirmed a bit, but his grip didn't loosen, and I felt cold suddenly, very cold, because I was pretty sure that I hadn't told him my name at all.

I squirmed harder and tried to pull away, and he grabbed my wrist in one hand. It wasn't too painful, I really don't think he was trying to hurt me, but he wasn't letting go, either. "Hold still, m'dear," he said, trying to sound stern and reassuring all at once. "We've got orders to bring you in if you turn up. Somebody wants to talk to you, that's all."

"Let go! I haven't done anything wrong!"

"Then you've got nothing to be afraid of," said the constable. "Stop that, girl, I'm not going to hurt you."

"Then let *go!*"

I kicked him in the shins. He grunted. "Now don't be like—"

He never finished saying what I wasn't supposed to be like, as two things happened simultaneously. Spindle slammed into the back of the constable's knees, and the gingerbread man launched himself off my shoulder and went for his eyes.

He fell down with a wild yelp, batting the enraged cookie aside. Spindle rolled out from under the man's legs and scrambled to his feet. I snatched my tiny gingerbread protector from the cobbles—the fall had knocked one of his icing buttons loose, but he was otherwise unharmed—and turned to run.

There was another constable hurrying toward us from down the street. He'd gotten close enough to see that something was happening. I turned the other way and Spindle grabbed my elbow and yelled "This way!"

We raced up Varley Street and across a footbridge. We had barely reached the far end when I heard footsteps pounding on it.

I looked back. There were *three* guards chasing us now.

"You were right," I moaned, as we ducked into an alley and ran down it, jumping over old boxes and broken crates. Rats scampered out of our way, chittering angrily. "Spindle, you were right!"

"Told—you—so—" he panted. "Probably—all got—orders—last night—"

There was a constable at the end of the alley. He said "Here, now—!" but Spindle went right and I went left and he missed both of us. I flung myself through a gap in a courtyard fence that was too narrow for a grown-up—it was almost too narrow for me—and Spindle was right behind me, while the constable growled and rattled at the gate.

"Over the back wall," said Spindle. "Hurry!"

Punching dough for hours a day gives you pretty strong arms, but it still wasn't easy to get over the wall. Spindle had to actually get under me and shove my legs upwards. It would have been embarrassing, but when you're running for your life, you tend not to worry about these things.

The road we came out on was clear, but I could hear, "Halloo!" and, "They went this way!" echoing down the streets.

They were between us and the Rat's Nest. I could tell Spindle wasn't sure where to go next, and my heart was hammering against my rib cage until I thought it might explode.

We skidded through an intersection, past the fiddle player, whose instrument let out a very unmusical squawk as we tore past her.

"I see them!"

"There!"

If only there had been more people about, we might have lost ourselves in the crowd. If it had been darker, we might have been able to hide.

If I wasn't a stubborn, hard-headed idiot, we wouldn't be in this mess in the first place.

Another bridge loomed out of the early-morning gloom.

"Down!" hissed Spindle, and wrenched me sideways. There was a water-stair there, a set of steps cut into the concrete, leading down into the canal. The water-stairs lead to tunnels where the sewer-workers can get into the drains, presumably to clear out rats and zombie crayfish and to make sure the sewers aren't going to collapse under us.

I know Spindle was thinking that maybe we could get into the drains and lose the constables that way. And it was a good plan, a really clever plan... except for the enormous locked grate under the bridge.

Spindle rattled the bars futilely. The padlock had a latch as thick around as my thumb. There was no way we were breaking through it.

"Can you pick that?"

"Sure, if I've got time—"

"Hallooo!" sounded directly over our heads.

"They're on the bridge," I whispered.

"They'll be down here in a minute," Spindle whispered back. "Can you swim?"

Urrrgh.

You don't swim in the canals. Not unless you're a duck, and even the ducks probably don't enjoy it much. Whenever it rains, the sewers overflow directly into the canal—at high summer, the city stinks in ways that even poets can't describe—and that's not even including the stuff that people dump in there as a matter of course. We get our water from wells, not from the canals. We don't even dig the wells anywhere *near* the canals. You jump in the canal if you're trying to kill yourself, not if you want to go for a swim.

"No," I said. "Can you?"

"Not really."

"Did you see them?" asked a constable at the far end of the bridge. "They didn't come by me."

"Can you magic us out, then?" asked Spindle, rolling his eyes wildly at the sound of the voices.

"Bread! I work with bread! *Only* bread!"

Spindle slapped his pockets and came up with the half-loaf I'd given him yesterday. "Okay, now what?"

He looked so expectant that I didn't know whether to cry or hit him. "Now *nothing!* I can't do anything—I mean, maybe if you could get them to *eat* it—" I had a sudden absurd image of Spindle throwing bits of bread to the constables and the men quacking like ducks as they fought for the floating scraps. I could feel hysterical laughter welling up in my throat and crushed it.

I'll have plenty of time to go mad with terror after *they've caught me.*

And then that stupid image of the constables in the water

and the scraps of floating bread caught me, and I didn't feel the urge to laugh any more.

Floating bread.

Floating bread.

"Give me the bread," I said.

"Check the water-stair," called one of the constables. "They might have gone to ground."

Half a loaf. Not sliced. Well, that was easy enough...

I held the stale bread in both hands and suggested that maybe it was tired of being in one piece. It resisted for only a moment, then fell apart in exactly even slices.

It took me a week last autumn to learn how to make bread slice itself. I made a lot of ragged stumps at first, and it's a good thing Aunt Tabitha believed in me, because we had to put about fifty mangled loaves on the discount pile and make a whole lot more into bread pudding before I got the hang of it. I still tend to leave pretty thick end pieces, but I'm a lot faster than using a knife.

I made five good-sized slices, and we'd probably only need four, so nobody would be stuck with the heel. And they were stale already, and as I held them, I told them to get even staler, to get so hard that they were practically stone. This bread wouldn't dissolve in water. This bread *hated* water. Water was the enemy.

Float, I ordered the bread. *No matter how heavy you get, float.*

There was a clatter as one of the constables started down the water-stair.

"Here," I told Spindle, handing him two of the slices. "I don't know how we'll stay on them, but it's the best we've got."

The constable peered into the gloom and cried "Hey! You there!"

"Come on!" I set the bread into the murky green water, took a deep breath, and stepped out onto it, one foot on each slice.

We were much too heavy, of course. It's impossible to float on bread, which is why magic had to get involved. *Hold us up,* I ordered the bread. *Don't sink.*

If you have ever tried to stay afloat on a pair of magic bread slices, then you know what it was like. Otherwise, all I can say is that I don't recommend it. The slices were from one of our big sourdough rounds, so they were a pretty good size, but my feet still stuck out a little over the crust.

Staying balanced was nearly impossible. It was like trying to walk on moving ice. One foot went one way and the other foot went the other way and I nearly went down into the sludge. Then I overcompensated and nearly went down the other way as my left foot shot out from under me.

Spindle caught on quicker than I did. He had both slices in the water and a foot on each slice before I'd managed to get my balance back.

The constable stared at me. He could probably have reached out and grabbed me, but he was too flabbergasted. His mouth hung open and his eyebrows were so high they'd vanished under his hair. You'd think he'd never seen anybody ride bread before.

The gingerbread man put his hands to either side of his head and made faces at the constable, as best you can when you don't have a tongue to stick out.

There is a river somewhere that flows into the city, breaking into all the canals, and that river flows eventually into the sea, which means that there is a vague current. It carried us away, not too swiftly, while Spindle and I flailed and rocked and tried not to fall in, and the constable stared after us as if we'd grown wings.

But it worked. That was the thought that kept going through my mind—*it's working, it's working, sweet Lady of Sorrowful Angels, it's working!* The bread was stale enough and my magic was strong enough. We floated on the surface of the water, and even though it splashed over the sides occasionally and soaked our shoes, the bread continued to float.

"Look out!" The current was pushing Spindle into me. I tried to get out of the way, but bread isn't very good at evasive maneuvers. At the last second, I leaned one way and he leaned the other and we passed with an inch or two to spare.

It didn't get any easier to ride, but we did get a little better at it. The best way was to crouch down with your knees close together, so that you didn't slide too far to either side and risk having your feet go out from under you. There were pilings in the water that were harder to navigate around, but you could grab onto them to steady yourself, so they were actually more help than harm. I think the bread caught on to what we were doing and tried to steady us, too. (I'm not saying bread is intelligent, mind you, but magic is.)

At one point, an eddy caught one of my slices, and it was either turn around with it or fall off completely, so I turned. A line of constables was just visible on the bridge, all staring after us with identical expressions of stunned dismay. One broke away and started running down the road, trying to keep pace with us, but the road turned and we floated between a row of houses that came right up to the canal's edge. The gingerbread man on my shoulder waved to our pursuer as we drifted out of sight.

"We're getting away!" Spindle cried. "We're really getting away! On bread!"

"We are!" I said. "But we should find someplace to get off soon—I don't know how long I can keep magicking this bread from getting soggy, and I don't want them to get any bright ideas about nets."

Spindle nodded. "Or crossbows," he said grimly.

Crossbows? They wouldn't shoot us, would they? I mean, we weren't... we hadn't...

Somebody wants to talk to you, the constable had said.

What if that somebody was Inquisitor Oberon?

What if nothing—*who else could it be?*

There was a grate ahead, where the canal ran under street level. The grates were wide enough for two kids to pass through, although I had a bad moment when each of my slices went on a different side of a bar and I had to grab the bar and swing awkwardly around it to keep from falling over.

The ceiling on the other side was low and furred with moss. I could hear dripping sounds from all directions. Spindle and I crouched over our bread and let the canal carry us down the tunnel of dark water.

THIRTEEN

"I'm sorry I called you a street rat," I said, flicking a pebble into the murky water.

"S'okay," said Spindle, hunching up inside his jacket. "You're not used to this sorta thing."

We were sitting inside the sewers, or at least some tunnels that had probably originally been dug as sewers. Now they were much larger, as generations of smugglers running goods up the river had used them as a landing point and illicit entry to the city. We'd nearly wound up in the river ourselves before our sliced-bread floats gave out completely. But there had been a tiny little beach—if you can call it a beach when the sand is mostly covered in bits of packing crates and stubbed out cigar-butts—and we'd abandoned our bread and waded up onto it.

It stank. I want to be absolutely clear on that. It could have been a lot worse—the river carried a lot of it away—but it still stank. Outhouse-at-high-noon kinda stink with wet green mucky stink mixed in and a faint patina of dead-thing-rotting stink on top. After wading in it, Spindle and I stank too.

The gingerbread man made a show of holding his nose.

"Quiet, you," I muttered. "I don't think you've even got a sense of smell."

He waved a hand in front of his face exaggeratedly, but even that wasn't enough to cheer me up.

I'm going to catch some kind of horrible disease. It'll kill me before the Spring Green Man gets the chance.

"Anyway," Spindle said, unrolling his sleeves so the grubby cuffs dangled over his fingers, "you got dropped into this sudden-like, you weren't born on the streets, like me." He jerked a thumb at his chest and sat up a little straighter. "So I guess it's not your fault you're a bit bacon-brained."

After this magnanimous speech, I didn't feel like arguing, although... *bacon-brained? Really?*

Actually, I would have killed for some bacon. Even the horrible stink wasn't enough to make me forget that I was really hungry.

I hoped I was the only hungry thing down here. If there were undead crawfish remaining anywhere in the city, it was probably somewhere nearby. I listened for the clicking of terrible tiny claws but didn't hear anything.

"So now what do we do?" asked Spindle.

"I have no idea." Truth be told, I had been hoping he'd have an idea. "Can we get back to Knackering Molly's?"

Spindle thought about it. "Maybe. Well, I can, probably. But you shouldn't be going out until it's dark. If the constables get sight of you, I dunno if we can give them the slip twice."

My stomach growled again. Spindle's growled in response. We both snickered.

"We gotta get some food," I said. "Or else I'll die down here, and I don't want to give the Inquisitor the satisfaction."

Spindle bounced to his feet. "Well... here's what I'm thinkin'. If we follow the smuggler's tunnels, we'll get to wherever they go to deliver their stuff, and I bet you anything it's a tavern."

"A tavern? Why a tavern?" I stood up and dusted myself off. The gingerbread man steadied himself on my earlobe and went back to picking bits of waterweed out of my hair.

Spindle gave me a superior look. "Because they smuggle booze. Don't you pay attention? They bring it up the coast and sell it to taverns."

"What, illegally? Really?" I tried to imagine smugglers selling rum to the tavern down the street from the bakery. The innkeeper had really bad dandruff and his shoulders looked like a powdered-sugar donut, but he was always very nice to me, so I tried not to look at his shoulders when I talked to him. I had to run down and arrange the order of dark ale for the beer bread, and once Aunt Tabitha had gotten a big order in for rum cakes and had to order a... half-keg... of... rum...

I put a hand over my mouth. The innkeeper had been breaking the law this whole time? Did Aunt Tabitha know about this?

Spindle laughed at me, but not unkindly. "C'mon, then." He started up the tunnel and I followed.

Sure enough, the tunnels came out at a tavern. Well, they probably came out at all kinds of places, but the one we followed, based on a few chalk arrows and squiggles that Spindle claimed were "thief-sign," came out in the alley behind a very seedy establishment called The Hanging Goat.

"Wait here," said Spindle, leaving me in the alley, and ducked through the open door into the back of the tavern's kitchen. The smells coming out weren't promising, but since the smell coming off me was truly apocalyptic, who was I to judge?

I hunkered down in the alley and fidgeted. I could see people walking past the mouth of the alley. They looked very normal. Nobody was trying to kill them. I'd been like that once. It seemed like a very long time ago.

A guard in a blue uniform went by the alley mouth, and I scrambled back farther into the piled trash. He didn't even glance down the alley. The gingerbread man patted my ear comfortingly.

Spindle re-emerged, clutching a lump of something wrapped in rags, and grabbed my arm. "C'mon! She'll notice they're gone in a minute! We gotta scarper!"

So, we scarpered, which apparently meant "run away very fast."

Two blocks over we stopped, climbed a metal staircase in yet another alley, and Spindle unwrapped his prize—a pair of meat pies. They were still burning hot and somewhat squashed.

"Nicked 'em off the cooling rack," said Spindle proudly, juggling his from hand to hand. "'Ere, be careful! You'll roast yourself!"

"Gmmrmgfff," I said. The filling was still boiling hot and scalded the roof of my mouth and the crust was deeply inferior compared to one of mine. The cook was letting the butter get too warm when she made it. The meat was probably horse.

It was *wonderful*.

"Thanks," I told Spindle, who was eating his rather more slowly. "You just saved my life. I was going to starve to death right here."

He rolled his eyes.

"So," I said, when he'd finished licking the crumbs off his fingers, "now where do we go? Back to Knackering Molly?"

"Best I can think of," he admitted. "But first we're stealing some clothes outta the poor box on Hanover Street."

I didn't much like the idea of stealing clothes out of the poor box, but desperate times called for desperate measures. "Do we need a disguise?"

"Disguise nuthin'," said Spindle, climbing down the staircase. He stopped at the bottom and looked up, wrinkling his nose. "We need clean clothes and a dip in a cistern. We *stink*."

FOURTEEN

Five days later, I sat in a church belltower, building a circus out of bread.

Knackering Molly had been hard to find. When Spindle finally tracked her down, I'd spent half the night hiding in back alleys and under bridges, shivering inside stolen clothes that were two sizes too big for me.

Molly didn't apologize for having left us for so long, or yell at us for leaving. I'm not entirely sure if she realized that she was a grown-up and we were kids, or if she knew and it just didn't matter to her in the slightest. Maybe that sort of thing didn't apply any more. If grown-ups were trying to kill you, did that make you an honorary grown-up? If so, I would have preferred to just grow up and get my period like a normal person.

"Got a theory," Molly said, when we had finished explaining our narrow escape. "Been talking to some people who saw the Spring Green Man workin', like you did, girl. I think he's magic too, but his talent's something to do with air and smells. Maybe not so good for killin' people, but good for sniffing out other magic. And he's got the knife for the killin' bit."

I remembered that strange, heavy smell around him, and how my brain felt foggy when I smelled it. "But why would he want to kill us?" I asked, pulling my over-sized coat tight around me.

"Maybe he's crazy," she said, shrugging. ("You'd know," said Spindle, not entirely under his breath.) "More like somebody's paying him. He talked about that Inquisitor fellow, you said, so I'm guessin' you don't need to be lookin' much farther."

"But why would the Inquisitor want to kill wizards?"

Knackering Molly shook her head. A moment later, Nag shook his, and stamped one bony hoof. "The answer to that question won't be found at street level, girl. I asked down in the Rat's Nest and at the Goblin Market, and they know about the Spring Green Man and somebody even saw him—and smelled him—but there ain't no telling what's behind him."

"What about Knucklebones?" asked Spindle. "Knucklebones knows all kind of stuff from up high. Used to be a lady's maid, she always says."

"Knucklebones is headed out of town on the first horse she can steal," said Molly. "Her kid's got a magicker daddy, and even if it don't normally breed true, she's runnin'. And Mona here's the only one who's tangled with the Inquisitor." Her lips twisted. "*Politics* is what it is."

Spindle spat on the ground.

"Now what do we do?" I asked gloomily. I didn't see a way of defeating politics with bread.

"They're talking about bringing in sniffers to look for you.

Don't think they will, but if they do, that's a lot of money on someone who wants you dead."

"Lot of work, too," said Spindle. "You gotta keep them wet."

"Sniffers are just like bloodhounds," said Molly, rather more cheerfully. "Track you for miles, but there's ways of throwing them off. And they can't get them in any closer than Delta City, so you've got a couple days. Grab hold of Nag's tail."

So we followed Molly again, and she led us to a little church, only a few blocks away from Our Lady of Sorrowful Angels, but not nearly so well-appointed. I hung back nervously (I'd just stolen clothes from a church poor box, I wasn't sure how good my credit was with the divine) but she rode Nag right up into the churchyard and urged Spindle and me toward a small door in the wall.

"The friar's stone deaf," she said, "and the lay brother's a good enough sort. They'll not trouble you, and they'll bring you two square meals a day on the strength of me asking." She frowned. "I don't know that the scent of hallowed ground'll cover over magic. Mayhap it won't. Maybe it's just a superstition, like making a magicker hold iron in court. But it can't hurt. If the Spring Green Man comes for you, girl, run for it. The folks here are priests, not fighters, and there's little enough they can do for you but die tryin'."

I gulped.

"I'll keep an ear to the ground. If I learn anything, I'll be in touch." She swung Nag around and clattered out of the courtyard without saying goodbye.

Spindle looked at me, and I looked at him, and then we went inside the church because we didn't know what else to do.

Well, I suppose I could leave the city—beg Spindle to take

me to the gate and just start walking—but what would I do? What would I eat? Even I can't make bread out of rocks and road dust. Not unless I get a bunch of extra ingredients.

And what about Aunt Tabitha? They said sniffers could find places you'd even thought of being, and that meant they'd be all over the bakery. What if Inquisitor Oberon decided to accuse her of something?

The church was small and very shabby. The pews looked worn, and the altar cloth had been eaten by moths until it was more holes than fabric. The lay brother was as good as Molly's word. He was a tall, craggy-faced man, and he didn't ask questions. He led me to a ladder and pointed up.

"The bell-tower," he said, nodding to himself. "We sold the bells long ago, you understand. The tower cannot be sold. There is little up there that will harm you. I would not go to the top room, where the bells were. There are bats."

After this inspiring speech, he nodded again and left. Spindle and I went up the ladder, and found that the room was almost claustrophobically small, not very warm, and the edges of the entry shaft were splattered with bat droppings.

"Cozy," said Spindle.

I peered out the single slitted window. I could see a number of roofs, and across them, the Church of Sorrowful Angels. "The view's nice." The gingerbread man hopped off my shoulder and stood in the window, gazing out.

And it was defensible, if nothing else: the Spring Green Man had only one way in, and if I kicked the ladder down, not even that.

Of course, that meant that I had only one way out as well.

"You're the one stuck here, not me," said Spindle. He stuck his hands in his pockets. "Can I do anything for you?"

"Tell Aunt Tabitha where I am," I said. "If you can get me paper, and deliver a letter—"

Spindle was shaking his head. "Knackering Molly already told me not to. They've got guards all over town and some of 'em got a look at me when we gave 'em the slip the other day." He frowned. "And you gotta bet that Spring Green Man's sniffing all over 'round there, and if he smells you on *me,* he could maybe track you back here."

I sagged. This was worse than I had thought. Aunt Tabitha had to be worried *sick.*

"Hey," said Spindle, "It's not so bad. It's only 'til they stop looking for you. I'll snitch you some food during the day, though. Place like this, it's nothing but gruel, gruel, and more gruel."

As it happened, he wasn't far wrong. It was gritty porridge for breakfast and half an onion and a slab of dark bread for supper. The onion was tolerable, although it did awful things to my breath. The bread was an affront to the baker's art. It took more energy to make it edible than I got from eating it. After the second day, I stopped even trying to eat it, and began molding it into tiny people and animals, which I tried to set into motion.

Believe it or not, I'd never spent a lot of time really working on my magic. I was always more interested in learning how to bake. Baking is much more rewarding. There are cookbooks to tell you what to do, and at the end you've got chocolate chip cookies to show for it. There aren't any books to teach you how to do magic, or if there are, they aren't available to people like me.

So when I do magic, it's more of an instinctive thing. When the bread is burning, I don't stop and think, "I must magic the bread so it doesn't burn!" I just *do* it reflexively, like when somebody hits a glass of water with their elbow and you grab for it before it goes over. You don't think, "I am going to grab that glass." I wouldn't have known that I could animate gingerbread men if I hadn't done it once already as a little kid, when you don't know stuff is impossible.

The magic I try to do deliberately doesn't work nearly as well, unless I'm panicked, like when I made the getaway-bread float, or brought Bob the sourdough starter to life. There's something about stark terror that really gets magic working.

Unfortunately, being stuck in a bell tower isn't quite the same thing. I was terrified, sure, but it was a boring sort of terror. You can't stay in a state of heart-pounding panic for very long. Your body just can't manage it. So I'd just sit there and stare out the window and think about being out in the city. Then I'd start to think about Aunt Tabitha and how worried she must be and then I'd remember all over again what was happening and I'd be angry and scared and tired. I slept a lot. Sleep was at least time passing that I didn't have to be around for.

Spindle brought me a pack of cards. That was fun for a bit, but I made the mistake of teaching the gingerbread man the rules of solitaire. After that, whenever I'd try to cheat and run through the discard pile an extra time, he'd kick me in the wrist and sit on the cards.

I taught him to play rummy, even though the cards were half as big as he was. He beat me eleven times in a row and then refused to play anymore. I think I bored him.

It was probably a good thing that we didn't have a checkerboard.

There was one good thing. Stuck up there for days with an

increasingly large pile of inedible bread, I finally had time to practice my magic.

I started by smooshing the bread together into balls, and molding little figures out of them, then making them walk around. It sort of worked. They weren't nearly as responsive as the gingerbread men. It felt like the chunks of bread didn't want to come together.

"Maybe I have to bake stuff into a human shape before it believes it's human?" I said to the gingerbread man.

He eyed my shambling bread-crust creature with disapproval and shrugged. He was building a house out of cards, which was a major construction project for someone his size.

My bread creatures also weren't very smart. When I made a couple of them and told them to march around the room, they stopped as soon as they ran into a wall. I sighed and took them apart again.

When Spindle came back that night, I had a request. "Hey, Spindle?"

"Mmmpgh?" His mouth was full. He'd gotten in the habit of eating a meal with me, and I felt almost pathetically grateful for the company. I knew that he didn't have to keep bringing me food, and if he decided to ditch me, it's not like I'd ever find him again. He'd probably be in a lot less danger, too, since he wasn't a magicker and the Spring Green Man might not even care that he existed.

"Can you get me some dough? Stuff that hasn't been cooked yet?"

He wiped his mouth. "It'd be harder than cooked stuff, but sure, I guess."

I was seized with a pang of misgiving. "Don't do it if it's too hard! I don't want you to get caught."

He gave me a disgusted look. "Girl, you're lookin' at the thief who pinched the socks off the feet of the head of the Jeweler's Guild. Too hard. Pfff!"

He was as good as his word. The next morning I heard a rattling on the ladder, and he came up carrying a sack which held an entire mixing bowl of dough (bowl included) and a number of battered onions.

I examined the dough. It was full of papery onion skin and bits of dirt.

"What?" asked Spindle. "You weren't gonna eat it, were you?"

"I guess not. Why onions?"

"Pretended to sell 'em," he said proudly. "Took a basket into the kitchen at the White Horse and offered 'em to the cook. While she was yellin' at somebody, I dumped her bowl into the basket and put onions over top."

"Very impressive. This is perfect, Spindle. Thank you."

I hugged him. He squirmed out and gave me a reproachful look, but his ears turned red, and I'm pretty sure that meant he was pleased.

FIFTEEN

The magic experiments went much better with dough than with bread. The dough was... well... smarter, I guess. More suggestible. The bread that had already been baked had a very clear idea that it was a loaf, it had always been a loaf, it would always be a loaf. The dough was willing to be little people or animals or anything else I wanted it to be.

They were gloppy people and animals, so I couldn't make them very large, and they were awfully sticky—I needed more flour, but I didn't want to keep making demands of Spindle, who was already being so nice. But if you told them to walk around the room, they'd walk around the room. When they hit a wall, they would turn around and walk in another direction. If I took a nap, when I woke up, they'd be in different positions.

One ran into the gingerbread man's card house and got thrown out the window. My cookie had a temper.

I could feel the dough, a little, inside my head. They were so small that I had to really pay attention, but it wasn't like I had anything else to do. It was just a kind of little mental tugging. It didn't do much but it did make me tired after a while, so I was careful to pull the magic out of them at night before I went to sleep.

When I concentrated, I could feel something similar from the gingerbread man, now that I was looking for it. It had been going on for so long, though, that I didn't even notice any more. If you wear really heavy boots in the winter, you stop noticing that they're heavy after a few days, and then when you take them off, your feet feel ridiculously light.

I was staring out the window one afternoon, when a couple of pigeons landed on a drainpipe at the corner of the roof below. One pushed the other off the edge, and it flapped frantically, tumbled a few feet, and then flew laboriously up to the roof.

Hmm...

I looked down at the dough in my hands. I'd made little dough dogs and horses. Could I make a dough bird?

I started to get excited by the thought. If I could make a bird out of dough, could I send it with a message to Aunt Tabitha? It was much too far for even my gingerbread man to walk, but a bird could fly! And bread was lightweight, wasn't it?

I hastily pinched out the shape of wings.

The end result was... gummy. It would undoubtedly have been better if I could bake it, but maybe with enough magic, it wouldn't matter. I held the lumpy bird in both hands and thought *Fly*.

It came alive like the others, flopping its wings. They stretched and drooped under the weight of the dough. This wasn't going to work if it kept being so heavy! Could I convince the dough that it was lighter?

You're light, I told it. *You're as light and flaky as the inside of a croissant. You weigh nothing at all.*

The dough bird flapped wetly. Did it feel lighter? I couldn't tell. Did it need more magic?

I tried to pump more magic into it, through that odd little link in my head. *Light!* I thought frantically. *You weigh nothing. You weigh less than air.*

It didn't exactly feel like pouring magic into the dough, like you'd pour milk into a mixing bowl. It was more like trying to *knead* magic into it, like kneading flour into a very stiff dough. The bird didn't want any more magic in it. It couldn't all fit.

My head was starting to hurt.

Light. Light. You can fly.

The dough strained, and very slowly started to rise into the air.

"Come on..." I said out loud. My vision was throbbing in time with my heartbeat. "Come on, you can do it..."

Slowly, lumpily, with holes opening in its wings, the dough bird flew.

"I did it!" I yelled, not caring if the lay-brother heard me. "I did it, I did... um?"

The bird was beginning to vibrate. It was puffing up to two and three times its original size. It spun around the ceiling, bits of dough flying off its wings and splattering against the stones. My gingerbread man threw himself off the windowsill and grabbed my pantleg, tugging me down.

I tried to grab for the little magical connection in my head. It felt... fizzy. And hot. This is not a nice sensation to have inside your brain.

The bird let out a whistle of escaping steam and exploded.

The room rained dough. I got a gob in the face. It was hot,

nearly scalding. The gingerbread man took shelter behind my calf.

When a couple of minutes had passed, and I had scraped the dough off the side of my nose, I surveyed the damage. The bird was gone. The stone walls looked as if they'd been caught in a very lumpy snowstorm. The inside of my head felt bruised. I sat down and clutched it, which didn't help at all.

"Let the record show," I said to the gingerbread man, "that bread was not meant to fly."

There wasn't much useable dough left. The bits of bird I managed to scrounge from the corners of the room were weirdly spongy, as if I'd set yeast dough out to rise and forgotten about it for a week. When I tried to give it magic, it wouldn't take. The magic just slid off it as if the dough had been oiled. I went back to trying the bread crusts again.

It got easier with practice. I found that if I only used crust from one loaf, it worked better. Two loaves that hadn't been baked together didn't want to cooperate at all. (There was no getting it to work with the remaining dough, either—the two rejected each other completely. Dough legs would walk off without the bread-crust body. One actually yanked its own bread-crust arm off and threw it at the wall. Baked and unbaked dough are *not* friends.)

I didn't try to make another bird. I had a feeling that I'd run up against the limits of what even magic bread could do. But I made tiny animals and people, and if I set them a repetitive task, they did okay.

The gingerbread man wasn't impressed. I couldn't blame

him. If I'd been able to bake my creations, I could have done a lot more with them.

Spindle, delivering the only edible meal of the day, stopped dead as soon as he climbed up the ladder. "Cor! What's that?"

"It's a circus," I said. The bread-crust elephant waved its trunk. "I'm bored."

"Never saw a circus for real," said Spindle, getting down on his knees. "Is this what they look like?"

"Well, they're usually bigger..." I said, grinning. He flapped a hand at me. "And a lot more colorful. And I couldn't do the trapeze. But this is sort of like it." He'd brought up another meat pie, this one cold rather than molten, and a lump of cheese. I devoured them while he watched the bread circus go through its paces—the elephant posing, the bread girl riding the bread horse (both rather lumpy, since I wasn't very good at horses) the lion shaking its crumby mane.

"Must've taken you hours," said Spindle, impressed.

I snorted. "I've got nothing but time. It's boring up here. And the gingerbread man gets very grumpy if I try to cheat at solitaire."

"Mmm. Brought you something." He reached under his jacket and pulled out a grubby sheet of paper.

"Hmm?" I took it and unfolded it, smoothing out the creases. "What is—"

I stopped.

I stared down at the paper.

My own face stared back at me.

SIXTEEN

"I found it on a lamp post," said Spindle. He stuck his hands in his pockets and stared down at the bread circus.

It was a cheap, flimsy sheet, the sort they print broadsides on. Someone had done a woodcut of me—not a great one, but enough like me to be recognizable.

"What's it say?" Spindle wanted to know. I looked up at him, startled, and he flushed. "Not like I can read. I mean, I know that word is "WANTED" but the rest is just gibberish."

"Wanted for questioning," I said numbly. "For murder and suspicion of treason—*treason*? I'm a *baker!*"

"The one doesn't let out t'other," Spindle said reasonably. I balled the poster up in my fist. I wanted to cry. What if Aunt Tabitha had seen it?

"How many of these are there?" I asked.

"A bunch," said Spindle, scuffing the floor with one foot. "You must have really made somebody mad."

I sat down. My stomach hurt in a way that had nothing to do with all the onions I'd been eating.

If there were a bunch of wanted posters, then everybody must have seen them. All the people who came to the bakery would think I was a traitor and a murderer. Some of them wouldn't believe it, but some of them would. *Miss McGrammar probably would. Heck, she'd probably be thrilled to know she was right.*

Hadn't she said something about broadsheets the last time I came in? "*You people,*" she'd said.

"I should have put *bugs* in your scones," I muttered, staring down at the poster.

Aunt Tabitha must have seen the posters. They probably would have put them up all over my neighborhood, and that meant that Aunt Tabitha might have to look at them every *day*.

I must have said something out loud, because Spindle put out a hand and patted me awkwardly on the shoulder. "It's not so bad as that," he said. "They got guards on the street, but they ain't done nothing to hurt your kin."

"How can it not be as bad as that!?" I cried, wadding the wanted poster up in my hands. "I'm a wanted criminal!"

"Yeah, but at least she knows if they've got the posters up, they don't got you," said Spindle. "Means you're alive, too. Ain't gonna put up posters if they've killed you."

The knot in my stomach loosened a little. "Yeah," I said. "Yeah, you're right." They wouldn't have put up posters if the Spring Green Man had killed me, or if I was in the dungeons somewhere. If that was the case, they'd want me to just stop existing.

I wondered why they wanted to get hold of me so badly. What did Oberon think I knew?

What *did* I know?

I wracked my brain. I didn't know anything. If anything, I knew a lot less than the other magickers in town. They'd all been smart enough to leave town. No, surely there was nothing I knew that Oberon would want hushed up.

Fine, if I didn't *know* anything, what had I done?

My kneejerk response was to yell that I hadn't done anything, but that wasn't right. I'd crossed Oberon by being innocent. Was that enough?

Hell, he must have known I was innocent. If he was working with the Spring Green Man, he knew perfectly well that I hadn't killed Tibbie. Was he really so petty that one insignificant bakery girl not allowing herself to be framed for murder was enough to hunt her to the ends of the earth?

The Spring Green Man had said something about being moved up the list. Maybe Oberon *was* that petty. Or... what if Bob had killed the Spring Green Man? Oberon would come after me for *that!*

"There's some others, too," said Spindle, pulling more broadsheets out of his coat. They had a curve where they'd molded against his body. "Wasn't sure if one of them might be about you, so I brought 'em."

I smoothed the papers out on the floor and began to read.

"This one says there's a curfew," I said. "Nobody on the streets between midnight and five in the morning, unless they've got necessary business." I frowned. Even if I hadn't been a criminal, a curfew would have bothered me. I had to walk between my room and the bakery every morning, usually earlier than five. Would the constables consider making bread necessary business?

"Heard about that," said Spindle. "They got criers all over town. People aren't happy about it."

"I bet." There were lots of jobs that happened between midnight and five. The nightsoil men came through, and the lamplighters. Those would probably be considered necessary business, but what about people who stayed out late? Widow Holloway, one of my favorite regulars, couldn't sleep the night through since her husband died eleven years ago. She usually went out walking in the middle of the night when she woke up. I met her sometimes on the way to the bakery. "It doesn't matter that I can't sleep, Mona," she used to say, in her piping little voice. "When you're as old as I am, you don't feel like wasting time sleeping anyway. Maybe that was true, but what would she do if the constables told her she couldn't go for a walk?

My eye travelled down the broadsheet. At the bottom, in smaller letters, it said "By Order of Inquisitor Oberon."

"You got a funny look," said Spindle.

"Ha-ha," I said hollowly, pushing the broadsheet away.

"What's this one?' asked Spindle, pointing to another sheet. "It's a couple days old, but people acted really weird when that one went up."

"Weird how?" I lifted the sheet. It had a woodcut of a soldier's helmet on top.

Spindle scratched behind an ear thoughtfully. "Well, some of them got really mad, and some of them seemed almost happy, in a mad kind of way. And Slug said that he'd always known it, and One-eyed Benji said that Slug was an idiot, nobody'd believe that was true, and Slug said if it wasn't true, why was it on a paper then?" He grimaced. "Stupid thing is that neither of them can read a word, so neither of them knew what they was talking about, not really."

Despite the fascinating saga of Slug and One-Eyed Benji, I turned my attention back to the broadsheet.

BE A PATRIOT!

Our courageous soldiers have marched out against the Enemy,
but there's a battle to be fought at home, too!
SPIES ARE EVERWHERE!

DO YOU KNOW YOUR NEIGHBOR?
Could THEY be a SPY or a WIZARD TRAITOR?
Report suspicious activity to your constables at once!

REWARD OFFERED
for information leading to the arrest of spies, wizard-traitors,
and those giving comfort to the Enemy!

"Good heavens!"

"What? What does it say?"

I read the broadsheet to Spindle, who listened with his mouth open.

"That'll set the cat among the pigeons," he said, when I was done reading. "Everybody'll be claiming that their neighbor's givin' comfort to the Enemy. Who do you figure the Enemy is?"

"Whoever the army went out to fight," I said. "Carex mercenaries, I think."

"Them weird people from up north who are always trying

to take over a city?" Spindle whistled. "How you gonna comfort them?"

"I think so." I didn't know for sure. It wasn't like I'd had a chance to keep up with gossip, up here in the bell-tower.

"What is it they want?"

"Their own city, as far as I know." I scratched the back of my neck. "They live out around the edges, but they'll go for a city if they think it's weak. Sort of like wolves watching sheep, you know?"

"Ain't never seen a wolf," said Spindle pragmatically. "And our city's a lot better than any smelly old sheep."

Metaphor was not Spindle's strong suit.

"What would they need spies for anyway? They just come up and attack a city, don't they? You don't need spies for that."

I propped my chin on one hand and watched the bread-crust elephant go through its paces. It walked in a circle, waved its trunk, sat up on its hind legs, walked in a circle again. The bread crust still didn't show much initiative.

I knew I was only fourteen, and I didn't know that much about politics, but Spindle's question seemed like a good one. Carex spies? In the city? Why? Carex are really pretty straightforward. They raid your farms so you don't have anything to eat, and then they try to take over your town. If they succeed, everybody dies and the Carex hang out there for a while and eat all the food and take all the money. Then they go find another town. (They've managed to do this to a couple of smaller towns over the years, but never to a real city with an army. They keep trying, though.)

It's horrible, but it's not complicated. It doesn't seem like it would require spies.

Plus Carex *hated* magic. It didn't make any sense that

they'd hire magicians to spy for them. The whole idea of wizard-traitors helping the Carex was ridiculous, but here it was on a broadsheet with the Inquisitor's name on it.

"I wonder if Lord Ethan knows about this." In the last war, when the Golden General got his reputation, I couldn't remember papers like this. Of course, I'd been much younger, but surely I'd remember a thing like that. And dammit, Riverbraid was always *good* to magickers. It didn't make sense.

"So that's why Slug was happy," said Spindle thoughtfully. "He always did hate magickers. Never wanted Tibbie in on a job, or Willy Thumbs either. He's all mean and happy now that the magickers are gone."

"Gone?" I asked absently.

"Ain't seen hide nor hair of one for days," said Spindle. "'Cept you and Knackering Molly. And Slug said he actually saw Big Mitch get dragged away by the guards, and there was a notice nailed to the door." He frowned. "'Course Big Mitch ain't much of a magicker, and he's a big drinker, so they coulda been hauling him away for being drunk and disorderly again."

I sighed. The papers were making me angry, and under the anger was a whole lot of scared.

The gingerbread man came down from the slitted window where he kept watch and stood on the edge of a paper. I wondered if he could read. Probably not. Reading's complicated. Then again, so's walking and circuses and stuff, so maybe I could enchant one to read if I tried.

"There's one more," said Spindle. "This one's new today."

This broadsheet was clearly new. The paper was still crisp, and hadn't blurred at the edges of the letters. "Pulled it down not five minutes after it went up," said Spindle proudly. "I was on m'way here anyway."

WIZARD TRAITORS ARE EVERYWHERE
It is VITAL for our SECURITY as a NATION
that we
PREVENT INFILTRATION by HOSTILE
MAGICAL ELEMENTS!

All loyal citizens with wizardly talents must register
with
the Loyalty Board within ten days FOR THEIR OWN
SAFETY.

The author, I thought gloomily, had clearly never met a capital letter he didn't like. I was surprised he hadn't printed WIZARD TRAITOR in red ink. Maybe it would have cost too much. I looked to the bottom of the page, and sure enough, in smaller block letters, it said "by ORDER of Inquisitor Oberon."

"This'll make people *really* mad," I said, when I had finished reading it to Spindle.

Spindle said "Um."

I looked up. "Um, what?"

He rubbed the back of his neck and refused to meet my eyes.

I waited.

"Might not," he said, all in a rush. "Lotta people are a little iffy 'bout magicker talents, even the little piddly ones. M'sister—lotta people didn't like her for it. Some of the kids. I knocked them down." He crouched down on the flagstones, looking curiously at the paper. "Couldn't knock 'em all down, though. And Slug's bigger than me, a lot, and he knocked me down."

It made no sense. No magicker with an ounce of brains would work for the Carex. I don't know what they do to grown-ups with magic, but presumably they don't just leave you on a hillside to die. Did people who weren't magickers *know* that, though? Was it the sort of thing you paid attention to, if you didn't have to worry about it yourself?

What if Spindle was right, and people were believing the broadsheets?

I didn't know what to say. Some of the people at the bakery... they liked my talent, didn't they? Making gingerbread dance? Most of them did.

"Some people might think it was a good idea," said Spindle apologetically. "Not to do anything bad to a magicker, you know, but just to know where they are. Might think a registry was a good thing."

"They wouldn't if they were one!"

"Hardly anybody is one, though. Or if they are, nobody notices. I don't know any more'n you and Molly right now." Spindle thought about it. "Told you about Big Mitch. And Spitter, but I ain't seen her in a long time either."

This was depressing. My hopes that the city would rise up in defense of their magical citizens were dashed before they'd even gotten started. I hugged my knees.

I'd been moved up the list. Where on the list had Tibbie been? Or Big Mitch?

Why would Oberon *want* a list of the magical talented, anyway?

Because then he'd know where they were.

And if he knew where they were, he could do something about it.

What else had the Spring Green Man said?

"You'll all be eliminated eventually..." I said slowly, remembering that awful night, crouching in the cellar behind Bob. "That was what he said. And something about a list."

Spindle cocked his head. The gingerbread man rubbed his hands together.

"Oberon wants to know where we all are," I said. "He's using the Spring Green Man to sniff us out, but that's not enough. Either he doesn't trust the Spring Green Man, or more people than me might have escaped. He wants the complete list so that he can destroy us all. And he's going to have people registering with this Loyalty Board and doing the work for him."

SEVENTEEN

The night I spent in the belltower after Spindle brought the broadsheets was one of the most restless I've ever had. Not the *worst*—it'd be hard to top having the Spring Green Man trying to kill me in the cellar—but the most restless.

I tossed. I turned. I tried to get comfortable, which isn't easy on a pile of straw, let me tell you. If you've got any notions that straw makes a good bed, just abandon them now. Straw is itchy. It pokes you. It's softer to sleep on than dirt or flagstones, sure, but the individual straws aren't soft at all. They stab through your clothes, and when you wiggle to move one out of the way, five more get into position to poke you.

Still, the straw was the least of my worries.

Sure, I was tired. You wouldn't think you could get tired cooped up in a belltower all day, but you can, particularly when you do eleven push-ups and run laps around the room for half an hour. (Those were good push-ups too, on my toes, not on my knees. My forearms were really strong from smacking all that dough around, as I've said, but my biceps were no slouches either.)

The posters were still there. I had shoved them to the far side of the room. They seemed to breathe malice into the air. I'd turned them over so that they were face down, otherwise I felt like the words were staring at me. Probably that sounds stupid, but that's how I felt.

The gingerbread man was standing sentry in the window again, and I watched his small, brave shadow travel across the floor as the night progressed. But I couldn't sleep. My thoughts ran over and under each other, stretching and churning, as if my brain were trying to pull taffy. I'd swear to myself that there was nothing I could do, that I was going to stop thinking and go to sleep now, and then ten minutes later my brain would be going again, jitter-flop, jitter-flop, like a three-legged frog on a griddle.

Oberon was planning to get rid of every magically-talented person in the city. He'd already gotten a bunch of us, and a bunch more had left. Spindle's friends, his sister... I didn't really believe that Little Sidney had run away to sea anymore. Lena at the market had said that everybody should get out, and like an idiot, I hadn't listened.

How many were gone?

Maybe that was the wrong question. Maybe I should be asking how many of us were *left*.

Great.

Jitter-flop, jitter-flop went my brain, stuttering around, trying to find solutions to problems that were so much bigger than me, it was laughable.

What could I do?

Well, not getting killed by the Spring Green Man was probably a good start.

And then what?

Stay up in the belltower for the rest of my life, living on Spindle's charity and the dour brothers below, until the Spring Green Man came sniffing up the ladder after me? No. Not an option.

Leave the city?

I rolled over in the straw, which fired a new volley of stickers into my legs and arms.

I could leave, I guess. Maybe that *was* the sensible and sane thing to do. I could go to another city, get apprenticed to a baker somewhere. It wasn't bragging to say that most bakeries would probably want me.

Oh, but that would be hard. I tried not to think about my parents much. They had died an awfully long time ago, but I still remembered how my mom smelled, and the way my dad chuckled, a furry sort of chuckle down deep in his chest. Losing them had been the worst thing ever. If I had to lose Aunt Tabitha and my uncle and the bakery... I mean, I might find another bakery, I might even love another bakery, but it wouldn't be *mine* in the same way.

That was assuming I got anywhere. The roads between city-states were well-travelled, and I wouldn't be eaten by bears, but being a fourteen-year-old girl on the road alone meant there were worse things than bears out there. And we were sort of cordially at war with a couple of other city-states, and what if I got all the way to one of them, and they turned me away because I came from Riverbraid?

And the army was supposed to be out dealing with the Carex mercenaries, which raided all the city-states with a kind of even-handed brigandry, but suppose the army didn't catch them all, and I stumbled into a Carex camp? They *ate* people. Probably.

It would be ignominious to escape the Spring Green Man only to get eaten by a Carex. I'd almost rather get eaten by bears. At least that was sort of normal behavior for bears.

And there was still the problem of being a magicker. If I got to a city, I still might have to leave again, or live in a wizard's quarter, or get registered by the government as a known magicker. That was what I was trying to *avoid.* It seemed like once you agreed that the government could put you on a list because of something you were born with, you were asking for trouble. Sooner or later somebody like Oberon would get hold of that list.

Jitter-flop, jitter-flop...

So. If I couldn't leave, and I couldn't hide forever, what did that leave?

Stopping Oberon and the Spring Green Man. Which I certainly couldn't do by myself.

Well, then. Who could?

I gave up on any effort at sleep and sat up, pulling my knees against my chest and picking malicious straw out of my pants. I felt so jittery that I wanted to get up and run—or go down and do... something.

The gingerbread man hopped down from the window and poked his head down the hole where the ladder came from.

A moment later he came back and waved to me.

I set a foot on the ladder and went cautiously down.

The door at the foot of the tower was closed, but the hinges were well oiled. I slipped into the church. Moonlight seeped through the cracks in the boarded windows. I heard a crier far off in the distance—*one o'clock and all's well... well... well...*

Maybe for *him*.

"Restless, my child?" asked a voice.

I whirled around with a yelp.

It was the old priest.

He was sitting in the second row of pews, so small and silent I had taken him for a pile of coats. He looked to be about a thousand years old, give or take a few hundred.

"S-sorry—" I said. I didn't know whether to run back up the ladder or try to get out of the church. He wasn't supposed to know I was there. Had I just given myself away?

He smiled and nodded vaguely at me. After a minute, I realized that he probably couldn't see me very well. His eyes had a dim, unfocused look.

He patted the pew back. "Come and sit down, child. If you are restless, prayer is good for the spirit and if you are tired, there is no harm in sitting either."

I crept closer. He looked so frail that I couldn't imagine that he could grab me. The gingerbread man lay close against the back of my neck.

I sat down on the pew in front of him, a little to one side.

"Is something troubling you, my child?" he asked, after a while. And before I could say anything, he smiled and added, "It doesn't matter if you tell me, you know. I am stone-deaf and cannot hear it anyway. It makes me very popular in the confessional these days."

It occurred to me that he probably would have a hard time turning me in, even if he wanted to.

"I'm scared," I said finally. "I miss my bakery. I'm scared and I'm sick of onions and porridge and I'm only fourteen and I shouldn't have to do this." I folded my arms around myself. "I'm scared that the people who help me are going to get hurt."

The old priest smiled and patted my shoulder. "There, there, my dear. I'm sure it's not as bad as that—or perhaps it is, in which case, I'm sorry. Or perhaps you were talking about the weather." He sighed. "Well, if nothing else, I find that you can rarely go wrong appealing to a higher power."

We sat in the pew, and suddenly all the things percolating in my mind came together. I had poured in all the ingredients and stirred, and the dough had finally begun to rise.

A higher power. I needed a higher power.

Not a spiritual one, but one right here in the city.

"*The Duchess*," I said out loud.

The gingerbread man moved restlessly against my neck.

Somehow, I would have to get word to the Duchess. She would give me a fair hearing, I was sure of it. She'd intervened on my behalf before. She didn't seem very warm, but she also didn't seem cruel. And she had wizards—*real* wizards, not just piddly little magickers like me, wizards who could do powerful things, and stop Oberon in his tracks.

Come to think of it, *her* name hadn't been on any of the posters. They were all issued "by order of Inquisitor Oberon." And I had a hard time believing that the Army wizards would be all that happy about a registry either.

Did the Duchess even know about the posters?

Nobody ever saw her outside the palace, except for during parades. There hadn't been a parade for a long time. And the Golden General was gone.

I was broken from my thoughts by a faint noise behind me. When I turned, the old priest was asleep with his head tilted back against the pew.

After a moment, he let out a very impressive snore. The gingerbread man came out and stared at him in awe.

I got up and crept back to the tower. My mind was a whirl.

Could Inquisitor Oberon be doing all this without the Duchess's knowledge? Why would he keep her in the dark? Could he be plotting against her as well as the magickers? Why did he even want the magickers dead, anyway? He couldn't just hate all magic, like some people, could he? Otherwise would he really use the Spring Green Man—a magicker himself—to hunt them down?

Could this be part of some larger plot?

Even if the Duchess *did* know about the posters, even if she somehow believed all this stuff about wizard traitors, someone had to tell her that Inquisitor Oberon was using the Spring Green Man to kill magickers.

So that was easy. I just had to get a chance to talk to the Duchess, with the understanding that all of her guards and ministers and functionaries would arrest me on sight and hand me over to my worst enemies.

Piece of cake.

"You want to break in *where?*" said Spindle, staring at me like I had suddenly grown antlers.

"The Duchess's palace. No, the Duchess's bedroom. The palace is too big. It has to be someplace where she won't have a lot of people around her."

"The Duchess's *bedroom?*" said Spindle, staring at me like I had suddenly grown purple antlers garlanded with daisies and marmalade kittens.

"It's the only way."

"You're out of your mind! Mad as a mudlark! Completely bonkers!" Spindle looked wildly around the tower room until his eye fell on the gingerbread man. "Tell her!"

The gingerbread man shrugged. He was displaying a lot of independent thought these days, but he still couldn't talk, which was good. There would have been something really unsettling about a talking gingerbread man.

"You'll get killed!"

"How is that different from doing anything else? I'm stuck in this stupid tower until either they catch me, or you get caught for something and stop bringing me food and I die of a porridge overdose! At least if I try to warn the Duchess, I'll be *doing* something!"

The nice thing about Spindle is that he didn't tell me to be patient. A grown-up would have told me to be patient, it'd all work out. Spindle didn't bother, which was good, because I was *done* being patient.

Instead, he stomped over to the slit of a window and glared over the rooftops. I let him alone and settled for braiding a couple of stalks of straw together.

Finally, Spindle said, "Getting into the palace shouldn't be too hard. They've got a lot of people going in and out, and that always makes it easy. But once we're in, we'd be in trouble. You gotta filch uniforms and stuff, or everybody stops you to ask who you are and why you're there. And there's no uniform in the world that'd get you into the Duchess's bedroom with her."

"Don't you think... like... a maid, maybe?"

Spindle gave me a withering look. "You don't know much about servants, do you?"

"Oh, and you do?"

"Sure. You gonna pick pockets, you gotta know your mark. If you're gonna break into a big house, you actually want the high-up servant's rooms—they got jewelry and stuff that's worth money, but not so much that you can't sell it."

"You can't sell something that's worth too much money?" This sounded bizarre to me. I mean, breaking into somebody's house to steal their stuff sounded kind of bizarre already. I was pretty sure my nerves would give out before I was even in a window.

Meanwhile, Spindle was still looking at me like I was an idiot. Mind you, he did this so often that I was starting to wonder if he just had an eyelid tic or something—surely I couldn't be that dense, could I?

"Steal a great lady's jewels and ain't nobody gonna fence it —you know, sell the stolen stuff for you," he said. "S'more trouble to you than it's worth, 'cos nobody can move it. It's too good, you know? No back-alley pawnshop would have stuff like *that,* so it has to be stolen, and the constables will get awfully interested, and nobody's gonna buy it, 'cos they don't have the money. Stealing jewels like that is like... high-level stuff."

I propped my chin on my hand. "So, what? You're telling me I'm not noble-looking enough to be a maid to the Duchess?"

"Nope," said Spindle.

"So what would *you* do?" I asked testily. Tact, in Spindle's world, was apparently something that happened to other people.

"I gotta think about it," said Spindle. "I gotta go look at the palace. This is crazy. I told you this is crazy, right?"

Which is how we wound up, five nights later, climbing out of the Duchess's toilet.

EIGHTEEN

So, in a palace, the toilet's called the "garderobe." It's basically a closet with a hole in the floor that drops straight down a couple of stories into a cesspit. In the nicer ones—and the Duchess's garderobe was very nice—you get a little carved wooden bench with a seat on it, and you can sit there and think about life or whatever you want to think about when nature is calling, and the point is that since it's three stories down and there are vents, it doesn't even smell bad. Much.

Well, comparatively speaking.

Regular people have to use chamberpots, but if you're rich or noble and you've got a castle with a spare closet and a straight shot to the ground, you get a garderobe.

There's a guy whose job is to shovel the cesspit out once a week. It's under a locked grate in a little stone hut with locked doors. (Who knew you had to keep *that* under lock and key? I mean, nobody's going to *steal* it... right?)

As far as I can tell, Spindle broke into the palace disguised as an ash-sweeper, then followed this guy around for two days until he got a chance to filch the keys, and then he made a wax imprint in a bit of old candle and returned the key before the cesspit cleaner even noticed.

I was very impressed by this and told him so. Spindle muttered something about how it was no different than any other second-story job, and there was no place in the world for a clever noddy who couldn't swindle some outhouse cove. (I think that was what they call Thieves' Cant.)

It occurred to me that Spindle's criminal experience was a bit wider than I had realized. I'm pretty sure "second-story job" meant that Spindle used to be a burglar, and presumably he was also the "clever noddy" in question, which would make the cesspit shoveler the "outhouse cove." I wondered what Spindle and his sister Tibbie had gotten up to, before the Spring Green Man had showed up and put an end to her career. Some hints that Spindle dropped now and again made me think he'd been part of a gang of child-thieves, but apparently they'd either broken up or he'd left when Tibbie died. It was weird to think that this sort of thing went on in the city, while I'd been at home, innocently baking muffins and wondering if we had enough sugar to get through the week.

At any rate, if you wanted to steal the keys to a royal cesspit, you couldn't ask for better than Spindle.

Once we had the key, though, it was... well, still not easy.

I have never climbed a three-story anything in my life. It's not like it comes up when you're a baker. You never have to climb a ladder and swan-dive into a vat of croissant dough or anything. I'm not afraid of heights—as far as I know—but I wasn't sure that even with a rope, I was going to be able to do it. And I was awfully worried about what the Duchess was going to think when we showed up smelling like the inside of a garderobe. If she just started screaming, we were going to wind up in the dungeon without a chance to say our piece.

I spent most of a day repeating my speech over and over in my head. *Your Grace, I've come to warn you of a plot against magickers, and maybe against you. Your Grace, Inquisitor Oberon is plotting against them, and I'm sorry, this is the only way I could close enough to warn you. Your Grace, have you ever heard of the Spring Green Man?*

Oh, this was madness. I was going to show up dripping sewage on the Duchess's rug and she was going to have me thrown in the dungeon and no one was going to listen and magic-folk were still going to die. The bit about Inquisitor Oberon plotting against her might not even be true. I didn't have any proof, anyway. I just felt really nervous with Inquisitor Oberon still in the city, and the Golden General and the army somewhere else. It seemed like a bad idea.

Was I really about to climb up a three-story toilet because the army being out of the city seemed like a bad idea?

Apparently so.

Well, even if they threw me in the dungeon, at least I'd be out of the bell tower. The room seemed to get smaller and smaller, once we had a plan. I paced back and forth for hours, twenty-five steps all the way around, and I kept expecting it to take less. Twenty-four. Twenty-three. It felt like the walls were closing in on me. I had to get up once in the middle of the night and measure it. It was still twenty-five steps. Probably that sounds nuts, but nobody was watching except for the gingerbread man and the rag-tag bread crumb circus.

Spindle came for me on the fourth night, and I went down the ladder without a backward glance, the gingerbread man clinging to my hair. I was glad to be gone. The lay brother had been giving me odd looks. It might have been nothing, but it might have been that he'd seen the wanted posters, and there was no use taking a chance. I left the bread circus behind. They'd almost run out of magic and were just crude little sculptures made of bread. I don't know what the priests thought of that.

We didn't go out by the main door, but through the back where the priests lived. I paused in the kitchen to tap each of the hard black loaves waiting on the counter.

You're good bread, I told them. *You're soft and you want to* stay *soft. And if I live through this, I'm going to make sure the priests get some of Bob's best sourdough from now on. Assuming Bob is still... oh, damn.*

"You all right?" said Spindle suspiciously.

I rubbed my nose and sniffed. "Yeah. I'm fine."

Being out on the street again felt like my birthday. I was giddy. I wanted to laugh and dance and hug strangers. I swung around a lamppost just because I could. Spindle had to thump my shoulder and hiss, "Settle down! People are looking!" before I stopped giggling.

It was a beautiful night. It had rained in the evening, but that was done, and now the mist was rising from the water and the cobbles were slick and shining with reflected light. I could hear frogs croaking in the canals.

I was still feeling giddy and light-headed when we passed a constable. That settled me down in a hurry. He was slouched against the canal railing with his hands stuffed in his pockets, and I doubt I would have even noticed him, except for being a wanted fugitive and all.

"Relax," muttered Spindle. "Don't tense up. They don't

notice you if you just walk along and pretend like you're going somewhere. Curfew isn't for another couple hours yet."

We went in a roundabout path, in case anybody was following us from the church. It didn't seem likely, but Spindle was paranoid and that suited me just fine. There were more broadsheets pinned up, talking about the curfew and registering magical talents.

There was one that said:

Do YOU know an unregistered WIZARD?
WIZARD TRAITORS COULD BE ANYONE!
They could be your FAMILY, your FRIENDS, even your CHILDREN!
Loyal citizens will REGISTER TODAY!

Well, that was depressing.

"You okay?" asked Spindle. "You've gone all fishy-colored."

"Nothing," I muttered. "It's fine." It wasn't that different from the others, but the notion of telling people to hand in their own kids for being magickers turned my stomach. I didn't offer to read the broadsheet for Spindle.

When we passed by Peony Street, I looked down at Master Elwidge's shop. There was a "For Sale" sign in the window, and someone had nailed a broadsheet to the door.

We didn't see any that had my face on it. Maybe those were only near the bakery, or maybe they'd forgotten about me. I could only hope it was the second possibility. The notion of

Aunt Tabitha having to go out and buy ingredients surrounded by all those printed faces...

Of course, sometime tomorrow I'd probably be in jail or exonerated, so they could take the broadsheets down one way or the other. The criers would have other news to shout. Hopefully it would be "Plot against magickers uncovered!" and not "Poop-covered assassin foiled in Duchess's bathroom!"

Really, of all the ways to go...

NINETEEN

All we had to do was get into the palace, make our way past the guards to the curtain wall, which was a kind of wall sandwich between the palace and the outer walls where they store all the stuff you don't want to keep right inside the palace, like stables. And cesspits. Then we'd wait until nightfall, sneak into the cesspit hut, and climb up the inside of the garderobe wall. Which was three stories high and covered in... um... nastiness. Also, according to Spindle, it had metal spikes.

"Spikes..." I said faintly.

"They're nuthin'," Spindle said, waving a hand. "You can squish right by 'em. And they're kinda handy, because we'll tie a rope to 'em so you can climb easier."

I did not feel convinced.

"I reckon they'd keep a grown-up out," he allowed. "That's what they're for, see, to keep somebody from climbing up and stabbing the Duchess while she's havin' a—"

"Right. *Thank you,* Spindle. I get the point."

The plan was for me to work in the kitchens until nightfall. The guards would notice a scullery maid trying to get into the palace late at night, but they probably wouldn't notice if one of the maids who had come in during the day didn't leave. I was afraid they'd notice a stranger in the kitchen, but Spindle snorted.

"That place? They wouldn't notice if you came in ridin' an elephant. Just act like you're s'posed to be there."

It turned out he was right. Getting into the palace was the easy part. Spindle had stolen an apron. I put it on and walked past the guards in the courtyard. I was clammy with sweat and my knees shook, but their eyes slid right over me.

I peeked into the kitchen. It was a crazy whirl of activity. The head cook was a red-faced woman who barked orders like a drill sergeant. People ran past carrying trays of food and buckets of water and great piles of dirty dishes. I was afraid to get in anyone's way—what if they noticed me? What if they knew I wasn't supposed to be there?

Then I saw a girl trying to cut out biscuits on a table and making a hash of it. She'd kneaded the biscuits far too long. They were going to be like rocks. I hurried over and nudged her aside. "You're overworking the dough," I said. "You want it to hold together, but that's all. If you knead it too long, they turn into bricks."

"Will you do it?" she asked, giving me a grateful look. "I've still got to cut up the ham and cheese for these, and there's the eggs—"

"Of course," I said. "Err—I'm new. My name's Mona. Is there anything I should do?"

"Just make the biscuits," she said. "I'm Jenny. I'll be back in a minute."

'A minute' in this case was nearly forty-five, but Jenny did come back. By then I'd finished three batches of biscuits. Whenever the cook looked in my direction, my knees quaked, but she didn't stop me.

I used a little magic to save the first set of biscuits. *You're fluffy,* I told them. *You're very fluffy and soft. You're like little fluffy lambs, only without the poop stuck to your tail because that's gross.* They agreed to be fluffy. Biscuits are very accommodating that way.

Probably this was a waste of time since I had much bigger worries than fluffy biscuits, but hey, once a baker, always a baker. If I was going to get thrown in the dungeon, at least I was going to leave a trail of quality pastries behind me.

"You did it!" said Jenny. She was about my age, with thin little bird-bone wrists. "Cor! I hate doing those. My arms get so tired. How are you at kneading bread?"

"What I don't know about kneading bread," I said, with great honesty, "isn't worth knowing."

It was five hours later before I managed to slip out of the kitchen. It had gone from bread to chopping vegetables, and then Jenny left for the evening, and since I kept explaining that I was new, the other girls stuck me in the scullery. That meant I had to wash dishes.

A *lot* of dishes. And magic couldn't help me with that.

There were four girls working in there, and they gave me the worst ones. I didn't really mind. It's never fun to wash dishes, but it's sort of satisfying to get a really bad one clean. Some of them needed to soak with lye, there was no getting around it. I finally excused myself to go to the bathroom and ran into Spindle on the way to the privies.

"Where have you *been*?" he hissed. He was wearing the

ash-sweeper rags and nearly vanished in the shadows around the low wooden buildings. "I been waitin' for hours!"

"I was doing dishes," I said. "I can't believe this! Nobody's asked where I'm from or anything! Anybody could just walk right in here!"

"That's 'cos most assassins ain't gonna waste time doin' dishes," said Spindle. "They're lookin' for scary people, not girls in aprons." He pulled me into the shadow of the wall. "C'mon, let's get moving. We wait much longer, it'll be morning again."

We passed two guards on the way to the garderobe, and neither of them so much as glanced at us. An ash-boy and a scullery girl weren't worthy of their notice. Spindle glanced around, made sure no one was watching, unlocked the garderobe door and waved me inside.

It stank. It stank a *lot*. I mean, the canals get pretty ripe in summer, don't get me wrong, but at least there was a lot of air for them to diffuse in. This was a little stone chimney with a couple of narrow slits in the walls, and the smell had etched its way into the mortar.

There was a rope hanging down. "Left it earlier," Spindle said. "While I was waitin' for you to get out. The first set of spikes is easy to get to, so I tied a rope to it." He gave me a patronizing look. "Well... easy for me..."

"Thanks, Spindle," I muttered. "You're just like a brother to me. In the most annoying possible sense."

He grinned and gave me a quick punch on the shoulder. For Spindle, that was an incredible display of affection. I got a little choked up, but that might just have been the smell coming off the cesspit.

So. Shoulders against the wall. Feet against the opposite wall. Grab the rope in both hands. Walk feet up a couple of steps, brace them, hitch shoulders up, hauling on the rope. Brace, hitch, haul. Brace, hitch, haul.

The stones were cold, but that was almost a relief, because I hadn't gotten more than two man-heights off the ground before I was dripping with sweat. It ran into my eyes and off the tip of my nose and down my back and it itched and tickled so that I thought bugs were crawling on me. Oh lord, I hadn't even thought about bugs. What kind of awful bugs did you get in a garderobe?

I also hadn't anticipated that there would be moss growing on top of the gunk on the walls. Moss is not good for climbing. It looks furry, but if you try to stand on it, it turns slick as ice in a hurry. When I passed one of the vent holes, the light coming in showed green streaks of moss along my hands, in addition to blackish streaks of something else that shall not be named.

Oh, this is delightful. I was going to get to the top and I would be covered in... stuff. Let's go with "stuff." I would pop out of a toilet covered in stuff and dripping sweat and maybe with bugs on me and expect the Duchess to listen to anything I had to say?

Soon I ran into the first row of spikes. I literally ran into them. My head whacked into one and thank goodness they weren't very sharp.

They were more like metal fenceposts than spikes, arranged in an X across the garderobe. Spindle had been right, it seemed they were designed to keep out grown-ups, so there was more than enough space to get by them. Spindle could get through without even touching the sides, and I managed well enough, although I had to sort of shuffle around the chimney until I was under a gap, and there was a bad minute when I hit a slick patch of moss and thought I was going to fall.

The gingerbread man stood on a spike, grabbed my sleeve, and pulled. It didn't help at all, but I appreciated the thought.

Spindle was waiting just above my head. He dropped down —the metal crosspiece made a muffled *bonnnng* that terrified me—and untied the rope, then scurried up the side of the garderobe to the next set of spikes. A moment later, the rope dropped down onto my head.

I went back to climbing.

Brace, hitch, haul...

I slowly passed two more sets of spikes and another row of vents. The vents were narrow, like arrow slits, but set horizontally. I stopped for a minute on the set of spikes just under it and put my face against it to breathe.

My legs were killing me. My shoulders were starting to throb. The problem was that I was stuck. Going back down was going to be just as bad as going on up, unless I fell, in which case I was going to hit a cross-piece and go "splat!"

"Here!" hissed Spindle above me. "At the top!" I looked up.

Light! I could see the light at the end of the... well, at the top of the... well, through the toilet seat... well, anyway, it was light. Spindle was silhouetted against it, like a spider. As I watched, the silhouette got an arm across the top and then hauled himself out.

I was nearly there. I went back to bracing and hitching with a will.

Fortunately, the last set of spikes was close enough to the top that I could put my feet on the cross-pieces and try to get my shoulders through the hole.

And then I promptly got stuck.

The spikes had... stuff on them. Stuff that made for bad

footing. So I couldn't push very well with my feet, and my shoulders were through, but that was about as far as I got.

Spindle grabbed my arm and hauled. The gingerbread man jumped down and pulled. The carved seat scraped at my waist.

"You been eating too many of your own pastries!" Spindle grumbled.

This was blatantly unfair, since I'd been at the church long enough to have dropped any excess pastry weight I might have been carrying around. "It's easy for you!" I hissed. "You don't have hips! Now pull!"

He pulled. I started to emerge. Unfortunately my skirt was rucked up under the seat, and while *I* was coming out, it wasn't coming with me.

The gingerbread man covered his face with his hands.

Great. I was going to be covered in poop, sweating like a pig, *in my underwear*, trying to make my case to the Duchess...

...And at that very moment, she opened the door to the garderobe and walked in. She had a book in her hand and obviously planned to spend some quality time in the garderobe by herself.

If the Duchess had been a screamer, the guards would have burst in and things might have turned out very differently. But she didn't scream. Instead she put a hand to her mouth and said "...oh."

"Your Grace, please listen to me!" I said, sticking half in and half out of the toilet. "I've come to warn you of a plot against you!" Admittedly, I still wasn't sure that the plot was against her, and not against all magickers, but I thought I had a better chance of getting her attention this way.

(Although in fairness, I suppose if a half-naked girl is being hauled out of your toilet by a boy covered in sewage, that garners plenty of attention, too.)

"Your Grace—please—" I was thoroughly stuck, like a cork out of a bottle, and now my feet were just barely touching the crosspiece on the spikes, so I couldn't push at all. The skirt had slid down another few inches. Fortunately my underwear was still holding up. Faithful, faithful underwear.

"My name's Mona, you saved me from Inquisitor Oberon a few weeks ago, I was in court and you stood up for me, so I came to tell you—you have to listen—*please*—"

"How did you get up here?" she asked. It was not exactly the response I was looking for, but at least she wasn't yelling for the guards. I probably didn't look like much of a threat, jammed into the toilet, and Spindle was awfully young and scrawny for an assassin.

"We climbed up," said Spindle. "Weren't hard. Well, 'cept for this bit." He gazed at me in professional disgust.

I took a deep breath. That was probably a mistake. I could smell myself, and it wasn't good. I tried to remember the speech that I had practiced all those nights in the tower, and for some reason all I could remember was the porridge and the way the straw poked me at night.

It was the gingerbread man that saved me.

He had clung to my ear for the entire ascent up the garderobe shaft, a lock of hair wrapped around one arm. I'd almost forgotten he was there.

He stepped forward, hopped down from my shoulder to the seat, then to the floor. When he was three paces from the Duchess—human paces, not gingerbread man paces—he dropped his cookie head and bowed deeply to the Duchess.

"Oh my," said the Duchess faintly. I suppose most people

aren't used to being bowed to by baked goods. It occurred to me too late that the Duchess might be one of those people who found magic unsettling, but no, she worked with all those army wizards, right? The Golden General was her right-hand man. Surely she'd gotten used to it by now.

Regardless, it gave me the time I needed to assemble my thoughts. I took another deep breath. "Your Grace, Inquisitor Oberon is sending out assassins to kill magic-folk, and I don't know where it's going to stop. I think it might be part of a plot against you. I think with the General out of the city, he's going to try something. I had to warn you. Your Grace, I think you're in terrible danger. I know we—magickers—are."

And then the last thing in the entire world that I expected to happen, happened.

"Oh, my dears..." The Duchess's face crumpled. "I know. *I know*. And I don't know what to do!"

And she burst into tears.

TWENTY

In that supremely awkward moment, Spindle came to the rescue.

"Right," he said, apparently unfazed by the fact that the ruler of our entire city was weeping in front of us. "If I grab this arm, and you grab that arm, mum, I think we can get 'er out."

The Duchess, to her credit, put down her book, gave a quick hitching sob, and grabbed my left arm.

They hauled. I popped out of the toilet with long red scrapes across both hips and tumbled headfirst onto the carpet. The gingerbread man dove out of the way. The carpet probably came off the worst in the encounter.

"Oh dear." The Duchess found a towel and draped it over my shoulders. It was the softest towel I have ever encountered, thick and fluffy, and it seemed criminal to use it to scrub... stuff... .off my skin, but I did anyway. Hopefully they could launder it or something.

"Errr. Thank you, Your Grace." I tried to arrange the towel

over my legs. Standing in front of the ruler of the city was one thing—standing in front of her in your underwear was something else again. Although in truth, she didn't look much like a ruler right now. She looked smaller than she did in the parades and when I'd seen her at court. Smaller and older and a great deal more tired. When she walked, there was a faint hint of a shuffle, as if one of her knees pained her. There were dark purple half-moons under her eyes, and her brief tears had made her nose red and shiny.

It was strange to think of the Duchess as old. She'd been middle-aged practically forever. I guess she must have been young once, but when you put "Duchess" in front of somebody's name, they become sort of permanently middle-aged. And she'd seemed... oh, not *unkind*, maybe, but stern, when I'd seen her before. Competent. Not like somebody who'd be crying in her bedroom and not knowing what to do.

"Are the guards going to come in...?" I asked. I was hoping for more than a towel if they did. Soap and water before they arrested me, maybe.

"No," the Duchess said firmly, dabbing at her eyes with the edge of her sleeve. "No, the guards are loyal to me at least, and will not act without my orders. I wish I knew who else was."

"*We* are, Your Grace."

Spindle, never a staunch royalist, scuffed his foot on the carpet and muttered something.

"Thank you, children," said the Duchess. "Although I cannot think how I came to fall so far that my supporters must climb up the garderobe to pledge their loyalty!" She took my towel absently and tossed it into a hamper. I tried to pull my shirt down over my legs, but she picked up a lap-robe and handed it to me.

"It'll get all dirty, Your Grace," I said, looking at the fine embroidery.

"Then it will get dirty," she said firmly. "We have bigger things to worry about."

"Could I..." I looked longingly toward the bathroom. I stank. I didn't want to ruin the lap-robe, but I also didn't want to smell like a garderobe. "It'll only take a minute."

"Yes, of course."

I pulled Spindle in with me and made him wash. He muttered. "This soap smells like roses."

"Yes, isn't it nice?"

"No."

I would have made him wash behind his ears, but we didn't have all night. I was half-afraid that when we emerged, the Duchess would have called in armed men to deal with her visitors, but she was still sitting there, picking at a loose thread on the arm of the chair. She smiled a little when she saw us, but there was a lot of sadness underneath it. "Much better, my dears. Now, tell me about this assassin."

So Spindle and I—interrupting one another and talking over each other more often than not—explained about the Spring Green Man, and the broadsheets and the curfew and the sudden disappearances of magic-folk.

I had to explain about Tibbie. Spindle didn't say anything, but the Duchess reached out and took his hand in her own and squeezed. Her hands looked older than the rest of her. The tendons on the back stood out, and there was a white band of skin around one finger where a ring had been.

"I did not know about the registration of magic-folk," she said soberly. "I would not have allowed it."

"There's posters up all over," said Spindle.

The Duchess gave a short, bitter laugh. "I do not leave the palace much, my dears, and only then with guards. There is always so much to be done here. And we are not at war, but we are not far from it, and the Council—Inquisitor Oberon chief among them—tell me over and over again that I must not risk myself outside, that all it would take would be one madman with a knife to throw the city into disarray." She ran a hand through her hair. "Without Ethan—the Golden General—here, it has become easy to listen. So I have seen no posters, and I suspect that the people seeking an audience are being screened, so that no one with such upsetting information would reach me."

"But you wouldn't have allowed the registry," I said, feeling something unclench. It mattered to me, a lot. When you're different, even just a little different, even in a way that people can't see, you like to know that people in power won't judge you for it.

"I would have tried to stop it. It has always been a great virtue of our kingdom that magickers are treated no differently than anyone else here. I would not see that end on my watch." She sighed. "There are a great many things I would not wish to see on my watch, though, and perhaps it will not be my watch much longer, if Oberon has his way."

"Can't you stop him?" I asked. "Countermand the order?"

She sighed again and pinched the bridge of her nose wearily. "It is not so simple. You must understand, Mona, the ruler of a city is not an absolute power. The Council also wields a great deal of control. Usually that's a good thing. It keeps a bad ruler from making things unpleasant for the citizens. But it can also lead to problems, particularly if someone on the Council has an agenda of their own. Oberon leads the Council and he is... skilled... at making other councilors see his way of thinking."

"But what does he want?" I cried. "What does he have against magickers?"

The Duchess paused. "Odd as this may seem, Mona, I don't think he does have anything against them. At least, nothing personally."

I clenched my fists in the lap robe. It certainly felt personal to *me*.

"What Oberon wants—what he has always wanted—is power." She stared out the window, but I don't think she really saw it. "He has long believed that we should be waging war on other city-states, using the power of our war-wizards to bring as many of the cities as we can together under one ruler."

"Cor!" said Spindle. "Does 'e want to be an emperor, like in the old days?"

"More or less," said the Duchess, sighing. "He wants the power, but he wants a figurehead on the throne. If the people are angry, it is me that they will come after, not Oberon."

"And the magickers—" I said.

"A power he does not control, and so must be removed. He has a good idea of the strength of the army, but there are so many minor wizards in the city, and who knows what they might be capable of? Clearly he has decided to force them out, or kill them if they will not leave."

This may sound strange, but that actually made me feel a little better. Somehow it's better to be a potential enemy than one of "you people." At least you respect your enemies.

"Well," said the Duchess. "At the moment, Oberon believes that I am unaware of much of what he does... and apparently he is right! He believes that I am a fool, and there is no need to act against a foolish old woman. The moment that I become dangerous, he will act to remove me."

I gulped.

"It will happen sooner or later." She rose and began to pace through the room, still limping a little on her right knee. "I am only convenient so long as I am a figurehead, and even a foolish old woman, sooner or later, will protest at what she is asked to do." She fisted one hand in a tapestry. "I should have done so long before now. The blood of the magic-folk is on my hands. Mona, Spindle, I am sorry."

I didn't know what to say. Grown-ups don't usually apologize to kids, not about big stuff like that. When somebody says, "I'm sorry," you say, "It's okay." Except that this time it wasn't. Tibbie was dead. So were a lot of other people. Maybe she could have stopped it but maybe she couldn't, and who was I, Mona the baker, a wizard of bread-dough and cookies, to accept an apology on behalf of the dead?

Apparently, she didn't expect an answer, because all she did was drop her chin to her chest and lean against the doorframe for a moment.

"If only Lord Ethan were here," she said sadly. "Sending the army out was a mistake, but what could I do? The Carex mercenaries are raiding the outer townships for supplies and livestock—at least, so we have heard—and we cannot simply abandon those people to their fate. But Oberon is here and Lord Ethan is not, and I do not know if I am strong enough to stand against the Inquisitor and however many traitors he has rallied to his cause."

"Can't you get 'im back?" asked Spindle. "Send 'im a message! Tell 'im to get back here double-quick and throw Oberon out!"

"There is a problem with that as well," she said. "It takes a mage—a wizard, like Mona, but specially trained—to send a message quickly. Otherwise we must fall back on riders carrying messages, which will take days. And of the three wizards left stationed at the palace, one has died quite recently of natural causes..."

She stopped. I watched the knowledge cross her face that those causes had likely been unnatural. She took a deep breath, and continued. "One is very old and I do not know if he has the strength to send such a message at all."

"And the third one?" I asked, feeling cold. Only three mages? Only *two* mages, if one had just died?

"The third," said the Duchess, "I very much suspect is the one you call the Spring Green Man."

TWENTY-ONE

"Well," said Spindle, speaking for all of us, "this is a right pretty mess."

"The Spring Green Man? In the palace? *Here?*" I squeezed my arms around myself tightly, feeling an urge to make myself as small and inconspicuous as possible. What if he could smell me already? What if he'd smelled me coming in through the scullery? He probably couldn't climb up the garderobe, but he had to know what room it led to. What if he was outside the door right now?

No. The guards would have said something. The guards were loyal, the Duchess had said.

Assuming he hadn't killed them.

Possibly reading my wide-eyed look of panic, the Duchess rose and went to the door. She opened it a crack and said softly, "Anything going on?"

"No, my lady," said a deep male voice from the other side. "All is well."

"Thank you," said the Duchess. "See that I am not disturbed." She closed the door again.

"This old wizard," said Spindle. "How old are we talkin'? Like *old*-old, or like senile and decrepit-old?"

The Duchess raised an eyebrow. "Well, fairly old. I don't know that he's senile, but he's definitely feeling his age. His loyalty, at least, is never in doubt. He was a dear friend of my father's."

"He'll have to do," I said. "If the Spring Green Man is here in the actual palace—Your Grace, he could come for *you!*" (*And me*, I thought, but I didn't want to say it out loud.)

I expected her to tell me that I was being silly, or that there was something else I hadn't thought of—you know, the sort of things grown-ups tell you when you're absolutely positively sure of something, that blows the whole thing out of the water and makes you feel like an idiot—but she didn't. Instead she nodded, and said, "Yes. You're right. Let's go speak to him."

"Um," said Spindle. "We're not exactly dressed for wandering around the palace with you, ma'am."

The Duchess smiled. It was a haggard sort of smile, but under the circumstances, it was pretty good. "Don't worry about that, young man. There are *some* advantages to being the Duchess."

She opened the door. The guards snapped to attention.

"Joshua," she said to the one on the left, "go and get me some page's livery. Two sets, one small and one large. If you can't get the shirts, at least get the tunics."

"Your Grace?" said Joshua, looking a bit startled.

"*Now*, Joshua."

"Yes, Your Grace."

Joshua left his post. The guard on the right, admirably

blank-faced, moved to stand in front of the door. The Duchess closed the door again.

"Won't he tell somebody?" asked Spindle, puzzled.

"I highly doubt that the Inquisitor is going to be woken in the middle of the night by news that I am requesting two page's uniforms." She ran a hand through her hair and paced around the room again. "If he's monitoring me that closely, we are probably already doomed."

Spindle nodded absently. His attention had been claimed by a plate of cheese and bread on a little side table. "Err... ma'am...?"

"Spindle!" I hissed, mortified. We were here to prevent a bloody coup, not eat a midnight snack.

"Help yourself," said the Duchess, amused.

Spindle carved off a hunk of cheese and went to work. His table manners were mortifying. Also, now that I was aware that the cheese was there, I could smell it.

My appetite had shut down in self-defense during our ascent of the garderobe, but there were some stirrings that indicated it wasn't quite gone. I helped myself to some bread and cheese.

It was great cheese. The bread was pretty good. Superior flour, very fine, but a bit too dense where it wanted to be fluffy. I could have done great things with that flour.

A few minutes later, the guard returned. He came into the room carrying an armful of clothes and stopped dead when he saw Spindle and me.

"Your Grace..."

"They're friends of mine," said the Duchess firmly. "I am making them royal pages."

"But Your Grace—we were on guard—how did they...?" He

sounded almost plaintive.

"Through the garderobe," said the Duchess. "Which was ultimately a good thing, but nevertheless, we shall have to have it looked at. Not everyone climbing up it may be so benign."

"I... yes, Your Grace. At once."

"Couple of extra cross-bars ought to do it," Spindle piped up. "The spikes aren't worth much, but if you weld on another set of cross-bars, ain't nobody getting through but rats."

"Let us hope there will not be rats," said the Duchess firmly. "I accept that rats are a fact of life, but I am not overly fond of them. Now, children, let us get you into uniform..."

The uniforms fit, sort of. My pants wouldn't button. Spindle thought that was hysterical. His required a belt to hold up, which Joshua very kindly donated, and which went around Spindle's skinny waist twice before they could get it buckled.

The tunics, however, were long and elegant and hid a multitude of sins. They couldn't hide Spindle's rolled cuffs, or the fact that neither of us were wearing the right shoes, but hopefully nobody would be looking that closely.

The gingerbread man, recognizing that we were in disguise, gripped the back of my collar and hid underneath my hair.

"Very well," said the Duchess, surveying us. "No one is going to be looking that closely at this time of night. I hope. Let us go to Master Gildaen's quarters." She flung a cloak over her shoulders. "Joshua, if you would."

"Yes, Your Grace."

Stepping into the castle hallway was almost as frightening as climbing into the garderobe. The Spring Green Man was somewhere in the castle. What if he came out for some reason? What if he had insomnia, or wanted something from the kitchen, or just felt like murdering a random page that was wandering around the hallways?

The Duchess, however, had no such fears. She swept down the hall as if she owned it. I suppose technically she did. Joshua followed behind her with his hand on his sword hilt, looking very warlike and protective. I wondered how much he knew about what was going on with the Inquisitor. Spindle and I scurried after them. I was convinced that my shoes were leaving mud stains on the carpet, even though I couldn't see anything when I looked behind me.

We turned and turned and turned again, went down a broad staircase, and through a doorway. Joshua threw open another set of double doors and waved the Duchess through it with a little bow. Our eyes met when I was going through. He looked thoughtful and a little worried, but not mad. That was a relief.

"Now," said the Duchess, as we entered a broad hallway lined with doors. "Which one is Master Gildaen?"

"The third on the right, Your Grace."

"Thank you." She approached the correct door and rapped on the wood with her knuckles.

Nothing happened for a bit.

"He is a bit deaf, Your Grace," said Joshua apologetically. "If I may...?"

"Please."

Joshua pulled a knife—both Spindle and I took a step back—and hammered on the door with the pommel. "Open in the name of the Duchess!"

"Well, really," murmured the Duchess, "that seems a bit excessive."

"*Very* deaf," said Joshua, putting his knife away.

Apparently Master Gildaen was not quite as deaf as all that, because we heard a faint "I'm a-comin', I'm a-comin'..." and a moment later, the door swung open a handspan.

"What's this all about, then?" asked the wizard, sounding cranky. "It's the middle of the bloody night! It's so late it's practically early! What are you doing pounding on an old man's door at this hour?"

Joshua pushed the door open, and Master Gildaen took a step back. "What?" he said. "Hey, you show some respect, young fellow! I'll turn your blood into pickled herring, see if I don't!"

"Master Gildaen," said the Duchess warmly, "the kingdom needs your help."

The old wizard blinked at her. "Oh," he said slowly. "Oh. Err. Your Grace. I had no idea... come in, come in..." He took a few steps back and flapped his hands at us.

His chambers looked more like something you'd find in the Rat's Nest than inside the palace. There were things piled on... other things... none of them terribly clear of purpose or definite in origin. There was a wingback chair with a thing in it that looked like a cauldron made out of a crocodile, with a big glass fishbowl full of sludge where the footstool would be.

Doors opened on every side, although the one in the far wall was only accessible by stepping over a jumble of what had probably been suitcases at some point in the distant past.

Master Gildaen looked around the room awkwardly. "Oh dear. Will you come this way, Your Grace? I think the sitting room is... errr... not so... um."

The Duchess, showing the sort of grace that you expected from a monarch, said "Truly, it is nothing, Master Gildaen. We have come for your magical services, not your housekeeping skills."

"Magic, eh?" asked Gildaen glumly. He pushed open the door to the sitting room. It was indeed better, although there were still stacks of books across the floor, and dust made a thick fur across the backs of the chairs. "Should get young Elgar to do it. Not that he's good for anything but air and smoke and smells. Young wizards today! No better than a hedge-wizard, if you ask me. But still better than a senile old magicker. Not as young as I used to be, probably only make a hash of it..."

"We have reason to suspect that Elgar is a traitor," said the Duchess, sweeping into the sitting room.

Elgar. So the Spring Green Man had a name.

I followed her, with Spindle close behind me. Joshua took up a post by the door. The Duchess settled into a chair and looked up at Master Gildaen, who was looking old, old, far older than he had a few moments ago when we opened the door.

And yet, when he spoke, there was no trace of querulousness in his voice, and it sounded stronger than I would have expected, coming from such an old man.

"I see. So it has come to this, then." He met the Duchess's eyes. "I do not know how much magic is left in me, Your Grace, but I served your father and your father's father, and whatever I have left is yours to command."

TWENTY-TWO

Less than an hour later, I was jammed into a closet with Master Gildaen and a large bowl of water.

"You can't *all* fit in here," said the wizard, when Joshua seemed inclined to argue. "It's my working room. I go in there to talk to the waters, not entertain guests. My young colleague here can come with me, if you're worried I'm going to summon up water demons to wash your bones clean, but the rest of you might as well stay in the sitting room."

"I can't watch the entrance to the working room and the Duchess at the same time," said Joshua. "Not unless we all want to stand out in the hallway, and I don't think that would be a good idea."

The Duchess told him that he could watch the door and she'd be fine by herself and Joshua pretended that she hadn't said anything. That surprised me. I guess it was proof of what she had said, that the ruler of a city didn't have absolute power. As far as Joshua was concerned, when it came to keeping the

Duchess safe, he was in charge. And the Duchess seemed to accept this.

She turned to me instead. "Mona?"

I knew that wasn't an order. She was asking me if I was willing to do it, in case Master Gildaen was also a traitor. I could have said no, and we would have worked something out.

"I'll go," I said. I didn't believe that Gildaen was a traitor. He'd listened to the entire story, and if he had been, he would have acted surprised when we told him about Elgar, to divert suspicion.

Instead, when we told him about the Spring Green Man, he only nodded. "Sounds like Elgar, all right. Nasty young fellow, the sort that pulls wings off flies when he's bored. Always wearing those ridiculous bright green robes, too. You'd think he'd stick out like a sore thumb, but he's got that weird talent with air, wraps it around himself so your eyes just slide off him half the time."

"Can you go arrest him?" asked Spindle. He was eyeing Joshua's weapons with intense interest. "Go chop him up for being a traitor?"

"We can try," said Joshua. He looked at Master Gildaen for confirmation.

"*Try* is the right word, young man. Elgar's not enough wizard to stop the breath in your lungs, but he'll get smoke in your eyes and tangle your brain, and after that he only needs a knife. And the days when I could summon a rainstorm and wash the air clean for you are long behind me." Gildaen glanced at the Duchess and sighed. "But I'll do what I can, Your Grace, if you ask. Though I strongly suggest that we send a message to the Golden General first, so that if we fail, you aren't short a wizard."

"Then by all means, send your message, Master Gildaen." The Duchess gave Joshua a quelling look. He looked as disappointed as Spindle, although he hid it better.

Gildaen himself was a master of water. (This is one of the major differences between really good wizards and me. They've got access to *big* stuff, like water or air or lightning. Being able to command any kind of water is a lot more useful than being able to command any kind of bread.) He insisted on bringing out a teapot and teacups, although there hadn't been a fire in the fireplace in a very long time, judging by the state of the hearth. I busied myself wiping out the teacups with the edge of my tunic while the wizard hunted for tea.

When I started to say something about heating the water, however, he touched the teapot and steam poured from the spout.

"Hot water for tea I can still manage, for all the good it does me. I can send a message—probably—but I wasn't lying, Your Grace. You'd be better off with nearly any wizard in the kingdom other than me. The magic isn't what it used to be."

"There *are* no other wizards," said the Duchess. "Oberon has seen to that. You and Mona are the only ones I can trust. The others are dead or fled or deeply in hiding. Or rode away with the army weeks ago." She sighed and ran a hand through her graying hair. "I have been a fool for too long, Master Gildaen, and now we are all paying the price."

"Ah," said Master Gildaen. "But it is safer to be a fool, is it not? Do you think I have not known that, these last few months? No one bothers an old fool." He dropped his hands. "Come, Mona. If we are the last wizards in the kingdom, let us see what we can do."

When he put it like that, I had to go with him. Maybe we

were the last wizards in the kingdom. You probably couldn't count Knackering Molly. The odds that getting rid of Oberon would hinge on dead horses walking seemed pretty slim.

Master Gildaen wasn't lying—there really wasn't room for everyone in the working room. Joshua and the Duchess and Spindle stayed in Gildaen's suite just down the hall. Magical workrooms weren't connected directly to living quarters, in case the spells got loose. It made sense to me. If I lose control of my magic, the worst you get is bad bread. If Gildaen lost control, you could have a sheet of angry, intelligent boiling water rampaging through the castle.

Unlike the rest of his chambers, Gildaen's workroom was completely bare except for a padded stool and a large bowl of water sitting on top of an old wooden milk crate. The whole room was perhaps five paces long and three paces wide. I think it might have been a hall closet at one point, which would explain why it was right down the hall from his rooms.

He sat on the stool with his back to the door. I squeezed myself around the other side of the bowl of water and sat on the floor.

"Have you ever done any message work?" asked Gildaen, stirring the water with a finger.

"Uh..." The question surprised me. "I work with bread, sir. Just bread."

He snorted, eyeing the gingerbread man sitting on my shoulder. "And I work with water—*just* water. I admit bread's a little more specialized, but I suspect you could work something out. Convince your message to appear on a scone or something." He frowned down into the water and stirred it again. "Come on, you... wake up..."

I thought about it. I could probably convince a scone to burn in a specific pattern, like a word, but not at any great distance. Certainly not as far away as the army. "I don't think I'm strong enough," I said. "I'm... err... not a very good wizard. There's no way I could reach the army's ovens. I wouldn't even know how."

"Ha!" Master Gildaen shook a finger at me. "Neither could I, youngster. Doubt very many of us could. This bowl is the mate of a bowl the army's carrying with them, made by the same hand in the same hour, and the water in it was drawn up from the same well in the same bucket. I couldn't reach across the city cold. The only reason I can send a message at all is because the bowl and the water remember each other." He poked the water a third time, and leaned back, apparently satisfied. "All the message wizards have something like this. There's a man in a tent wherever the army's camped who has the bowl out, and a stick of Elgar's incense, and a tray of sand for poor Dalthyl..." He sighed. "Although I suppose they've taken Dalthyl's tray down, now."

"Maybe not," I said. "Elgar would have sent them the message that he was dead, right? Maybe he didn't. Maybe they don't know." Somehow that seemed likely to me. If things were coming to a head, would Oberon want the Golden General to know that the city was short a wizard?

Gildaen grunted. "You may be right. Anyway. We could probably arrange a mated pair of ovens, and dough from the same batch, and you could send messages that way. It'd be a little more awkward, but there's never enough wizards available, so people are always willing to find a workaround."

I'm pretty sure I blushed. The army was probably the only place in the city that wanted *more* wizards, particularly now.

"Err... honestly, sir, I'm really not that much of a wizard. I mean, I bake stuff. It's nothing special."

He made a rude noise. "You've got your head stuffed full of stories about wizards smashing mountains and hurling fireballs. You're not that weak, youngster. Wizards have done more with less."

"It's *bread,*" I said.

"Kilsandra the Assassin grew roses," he said, bending over the bowl. "That was all she could work with. She convinced them to grow deadly poisons and sleeping powders in their pollen, and to carry messages along their stems so that she could eavesdrop on her enemies. She nailed up a few people in rose thickets with thorns as long as your arm. There are a couple of kingdoms where they still won't grow roses within a hundred yards of the palace or the army barracks, just because of her, and she died eighty years ago." He tapped the side of the bowl with a fingernail. "Mind you, I don't suggest that you'd want to follow in her footsteps, but with a little imagination... ah, here we go."

The water rippled and sloshed, and a tinny voice said, "Gildaen? Is that you?"

"Don't sound so surprised, Hagar. I'm not dead yet. Not like poor Dalthyl."

I peered over the edge of the bowl of water. It showed two sets of reflections, like two panes of glass laying on top of each other. One was of Master Gildaen, and the other was of a woman with frizzy blonde hair. Apparently this was Hagar. Due to the angle, I could see directly up her nose.

She frowned, which changed the view somewhat. "*Dalthyl?* What are you talking about?"

Gildaen and I shared a long look over the top of the bowl of water.

"Listen to me," said Gildaen. "Dalthyl's dead. Elgar's a traitor. Oberon's planning something. You have to get the army back here as soon as possible."

Hagar's nostrils flared. I think she probably furrowed her brow, too, but mostly what I saw was the flare. "What? *Elgar?* Are you sure?"

"Of course I'm sure, nitwit!" Gildaen pounded on the milkcrate with his fist, which sent ripples across the water and temporarily broke up Hagar's reflection. "The Duchess told me herself! You've got to do somethi—"

It was the ripples. The ripples distorted everything. The flicker of pale green that appeared behind him was too broken up for either of us to notice it until the Spring Green Man put a knife into Master Gildaen's back.

Gildaen gasped. It was a wet, unhappy sound. Through the water, faintly, I heard Hagar shriek. I jerked my head up and saw the Spring Green Man—Elgar—pull the blade out of the old wizard's back.

Time shuddered and juddered to a halt. We might have been a trio of statues, me and Gildaen and the Spring Green Man standing over us. All I could think for a moment was that the blade was clean, there was no blood on it, surely that meant that this was all a mistake, Gildaen hadn't *really* been stabbed, when people got stabbed, the knife was all bloody, wasn't it?

Then Master Gildaen slumped forward over the milk crate, and his breath rattled in his chest like Nag's bones, and time started up again.

"*You* again," Elgar said, looking down at me. "Stupid child. I lost your scent and I thought you'd fled weeks ago. Coming here to the palace, right under my nose? Thought I'd puke from the smell of you." He shook his head. "I suppose the game is up now that I had to kill Gildaen, but at least it lets me wrap up one more loose end."

Oh god, I thought. *Oh god, we're in the magic wing of the palace. Of course Elgar could smell us. He probably lives right down the hall, and everybody's so used to being in a palace they didn't even think about it. Oh god, we actually thought that if we didn't knock on the door, he wouldn't know we were here.*

The room was too narrow. Elgar had come in through the only door, but now he had to come around one side of the milk crate or the other, but I couldn't get any farther away. If I tried to bolt down the other side, he could just reach across the crate or knock it over and grab me.

I was trapped.

"I owe you, anyway," snarled Elgar. "Throwing your damned acid-beast on me."

It was then that I noticed the shiny pink scars across the side of his face. Apparently Bob had done some damage. A small, bitter satisfaction bloomed in my chest, inside the terror.

Elgar took another step forward and pushed Master Gildaen aside with his knee. I could smell that thick, spicy scent that I remembered from the first time he tried to kill me. My stomach churned.

His feet didn't make any sound on the floor. It must have been more of his magic. If you can control air, maybe you can control the sounds that move through it. No wonder he'd been so good at sneaking up on people.

I pressed myself flat against the back wall. The gingerbread man crouched on my shoulder, icing eyes narrowed.

Two more steps and he'd be on me.

I'd have to try to bolt. There wasn't any other option. It wasn't going to work, and I knew it wasn't going to work, but the alternative was to stand there and be stabbed. Maybe if I could get to the door, I could yell a warning to the Duchess—

Dear Lady of Sorrowful Angels, the Duchess!

They were all in the sitting room. Still. The Spring Green Man must have snuck past the front door and gone for the working room, and meanwhile the Duchess and Spindle were just sitting in the other room a few feet down the hallway, drinking tea and waiting, with only a thin wooden door and a single guard to protect them.

I took a deep breath and screamed as loud as I could.

It didn't seem very loud. It seemed like a thin little wail. Elgar snorted and lifted his knife. From the bowl of water, I heard Hagar crying, "What's happening? What's going on?"

Master Gildaen, with what had to be his very last strength, got a hand under the bowl of water and flipped it onto Elgar's legs.

Elgar screamed, much louder than I had.

Whatever Master Gildaen had said about his fading skills, I'll swear that water was boiling when it hit the Spring Green Man.

He scrabbled at his robes, hissing in pain, and I lunged for the door. I wanted to grab Master Gildaen but I wasn't strong enough to haul him out. As it was, I just tried not to step on him, and then the Spring Green Man, half-weeping from his burns, clubbed me in the back of the head with his elbow and knocked me down.

I landed in a sprawl across Master Gildaen. My head rang and I knew that at pretty much any second there was going to be a knife stuck in me. The gingerbread man was thrown free and rolled, shedding bits of icing.

"I'll kill you," said Elgar, almost sobbing, stumbling as he turned toward me. I tried to crawl forward, away from him, but it was so slow and the stupid page's pants were too small and seemed to have my hips in a vise and my left hand hurt where I'd landed on it and Master Gildaen was under me and he wasn't breathing any more...

I squeezed my eyes shut—it was going to be a cold bright pain, I just knew it, and then I was going to die, and that would be the end of a bread wizard named Mona who just wanted to make really good sourdough and muffins and not get messed up with assassins and politics and—

There was a thud of impact. Something heavy hit me. It didn't feel like I had imagined that the knife would feel, but it was definitely heavy and knocked the wind out of me. *Maybe this is what being stabbed feels like,* I thought, *maybe you don't even feel it, it's just like something really heavy hitting you—*

"Mona," said Spindle, sounding frantic, "Mona! Get up! C'mon, get up!"

Spindle?

I opened my eyes.

Joshua dragged the Spring Green Man off me. He had clubbed him over the head with a chair. I gulped air, trying to get that spicy, head-clogging smell out of my lungs.

Except for a skinned palm where I'd tried to catch myself when I fell, I was unhurt.

Master Gildaen was dead.

And that meant that I was the last loyal wizard left in the palace.

TWENTY-THREE

"We must move quickly," said the Duchess. "The army is at least ten days away, and Oberon knows it as well as we do. We move against him now, tonight, before he is expecting it."

She made this announcement while we all stood in a circle around the Spring Green Man, who had a massive bruise across his forehead and was trussed up like a turkey. Joshua had tied him up with several belts and one of Master Gildaen's dressing gowns, torn into strips. It was a haphazard binding, but it didn't *look* haphazard.

Actually, it looked like he'd strangle himself if he so much as sneezed.

Spindle had wanted to kill him outright, right then and there, for what he did to Tibbie. The Duchess talked him out of it. "There will be a trial," she said. "We will not compound murder with murder. We will see justice done so that everyone in the city knows that magic folk cannot be killed with impunity." I'm pretty sure that's the only thing that convinced Spindle. That, and the fact that Joshua had a much bigger sword.

"Tonight," said Joshua, nodding. "We do not have time to delay."

"How we gonna do that?" asked Spindle.

"And what about Master Gildaen?" I wiped my nose. I was trying not to cry for the old wizard. We had set him in the other room with his arms over his chest and the sheet off his bed thrown over him for a shroud.

I'd known him for less than an hour, but I wanted to bawl my eyes out. He'd been kind to me, and he hadn't acted like I was just a little two-bit magicker, and he'd sent the message that might save us, and if I'd just been looking *up* instead of into the water—

The Duchess put an arm around my shoulders. "I know," she said softly. "I know. We'll give him a hero's burial. But we can't do it tonight. It won't do him any good, and if we don't act now, we'll waste what he did for us."

I took a deep, shuddering breath. She was right. I tried to cram the sad bits into a ball and squash them into the hollow place inside my chest. Later. I could cry about this later.

The gingerbread man, who had lost most of his buttons but was otherwise unharmed, reached up a hand and patted my face. The Duchess squeezed my shoulder and let go. "Joshua, how many guards are still loyal to me, personally?"

"Almost all of them, Your Grace," said Joshua immediately. "The ministers and lords I can't speak for, but the guard is yours. Oberon's personal guard would fight for him, but there aren't many else."

The Duchess nodded. "Lords and ministers we'll deal with later. Go and assemble the guard, Joshua. Get as many men as you can and do it quietly. Bring them to the great hall. You have thirty minutes."

"But—Your Grace, I can't leave you alone!"

She sighed. "Go and get Harold from my chamber guard, then, and send him here."

Joshua fidgeted inside his armor. "Your Grace, that would still leave you alone for a few minutes, and with this"—he nudged the Spring Green Man with his boot—"and no one to protect you. What if he comes to?"

The Duchess reached under her dressing gown and pulled out a knife. It was as long as the big butcher knife that Aunt Tabitha used to cut up pork for our pork buns. She sat down next to the Spring Green Man and held the knife a few inches from his throat.

"Whoa," said Spindle, with obvious approval. I blinked. This was a side of the Duchess I had not expected.

Joshua wrung his hands. "He's a *wizard*."

"So is Mona," said the Duchess. "Joshua, *go*. The sooner you go, the sooner this is all over and the less chance that he'll wake up."

Joshua went.

If you have never tried to make conversation with a monarch, over the hog-tied body of an evil wizard, with a dead man in the next room, it is *not* easy. Talking about the weather didn't seem appropriate, and "So, do you think this will work, or are we all going to die?" didn't strike me as very good either.

"Think this'll work, or are we all going to die?" asked Spindle, who was not troubled by social niceties. I sighed.

"Normally, I would say something reassuring," said the Duchess dryly, gesturing with her knife, "but you are not ordinary children, are you? So—I don't know if it will work. We have already gotten farther than I expected. I am hoping that if a troop of the guard throws Oberon bodily out of the city tonight, we may buy ourselves time enough for the army to return."

"If Oberon's gone, though, that's it, right?" I asked. "It's over. We got the Spring Green Man. We don't need the army."

The Duchess exhaled. "I don't know, Mona. I hope so. But Oberon has allies. That's why I don't dare kill him outright." She smiled, but it was an unhappy, twisty smile and it looked like it hurt a little. "I know that he should be allowed a fair trial and all that, but I will be honest, my dears—I would have him executed without any of the niceties if I dared. I have seen enough to convince me of his wickedness. But the lords and ministers that have allied themselves with him might rise up in revolt."

This was depressing. I had thought that if we just got rid of Oberon and the Spring Green Man, everything would go back to normal. It hadn't occurred to me that we might be able to throw Oberon out and still have more problems.

There was a knock on the door. I jumped. Spindle got up and opened the door a crack, leaning his whole body against the wood to keep it from being thrown open. "Who's there?" he growled, trying to make his voice sound deeper.

"Harold, for her Grace."

The Duchess nodded. Spindle opened the door, and the other guard from her chamber door came in. He looked from Spindle to me to the Duchess to the trussed-up Spring Green Man, and back to the Duchess. His expression didn't change in the slightest. "Your Grace," he said.

"Still the best poker face in the kingdom," said the Duchess warmly.

The new guard, Harold, sat down next to the Spring Green Man and drew his sword, laying practically on top of the mage's neck. It looked rather absurdly like a knighting. The Duchess stood up and began prowling around the room. I found some tea, still with a little warmth left from Gildaen's spell, and that made me cry again, but I did it in the corner and I don't think anyone noticed.

Harold was even less talkative than Joshua. The Duchess chewed on her lower lip and stared through chairs and bookcases, looking at something only she could see.

It's kind of sad when you've got an evil wizard tied up at your feet, a dead man in the next room, the monarch of the kingdom pacing the floor and you're waiting to instigate a coup that will throw out a traitor to the kingdom... and you realize you're *bored*.

Waiting is never very interesting, I guess. I was feeling a sick dread at the thought that I might have to see Oberon again, or that he might win, in which case we were probably all going to die or end up in the dungeons and *then* die—but I was still restless. If I left my mind alone, it wanted to start replaying Master Gildaen's death over and over. Minds are not our friends.

I wandered over to the bookcase and ran my fingers over the row of spines, wondering if there was something to read. Most of them were thick, heavy, leather-bound books that looked even more boring than waiting. My fingers left long trails in the dust and I had to wipe grime off. (*Not* on my clean tunic. I used the too-small pants. I was starting to get a real loathing for those pants.)

On the third shelf, eighth book in, my fingers stopped. The binding was just as dusty as all the others, but it had an interesting pattern of leaves and spirals on it. Also, it was a *lot* thinner. I pulled it down.

The title said *Spiraling Shadows: Reflections on the Use of Magic*. An embossed fern wove in and out of the letters. There was no author listed.

I looked around. Harold was glaring at the Spring Green Man, who had started—unbelievably—to snore. Spindle was flopped over in a chair upside down, picking at a bare spot on the arm of the chair. The Duchess gave me a vague smile in passing and kept prowling.

So. Nobody was stopping me. And it would probably be too dense to read anyway. I was an okay reader—I mean, compared to somebody like Spindle, who couldn't read a broadsheet—but mostly for recipes and stuff like that.

I'm not sure why I hesitated. It'll probably sound weird to say that the book felt different in my hands. Not hot, not cold, not even really magic, just... *kind*. It felt like a cup of tea on a cold day, or a warm scone left by the oven. Could a wizard's books feel like that? I'd never really thought about a wizard's library much. Mine was all cookbooks and none of them were magic. A *real* wizard's library would presumably be much grander, and have books with curses on them that you had to chain to the shelves or they would blast any mortal who touched them.

I glanced along the shelves. None of them were chained. Most of them just looked old and tired, rather like Master Gildaen himself had. *Spiraling Shadows* was the only one that seemed different. Would a cursed book really feel kind when you held it?

Well, if I were going around cursing books, it would probably be a lot easier to get people to pick up one that felt nice rather than one covered in skulls that you had to chain to the shelf.

I couldn't imagine Master Gildaen keeping cursed books lying around, though. He hadn't seemed like the type. And Elgar seemed less interested in curses than in knives.

I cracked open the cover. The first few pages were blank. I flipped to a page at random and read:

> *...I say again, giving magical life to inanimate objects is not a function of size but of intelligence and duration. The life force of an elephant is no greater than that of a mouse, merely it lasts longer and is greater in intellect. If you would give life to the unliving, it matters not whether it is as large as a mountain or as small as a housecat, the spark of life differs not in power. The weakest may command a mountain, if they have the gift of it, but the mountain will be mindless and remain living only a moment's time.*

The text was old and had some odd confusion between the f's and the s's, and a couple of the words gave me trouble —"inanimate" doesn't come up often in cookie recipes. Still, it was readable. I just wasn't sure it made sense.

Was it saying that if you were making something come alive, it didn't matter how big they were?

And what did it mean by "alive"... was it talking about things like my gingerbread man?

If that *was* what it meant, did that mean I could make a gingerbread elephant come alive?

I grinned despite myself. That couldn't be what it meant. I mean, I'd never *tried* to make a full-size gingerbread elephant, but surely that was impossible. Otherwise minor talents like me would be setting gingerbread monsters running through the streets... wouldn't we?

Not that *I* would.

Probably.

Well, maybe *one*. Just to see if I could.

Can that be right? The breadcrumb circus took a lot less power than my little gingerbread friend here, and they were so much smaller.

Although the breadcrumb circus hadn't been intelligent at all. They could only do one thing each. The little bread lion tamer waved his little chair and that was it, and the little tigers paced around and jumped on the little platforms, but that was all. They only did more elaborate tricks if I was actively directing them. It had gotten better when I used the single loaf of bread apiece, but they still weren't smart. But my gingerbread man *was* pretty smart, and he'd lasted a really long time, whereas the circus had probably fallen apart an hour after I'd left.

Hmm. Did it matter that I'd baked his dough myself? Had my hands in it? The unbaked dough had been a lot more responsive to me, too. And I'd always known that I might make the gingerbread men dance when I made up a batch. If I mixed up a load of dough, knowing what I wanted to do with it...

Oh, probably this was ridiculous. But I suddenly found myself wanting access to a really big mixing bowl and an oven the size of a house, just to see if I could make a gingerbread elephant.

The door rattled. Harold jumped, and Spindle sat up in the chair. The Duchess froze, and even though she was still an ordinary-looking middle-aged woman, she reminded me suddenly of a tiger—a real one, not made of breadcrumbs. A tiger waiting to pounce.

I was proud of her, but strangely, it also made me angry. Why couldn't she have been like this before any of this happened? Why had it taken two kids and a wizard so old he could barely stand to make her find her courage?

Why hadn't anyone *done* anything?

The door opened. It was Joshua.

"Your Grace," he said, and bowed low. "Your men await."

TWENTY-FOUR

I really didn't want to be around when they arrested Inquisitor Oberon. The Duchess said that she was going to throw him out of the city, and that sounded like a great idea, except that there was a whole lot of city between here and the gates and what if something went horribly wrong?

I couldn't shake the feeling that even now, somehow, Oberon could win. And that meant that I had to go with the Duchess, because however bad it would be if something did go wrong, it would be a lot worse to not know about it until the guards broke in and Spindle and I got dragged down to the dungeon. (Not by Joshua and Harold, of course. Other guards. The constables, maybe. Joshua seemed more like the Duchess's bodyguard than like a constable. I was never going to be easy with constables again, no matter how many scones they bought.)

Speaking of dungeons, the Spring Green Man was already on his way there. Harold was carrying him like a sack of meal, and he was still snoring occasionally. I don't think it's very safe to sleep when someone has hit you over the head really hard, but I confess, I was having a hard time dredging up any sympathy for the assassin. Besides, they said that they had cells to keep mages in, but I wasn't sure how that would work, and if Elgar woke up woozy and concussed, it was probably safer for everybody if he was in someplace where he couldn't do anything terrible.

Come to think of it, even if he woke up in a great mood and full control of his faculties, it was probably safer for everybody that way.

Spindle, who never had mixed feelings about anything, was delighted to come along with the guards and see Oberon "get it," as he put it. The Spring Green Man might have killed Tibbie, but Oberon had been the one to set him loose, and Spindle was thrilled right down to his toes.

"Maybe he'll resist, and the guards'll whack 'im!" he hissed to me, as we followed Joshua down the hallway.

"Maybe he'll say something political and grown up and the guards'll turn around and whack *us*," I whispered gloomily back.

"Well, ain't you a bright ray of sunshine..."

I sighed. Spindle's natural distrust of authority seemed to break down a bit when authority was fighting with itself, or maybe the Duchess had won him over when she pulled out that knife. I stared down at my not-standard-issue-for-pages shoes. My pants still didn't fit, but I'd wedged the book Spiraling Shadows into my belt, and something about the cover pressing against my belly made me feel a little better. I was still half-sick with terror—*what if Oberon sees me? What if he recognizes me?*—but it was a walking around and doing stuff terror, not a curl up in the corner and whimper terror. I guess that's something.

"How many men did you bring?" asked the Duchess, as we turned toward the main hall.

"Thirty-seven," said Joshua. "Nearly all the palace guard. There were four or five who were not... quite right in their reaction. Almost, but not quite. We locked them in a pantry. They may be innocent—I think it likely that some are—but I would not be surprised if one or two of them are in Oberon's pay, and it seemed better that they not have a chance to carry tales."

"Thirty-seven should be enough," said the Duchess. "The nobles have their own guards, but they cannot keep all of them in the palace. Oberon has no more than six men of his own, and he must see that they cannot stand against so many." She chewed on her lower lip. "I hope that he must see..."

Joshua pushed open the door to the great hall.

Thirty-seven men doesn't sound like a lot, but they can *really* fill a room.

Most of them were wearing armor and carrying swords, and a couple had those big halberd things that look like an axe and a spear got together and had really scary babies.

Spindle and I both stopped in the doorway. That's a whole lot of guys with swords, and no matter how much I liked the Duchess, up until a couple of hours ago, people like that had been trying to capture me and throw me in a dungeon. I guess Spindle felt the same way. He shoved his hands in his pockets and said, "Cor!"

The Duchess sailed into the room, and every man put his fist over his heart in salute to the monarch. It was amazing to watch her. Suddenly the tired, timid woman we'd met was—oh, not gone, but covered in a kind of shell. She smiled at them, and

I bet every single one of them thought that she looked him specifically in the eye when she smiled. I guess that's something you learn when you're royalty, or maybe that's why some people get to be royal and the rest of us make bread or carry halberds for them.

"My friends," she said, in a low, carrying voice. They all leaned forward, just a little, when she spoke. "I realize how strange it is that you have all been called together in private here. But we go tonight to roust a traitor from our kingdom, a man who wishes to—" she paused, "—to *overthrow* me and set himself up as ruler of our city."

A low growl rose from the guards, like a great dog on a chain. It was obvious to everyone that *overthrow* wasn't the word that she had planned to use. Somebody wanted their Duchess dead, and the guards were *not happy*.

"I cannot tell you, my friends, how grateful I am for your loyalty. In these times, it is the only coin in our kingdom of any worth, and I thank you, from the bottom of my heart." She put her hand over her own heart and saluted them, and I swear that every guard in the room stood an inch taller when she did.

"Ain't that somethin'," said Spindle softly.

Joshua stepped in then, and took command of the operation. "Halberdiers to the fore. Every man look to the other members of your watch. We go to confront a traitor, and treachery spreads like wildfire. Let no one slip away unnoticed. I trust you all, or I would not have called you here, but the life of the Duchess and the welfare of the kingdom is too important to place on my judgment alone."

I saw nods here and there, and set expressions. Spindle and I weren't going to be able to leave, even if we wanted to.

"Move out!" called Joshua, and at the head of a column,

with the Duchess striding on his left hand, they turned and made for our doorway.

We fell in with the column, next to the Duchess. There didn't seem to be any other option. Spindle gave me a look I couldn't read and I shrugged helplessly—we were in this way too far to pull out now.

The Duchess reached out and took both of our hands.

"What happens now?" I asked. I nearly had to shout over the tramp of booted feet.

"Now we throw the dice," she said.

It didn't seem like a very stealthy approach. Half the castle had to have known we were coming. I saw a couple of maids peeking around a corner at us, their mouths hanging open. But we arrived at a door that looked like any other door, and four halberdiers lowered their weapons and stood in a semicircle with the blades pointing at the doorway. The Duchess stood behind them, with Spindle and I on either side of her, and Joshua stepped forward and hammered on the door.

The door opened a crack and Joshua threw his shoulder against it and said "Duchess's business. Open up!"

"What?" said the guard on the other side.

"Duchess's business!" Joshua said, shoving harder. The Duchess's hand tightened on mine. We both had sweaty palms.

There were muffled voices inside, and then I heard *him.* Inquisitor Oberon.

"—well, open up then, fool, if it's Duchess's business—"

"But sir—"

The door was flung open, and Inquisitor Oberon stood in it, flanked by a pair of guards.

He seemed smaller. I suppose having a whole bunch of sharp objects pointed at you makes anybody shrink a little. His robes weren't quite perfect, or maybe people look less scary when you're standing with a small army around you. But the eyes—the eyes were the same.

I realized that I was squeezing the Duchess's hand in a death grip, and that she was squeezing back.

"Your Grace," said Inquisitor Oberon, and even now, I'll give him credit, it's not easy to ignore thirty-seven guards, particularly when there are halberds pointing at you. He managed somehow. The guards might as well have been invisible. "To what do I owe the honor of this visit?"

"On suspicion of treason to the crown," said the Duchess, her voice clear and ringing, "you are being exiled from the city."

Oberon's eyes widened just a little. "May I ask to know the source of these charges?" he asked.

Nobody but me knew how bad the Duchess's hands were shaking, when she said "You have condemned yourself by your own hand, Oberon. The curfews and registration laws against the mage-folk were done without my orders and without my knowledge. This is a blow against the very heart of our people, and a presumption of authority that you do not possess."

Oberon's eyes did not flicker at the charge. His gaze travelled over the Duchess, dismissed Spindle, dismissed the guards... and landed on me.

"Your Grace," he said, "for any presumption I have made, I beg your pardon. But I fear that you are being misled. The mage beside you is the true traitor. We have been trying to apprehend her for assault upon her fellow magic-folk for some weeks now."

My stomach felt like it was being kneaded by a baker with a savage grudge against the dough. The gingerbread man clinging to the back of my collar moved and patted my neck, as if I were a nervous horse.

"Mona is a loyal subject of the crown," said the Duchess. "The false arrest orders you have issued will be dealt with summarily. You, in the meanwhile, will be leaving the city at once."

Oberon chose to ignore this last statement. "Your Grace," he said smoothly, "while your judgment is far superior to mine, I would be remiss as your subject if I allowed this to pass. That is a mage and a traitor. She may be clouding your mind even now. If you will not take my word, the mage Elgar—"

"Is rottin' in a cell right now!" said Spindle, who had been about to burst this whole time and clearly couldn't take it anymore. "He stabbed that other fella in front of us, an' he killed my sister Tibbie, so shut your trap!"

Swords and halberds hadn't impressed Oberon, but that rocked him back on his heels. He opened his mouth and then closed it again and was so plainly at a loss that the Duchess released my hand and stepped forward between the halberdiers.

"Exile," she said again. "Now. At once. You will not taint this city a moment longer with your presence."

The Inquisitor pulled himself together. "If Your Grace will allow me a few moments to pack—"

"No," said the Duchess. "I do not trust you not to try to wiggle away. You are coming with us now. Joshua, see to it."

Joshua drew his sword. The scrape of steel was very loud in the corridor.

Oberon's guards drew together in front of him. Joshua looked past them to Oberon. "Do not waste your men's lives," he said. "There are a great many of us, and in the confusion, I cannot swear that you yourself would go unharmed."

Oberon inhaled sharply through his nose. I held my breath. Even now I was nearly sure that there would be something he could say that would turn the tide.

"Very well," he said.

He stepped forward. Our guards relieved his guards of their swords, and the two men joined him in a little wedge of prisoners.

Joshua went first, with three men behind him. Then came the prisoners, then the halberdiers, then the Duchess and Spindle and I, then a whole mass of other guards, and the entire parade went down the corridor and into the great hall and out into the courtyard.

There was a prison wagon waiting. I'd only ever seen one from a distance. They're great rough things with iron bars and strapped iron wheels, and they don't look any better up close. But Oberon stepped up into it with the same haughty expression he had worn stepping into his official gilded carriage. His guards got in as well, although the second one paused and looked at the Duchess.

"Your Grace, I have a wife..."

His tone was pleading. The Duchess nodded. "I cannot allow you to stay," she said. "But Joshua will see to it that she is given a pension, or coin enough to travel to find you again."

The guard nodded. My heart ached for him. What if his wife couldn't find him again? What if she didn't want to leave the city? What if he wasn't a traitor, and we were punishing him for no reason?

It's hard to rule a city. I wouldn't want to have to do it.

Joshua stepped up onto the wagon's seat. Two more men

joined him, one standing on the wagon's back to watch the prisoners. Another two wagons—open farm wagons, by the look of them, Joshua must have commandeered someone making deliveries to the kitchen—pulled up alongside, and even more men, including all the halberdiers, climbed into them.

The Duchess went up to the back of the prison wagon and gazed inside at Oberon. I felt an intense urge to grab her and pull her back, away from the bars, the way Aunt Tabitha used to when I got too close to the animals in the menagerie. What if he was hiding a knife in his socks, or had one of those rings with poison needles in them that assassins carry? What if he'd thought of something to convince her that I really was a traitor?

But he only looked at her, and said, very calmly, "You could have ruled a dozen cities, if you had the stomach for it."

"I have no desire to be responsible for so many lives," said the Duchess coolly.

He nodded once. "You always did lack vision. It does not matter. You will regret this night's work."

He didn't add, "Your Grace." The Duchess nodded to Joshua, and the prisoners and the guards rattled out of the courtyard, towards the edge of the city.

"Spindle," I said, as the sound of the wagon wheels faded.

"Eh?"

"Did you have to start yelling at Oberon in the middle of the arrest?"

"Hey, it worked, didn't it?"

I sighed from the bottom of my toes. Yes. It had worked.

And the Duchess hadn't pitched Spindle out of the city alongside Oberon for speaking up out of turn. Still.

"Your Grace—"

"It's all right, Mona," the Duchess said, and managed a weary laugh. "It all worked out for the best anyway."

"What happens now?" I asked.

"Well, Joshua deposits him on the other side of the Exile's Gate, I call an emergency meeting of the council to inform them of the events before gossip gets to them, we spread the word that Oberon's been convicted of treason in absentia, and then I buy off the nobles who would otherwise protest his loss by handing out his lands and titles as bribes."

I gulped. That sounded like a lot of work, and I was already bone-tired. In one night I'd climbed a garderobe, met a monarch, talked to a mage, seen him killed, nearly gotten stabbed myself, and helped evict a traitor. I could use a nap. For about six months or so. "Do we have to be there for all of that?"

The Duchess laughed. "No. Your job is done, my dears, and you have done it better and more faithfully than anyone could ask. I will probably have to give you medals, and perhaps a knighthood."

I gulped again. A knighthood? That *also* sounded like a lot of work. I'd have to get armor or something. I just wanted to go home to the bakery and make scones. Or muffins. Or cinnamon rolls. Or all three.

"Cor!" said Spindle. "Sir Spindle! Can you see it? I'd get a horse the size of an elly-phant, and wear armor and—"

"Time enough for that in the next few days," said the Duchess, amused. "Luke—" to one of the guards hovering around the courtyard, "—these two are heroes of the realm. Find them someplace to sleep and see that they have a late dinner or a very early breakfast or whatever it is we're up to now."

Luke bowed to her, and then to us and led us to bedrooms. The bed in mine was gigantic and the sheets were really cold, but a girl came in and built up a fire in the grate. I guess things must have warmed up, but I was already asleep, with the copy of *Spiraling Shadows* on the bedside table.

TWENTY-FIVE

I went home to the bakery the next day. There was an honor guard with me, and when we all walked in, Aunt Tabitha stared at us all blankly for ten seconds and then said, "Mona?" and burst into tears.

I threw myself into her arms. She smelled like flour and she put her arms around me and the horrible weeks I'd spent on the run got a little farther away. Then I cried a bit, and my uncle cried, and Spindle, who was lounging in the corner getting fingerprints on the glass of the bakery case, snorted and rolled his eyes.

"We thought you were *dead*," said Aunt Tabitha, once she'd gotten herself under control. She started pressing cinnamon rolls into the hands of the guards. "There was all that mess in the basement. But then they put up the posters, and I knew you weren't dead, because they wouldn't be trying to arrest you otherwise. I *knew* it!" She put her fists on her hips. "And I knew that it had to be a mistake, because

I've had the raising of you for years, girl, and I knew you were no criminal, no matter what some ridiculous constable said!"

She glared at the guards, as if she planned to take the cinnamon rolls back. They tried to look meek and not as if they were covered in bits of icing.

"It's okay, Aunt Tabitha," I said. "It was all a misunderstanding, and—oh, I'll tell you everything! But Bob! Is Bob...?" I steeled myself.

"Bob?" asked Tabitha blankly. "Oh! He was a right mess, and half of him gone, but a little flour and water and he perked right up again." She leaned in and murmured, "I gave him a bucket of dead sardines from the fishmonger. Don't tell your uncle."

When I went down to the cellar, Bob was so excited to see me that he crawled half out of his bucket, reared up, and wrapped himself around my leg. He'd never done that before. I rubbed his back as best I could, given how sticky he was, and he glorped and burbled happily.

The gingerbread man rolled his eyes. I think he was a little jealous.

So that was pretty much that.

Well... that should have been pretty much that, anyway.

For three days, everything was normal. I wandered around the bakery singing and taking delight in even the most mundane baking activities—dough rising! How marvelous! And the way the steam burst out of the blueberry muffins when you tore into one right out of the oven! Was there ever anything prettier?

Aunt Tabitha hugged me rather more than normal, and the regular customers had to hear the story ten times over.

And then at night, I'd lie in bed and wouldn't sleep.

It wasn't that I wasn't tired. I was. And it should have been easier to sleep now than it had been in the church, shouldn't it? All the posters had been taken down and the word had gone out that we did *not* register magickers in Riverbraid and the people responsible were in a lot of trouble. And Oberon was gone and Elgar was presumably in a cell under the palace on bread and water. Not even good bread. It should have been easier now.

It wasn't. I wasn't afraid, exactly. I just stared at the ceiling and sleep didn't happen and my mind replayed all the moments that it could have gone wrong. I cried for Master Gildaen. I stared at the ceiling some more.

I remembered the Widow Holloway saying that she couldn't sleep after her husband died, walking back and forth in the small hours of the night. I wasn't quite that brave. So mostly I stared at the ceiling.

When I gave up trying to sleep, I lit a candle and read a few more passages of *Spiraling Shadows*. The Duchess had said I could take it, since Master Gildaen hadn't had any kin or heirs. She hadn't cried, but her eyes had been a little too bright. Probably mine had been, too.

The book was interesting. Parts of it were much too complicated for me, and there was a lot about the philosophy of magic that didn't make any sense at all... something about magic rising up out of the earth like water from a spring and ley lines and its tendency to concentrate in certain vegetables like eggplants. The author devoted a whole chapter to eggplants. I skimmed that one.

But there were also sections about the magic of sympathy, which was what Master Gildaen had been talking about—how two things that are joined together once are joined together always on some level, and how a wizard can use that to her advantage. It made me want to perform experiments. Thinking about those experiments got me through the worst of the nights, and then I'd get up early and go and bake them.

The first few were pretty straightforward. I'd already figured out that if I made a little bread-crumb creature, it wouldn't hold together well unless the material was all from the same loaf. I spent hours with the day-old pastries, trying to work out the limits. It turned out that things all baked at the same time, on the same sheet, generally got along okay, too.

From there, it was a short step to holding one cinnamon roll and trying to make the rest of the pan do... something.

"Mercy!" said Aunt Tabitha, the first time she walked in and saw me standing over a pan of cinnamon rolls that had caught fire. She grabbed for the flour and dumped it out over the pan, smothering the flames. "What are you *doing?*"

I looked gloomily at the cinnamon roll in my hand. "Failing, mostly." I'd tried to warm the one on the pan up, that was all, pushing the magic through the cinnamon roll in my hand to its kindred. There'd been some resistance along that weird little mental conduit, so I pushed more magic at it.

Between the exploding bird and the burning cinnamon rolls, I was coming to the conclusion that *more* magic was not necessarily the solution.

These experiments made my head hurt, but in a good way. It was like whipping cream with a whisk. By the end, your arms ached and there was sweat dripping off the end of your nose, but you had all this lovely smooth whipped cream. Your arms feel better in five minutes anyway, and if you do it often enough (and during shortcake season, I do it a *lot*), you get muscles in places you never expected.

I felt like I was starting to develop mental muscles.

The first experiment that went really well was one that didn't involve me trying to make the dough *do* anything. I set a scone out on the counter and went downstairs with a scone from the same batch. Master Gildaen had said that war-wizards developed ways to communicate through their various items, and while I couldn't quite figure out how I'd do that—it's not like I could make a scone *talk* to somebody, and you wouldn't ever eat a scone again if one did—but I thought maybe I could listen *through* the scone.

I'm not saying it was easy. Scones don't have ears, for one thing. But I sat in the basement, with Bob glopping happily beside me, and concentrated on the pastry in my hands, and the one just like it upstairs...

Warmth. Vibration. These things showed up in my head along the little conduit. They were faint, and felt almost like thoughts, except that I wasn't thinking them.

The door opened and closed. The counter rattled a little.

It was kind of like the most boring daydream ever.

Aunt Tabitha said something. Uncle Albert said something back. I couldn't make out the words, only a distant *hmmmahmmmummh*. Scones aren't good with language, I guess.

Thud. Footsteps. Something plonked down on the counter. The voices came closer. I concentrated very hard, digging my fingers into the crust of the scone.

"...still wondering if we should leave," said Uncle Albert. He sounded distant and garbled at the edges.

"Leave?" said Aunt Tabitha sharply. "Leave the bakery, you mean?"

"It might be good to take Mona away from here," said Uncle Albert meekly. "After the unpleasantness. They never did find Elwidge, you know."

"That's over now," said Aunt Tabitha. "They caught the man doing it. He's in the dungeon up at the palace."

Uncle Albert said something more garbled than usual. I squeezed the scone until it started to break apart in my hands.

"...they say. I don't know. First they're looking for traitors and then they're looking for wizards and then they found a traitor and now they want wizards again. I don't trust any of it—"

"Mona's here. She's safe now. She's *fine*," said Aunt Tabitha, in a voice that brooked no argument.

Then a swooping, stomach-churning flight, pressure—oh god, Aunt Tabitha had picked up the scone! What if she took a bite out of it? What would I feel?

What had Uncle Albert meant?

I dropped the scone and the connection ceased immediately. When I picked it up again, gingerly, it was completely inert, but I could feel the connection there, just waiting for me to dribble a little magic into it. Probably I'd feel nothing more threatening than the inside of the day-old case, but what about the rest of the batch of scones? What if I connected magically to one that somebody had already eaten? Would I feel myself being digested or...?

Well, best not to dwell on that too closely.

I dropped the scone into Bob's bucket. He glopped happily over it. I think that might have been cannibalism.

As spies go, scones were probably not going to be that effective. I might do better with gingerbread men. I was already more sensitive to where my gingerbread man was, and sometimes I got odd flashes through our connection. I suspect I could have seen—or heard—a lot more through him, but I didn't want to risk damaging the link. He'd been with me for too long.

With a more expendable batch of gingerbread men, I figured out that I could indeed give one orders across the bakery, if I had a scrap of the original dough in my hand. It was simple stuff, nothing too complicated—walk to here and stop. I ran up and down the cellar steps a dozen times a day, checking to see if they'd obeyed orders.

My gingerbread man got very jealous. I went downstairs and found him giving orders to the lesser gingerbread men. One by one, they climbed up a shelf and did a swan-dive into Bob's bucket.

"Hey!" I said, snatching one up in mid-air, as it executed a beautiful triple back flip. "What are you doing?" And after a minute, while Bob slurped hungrily around the edge of the shelf, "*How* did you do that?"

He folded his arms and stuck his icing nose in the air. I resolved to pay more attention to him in the future.

Aunt Tabitha didn't say anything about it, although I caught her eyeing the gingerbread men warily, as if she thought they might do something unexpected at any moment.

To do a really dramatic experiment, like trying to control something across the city, I would have needed Spindle's help. Unfortunately, he had made himself scarce.

I couldn't blame him. When Aunt Tabitha heard how he had saved my life and helped pull the city's collective baguettes out of the fire, she would hear of nothing but that he would come to live with us. She made Uncle Albert clean out the storage room upstairs, and told Spindle to consider it his own.

Spindle took one look at the room—rose-pink quilt, lace on every available surface, a stitched sampler that read "Today Is The Tomorrow You Worried About Yesterday," and promptly went out the window, down the rain gutter, and was gone up the street before Aunt Tabitha had time to turn around.

"The poor little mite," she said, jamming her fists onto her generous hips. "He's like one of those shy wild birds. Well, we'll just have to win him over with kindness until he feels safe here."

Privately I thought this was laying it on a bit thick. Spindle had a lot of flaws—I would argue that he was primarily *composed* of flaws—but shyness was not one of them. Still, it didn't pay to argue with Aunt Tabitha.

"I wonder if he could learn a useful skill," she mused, going back downstairs to the bakery.

"He's a really skilled pickpocket," I said, opening the oven door to check on the muffins. The tops were rising and browning nicely but hadn't yet cracked open. Sugar glittered from their crests.

Aunt Tabitha ran a finger under her lower lip. "Hmmm. I suppose that's a skill of a sort. Not really *useful,* though, is it?"

Since that particular skill had kept me from starving to death and had gotten us the key to the garderobe, which turned out to be the keys to the kingdom, as it were, I could have mustered an argument, but I didn't feel like fighting with Aunt Tabitha.

TWENTY-SIX

My resolve was tested the next day. I was in the back, waiting for a pan of muffins to come out, and she bustled in. "Mona! Why are you hiding back here? People want to see you!"

I grimaced. There had been a lot of that. I hadn't minded the regulars that first day, but people I didn't know kept showing up and wanting to hear the story. I didn't want to keep telling it. I wanted it to be over. I wanted people to buy scones because they were good, not because it was a chance to gawk at me. "I'd rather not, Aunt Tabitha. I'm sure they're just here for bread."

"No, they're here for you. Because you're a hero!"

She said it so nicely. She really meant it. But the word *hero* twisted up in my chest and I couldn't seem to breathe around it. I mumbled something about the muffins and fled down the stairs to the cellar.

I sat on the steps with my head in my hands. *Hero.*

I was *fourteen.* People had been trying to kill me. I hadn't done anything heroic. I'd been terrified and yes, I know that line about how courage is going forward when you're scared, except that I hadn't even done that. I hadn't gone forward. I'd run away and run away and the only reason I'd gone to the Duchess was because I'd run out of ways to keep running away.

Hero.

It should never have come down to me. It was miserably unfair that it had come to me and Spindle. There were grown-ups who should have stopped it. The Duchess should have found her courage and gone to the guards. The guards should have warned the Duchess. The Council, whoever they were, should have made sure the Duchess knew about the proclamations. The Duchess should have had people on the street who reported back to her. Everyone had failed at every step and now Spindle and I were heroes because of it.

The door creaked open. I sniffled. I didn't want to talk to Aunt Tabitha. She meant well. She was proud of me. I didn't know how to explain that she shouldn't be proud, that it wasn't anything I'd meant to do, it was just that the whole city had fallen down on the job.

But it wasn't my aunt. Uncle Albert came and sat down on the step next to me. I scooted over to make room.

"Uncle Albert? You never come down here." I wiped my eyes, probably leaving smears of flour. "Bob's down here."

"Yeah, well. I heard your aunt talking to you. Thought I'd come down."

I sighed. "Do you want me to go apologize?" Uncle Albert was always the peacemaker, in the rare events that Aunt Tabitha and I argued.

"No," he said. That surprised me. A lot. I don't know if when you're an adult, you can argue and be right, but if you're a kid and you argue with an adult, you're automatically wrong. Always. It's a law of nature or something. On the other hand, I'd been right about Oberon, so maybe the laws were in flux right now.

"She thinks I'm a hero," I said, when the silence had stretched out. "But I shouldn't have had to do any of it. There should have been so many grown-ups who should have fixed things before it got down to me and Spindle. It doesn't make you a hero just because everybody else didn't do their job."

Uncle Albert leaned back and put his elbows on the step behind us. "I was in the army when I wasn't much older than you," he said.

I glanced over at him, surprised. I knew this, but he didn't talk about it. Not in a deep dark secret way, though. The one time I asked as a kid, he laughed and said it was mostly boring and people yelled at you a lot.

"The one time we really got in trouble was against Delta City," he said. He stared down the steps into the dimness. "We were sort of at war then, I guess. Nobody was real clear on it at the time. Probably they still aren't. Anyway, a bunch of us were stationed way out at the end of a peninsula, and we were cut off by the enemy. They didn't send us any help. Nobody attacked us, not really. Occasionally we'd throw rocks over the walls at each other, just to, y'know, remind ourselves there was a war on. But we ran out of message pigeons and we ran out of rocks and then we ran out of food. And still nobody came to save us. We thought there must have been a pitched battle or something, and maybe Riverbraid was overrun. Maybe no one was left to come save us. Eventually, the commander surrendered, because it was that or we'd all starve." He tilted his head back, looking at the ceiling. "Delta

City was very polite about it. They ransomed us back, and it turned out that nobody knew we'd been in trouble. A couple of quartermasters had been siphoning off supplies that the brass thought was headed our way. All the messages we'd sent were sitting at the bottom of a stack of papers on somebody's desk."

I stared at him in horror.

"Well, you can't really have that happening. It looks bad when people just forget you're there. So they decided it had been a siege. Called it the Siege of Dusk End, I think. They gave us medals for surviving, and we all went home heroes of the war."

"That's terrible," I said.

"Yeah." Uncle Albert glanced over at me. "But as long as they gave us medals, that fixed it, as far as the army was concerned. You expect heroes to survive terrible things. If you give them a medal, then you don't ever have to ask why the terrible thing happened in the first place. Or try to fix it." He made a flicking gesture with his fingers. "How else are you gonna have heroes?"

I rubbed my face. "I'm sorry," I said. Suddenly, my days in the church tower didn't seem so bad. How long had Uncle Albert and his men been trapped, watching their supplies dwindle, waiting for help to come?

"Yeah, me too. I'm sorry we failed you, Mona. We tried to go to the Duchess, but I'm not even sure if they told her we were there. Probably they didn't. Should have occurred to me to try climbing a garderobe."

"You didn't fail," I said. "They wouldn't let you succeed. It's different."

He put his arm around me and squeezed. He's not much of

a hugger, not like Aunt Tabitha, and it was awkward, but I felt better.

"I'll talk to your aunt," he said. "We heroes gotta stick together."

It got better after that. I don't know what he said to Aunt Tabitha, but she stopped asking me to talk to customers as much. Perversely, because she wasn't asking, it got easier to do. I even slept a little more at night, although not much.

That mood continued up to the end of the week, when the doors were thrown open and Joshua and Harold marched inside.

I say "marched" because it was pretty clearly official. They were both wearing swords and they stopped on either side of the door. Widow Holloway, who had come in for her blackberry muffin, leaned toward me over the bakery case and whispered, "My! Such handsome young guards they have these days!"

Widow Holloway is going exceedingly deaf, so her whisper could have been heard halfway to the palace. Joshua grinned and the tips of Harold's ears turned pink.

"Her Grace, the Duchess," Joshua intoned, "to see Mona, the Wizard of the Bakery."

Wizard of the Bakery. Now *there's* a title.

Aunt Tabitha came out of the back to see what the commotion was, just as the Duchess came in the front door.

"Mona, what's all this—?"

"Mona, my dear, forgive the disruption—"

They stared at each other over the bakery case. I could see

wheels turning in Aunt Tabitha's head, probably *she looks familiar, but where have I seen OH GOOD LORD—*

She dropped into a curtsey, apron flapping. "Your Grace!"

"You must be Mona's Aunt Tabitha," said the Duchess, smiling warmly. "How wonderful to finally meet you. I am so very sorry for the agonies you must have suffered while she was missing."

Aunt Tabitha tried to say "It was dreadful," and "It was nothing," at the same time and produced a garbled sentence that sounded vaguely like, "Notherful! Fing!"

"I hope to have leisure to sample some of your delightful pastries soon," said the Duchess smoothly. I suspect she was used to over-awed people. It probably happens a lot. "Unfortunately, duty calls, and I must beg your leave to borrow Mona to consult with her on official business."

Official business? *Me?*

I didn't like the sound of that. It might be nothing—probably it was just the knighthood she had threatened me with—but despite her smile, there was a kind of tightness around the Duchess's mouth that I didn't like.

Still, it was the Duchess. I took off my apron. Aunt Tabitha levered herself to her feet, holding onto the edge of the bakery case. "Begging Your Grace's pardon, but... you'll bring her back?"

"I promise," said the Duchess, and the smile slipped a bit, "Mona is not in any trouble. Indeed, I am hoping that she will be able to help us in our hour of need."

"Oh, well, then." Aunt Tabitha gave me a quick, ferocious hug. "Mind your manners," she whispered in my ear, and then, "and be *careful.*"

Then she swept up a box full of muffins (which were

supposed to go to the knitting circle on Fourth Street) and forced them into my hands. Maybe she thought they didn't feed people at the palace.

I walked out the door between Joshua and Harold, following the Duchess. Through the open door, I could hear Widow Holloway shout, in what she doubtless thought was a conspiratorial whisper, "That was the Duchess? Hmm. Didn't get her father's height, did she?"

"It's true," said the Duchess mournfully. "Father was six-foot-two. One of my great sorrows. It is easier to be imposing when you are tall."

"You seem to do all right, Your Grace."

We were settling ourselves into the Duchess's carriage, which had less carvings and gilt than Oberon's, but still looked a bit like a cake on wheels, when a small, ragged figure launched himself from behind a water barrel on the corner. Spindle hit the door and clung to it like a squirrel.

"If you're goin' somewhere with Mona, I'm comin' too!" he announced.

Joshua came around the side, sighed heavily, and picked him up by the scruff of the neck.

"We should not dream of leaving you behind," said the Duchess. "You may stand as surety of our good behavior." Spindle was dumped into the carriage. He straightened up, nodded to Joshua, and sat down on the bench next to me.

"What's going on, Your Grace?" I asked, as the wheels creaked into motion over the cobbles. "What's all this hour-of-need business?"

The Duchess stared at her fingers. "Do you know—no, you could not know, of course. Well. When someone is exiled from the city, we have them followed for a little time. We do this to make sure that they do not immediately turnabout and try to sneak back inside."

"Wondered about that," said Spindle. "Couldn't figure that you'd just let 'em go and not keep an eye on 'em."

I was embarrassed to admit that I hadn't thought about it, so I just nodded.

"Well." The Duchess leaned back against the cushions. "Our man followed Inquisitor Oberon. He travelled quickly, clearly with a direction in mind... and came to an encampment of Carex mercenaries."

I sat bolt upright on the seat. "But I thought the army was supposed to be out fighting them!" I said. "Aren't they days and days away?"

"Apparently not," said the Duchess grimly. "I suspect that the army's intelligence has also suffered from Oberon's influence. As near as we can tell, the army was chasing a small group of Carex, and the main body of the mercenary troops are currently two days' ride from here."

"Two days!"

"Cor!" said Spindle, who had broken into Aunt's Tabitha's muffins.

The bottom seemed to have dropped out of my stomach and been left somewhere back on the cobblestones. "What—two *days*—"

The Duchess nodded grimly. "We're trying to avoid a panic while we wait for confirmation, so there has not been a general announcement. But yes. I believe in two days, we will be in a state of siege. Oberon has found them—he must have been working with them all along—and informed them that the army is gone, the mages dead, and the city ripe for the taking."

Spindle has a quicker and twistier mind than I do. "Must

'ave planned to take over in here first, then use the mercs to deal with the army. Then he'd get a whole city without fighting for it. Now he ain't gonna get that, so he figures he'll burn it down and take what's left." He took a huge bite of muffin.

The Duchess regarded him with a kind of weary amusement. "There may be a place in my cabinet for you, young Spindle. That is exactly what we believe he planned. It is a shame that none of us saw it sooner. Perhaps it never occurred to us that he might watch his own city sacked." She leaned back against the cushions. "We sent riders out to find the army the day he was ousted, but without mages we no longer have instantaneous communication. It is to be hoped that when Master Gildaen died, Lord Ethan will have realized that something was amiss at home, but even at our most hopeful estimates, they are at least five days away."

Five days.

The Carex were two days away.

In two days, the Carex could overrun the city. They say that when a Carex goes past, his footprints fill up with blood. If what the Duchess said was true, the blood was going to be ours.

"But what do we *do?*" I whispered.

"We have the palace guard," said the Duchess. "We have the city walls. And we have one wizard left."

One wizard left? But who—

Oh.

Right.

Me.

I spent the rest of the ride to the palace coming up with reasons why I couldn't possibly save the city, why I probably couldn't do anything at all, why I was no kind of wizard at all.

The Duchess listened to this with a faint smile on her lips. "My dear," she said finally, "without the use of magic, you have managed to bring down a powerful traitor and recall a negligent ruler to her senses. I shudder to think what you might accomplish *with* the use of magic!"

"Your Grace, I work with bread!" I cried, for about the twentieth time, as the carriage trotted into the palace courtyard. "Just bread! Aren't there other wizards?"

She shook her head sadly. "I am sure that there are others in the city, but they are hiding. All the talk of the curfew and a registry has frightened them badly—and no wonder! And now we are asking them to come to the palace? Why should they believe this is any different?"

I slumped back in the seat, defeated.

The Duchess leaned forward and patted my knee. "My dear, I am certain that you can go on about how unworthy and incapable you are for hours yet, but we have very little time. Let us pretend that we have done all that and that I have nodded correctly and made the proper noises, and skip to the point where you say, "I don't know what I can do, but I'll try."

Spindle snickered. I said "I... but... *bread!*"

"The palace kitchens are at your disposal," said the Duchess. "I assume that you will need dough for whatever you do. We will set every bakery in the city to producing as much as they can for your use. Do you have any special instructions?"

She got out of the carriage on Joshua's arm. He helped me down too—Spindle jumped—and I handed him the rest of Aunt Tabitha's muffins. My mind reeled with images of the enormous palace ovens that I had passed during our trip to the scullery. You could bake huge things in there.

Really huge things.

The weakest may command a mountain, the book had said.

Well. I'd *wanted* to make an elephant out of dough, hadn't I?

"Tell the bakeries to let the bread rise much farther than they would otherwise," I said, surprising myself with how steady my voice sounded. "Let it overflow the pans. We need size. Spindle, I need you to go back to my room and get the book on the nightstand, and a change of clothes for me. Tell Aunt Tabitha I'll be gone overnight. Your Grace, I don't know what I can do, but I'll do my best."

TWENTY-SEVEN

If you have ever prepared for a siege in two days, then you know what the next few days were like. If you haven't, then you probably don't. Well... a big formal wedding is about the same (and because we do cakes, I've been on the periphery of a few), except that if things go wrong in a siege you'll all die horribly, and in formal weddings, the stakes are much higher. We had a bride threaten to set the bakery on fire once when her buttercream frosting came out the wrong color.

My plan was simple. I was going to make gingerbread men —or at least bread men, they probably didn't need more than a token amount of ginger—except that instead of being four inches tall, they'd be fourteen feet tall.

Even the big palace ovens couldn't do bread that size, so the blacksmiths were creating a kind of giant outdoor vaguely humanoid cookie sheet. Twelve enormous shields, hammered flat and bolted together, resting on top of a trench filled with coals and manned by teams of apprentices with bellows.

The result wasn't pretty, and I had no idea if it was going to work—I suspected that my bread warriors would be black and burnt on the bottom and raw in the middle—but I pretended I knew what I was doing.

The head blacksmith was a swarthy man named Argonel, and he was brilliant. He had a voice like stones grinding wheat, and his hands were scarred and hideous and he didn't act like it was strange at all to take orders from a fourteen-year-old girl. He was the one who suggested the outdoor cookie sheet. I was trying to figure out whether I could bake them in parts in the oven and then cement them together somehow—icing, maybe, although if working with icing gives me a headache normally, that would probably have sent me into a ten-day migraine—and Argonel listened carefully and said, "We can do this. Show us how large you want your golems, and we will make your oven."

Golems. I hadn't thought of them that way before. I'd run across the word in *Spiraling Shadows* but I hadn't connected it to my cookies.

When I had a moment, I pulled out the book and looked up the section on golems.

> *An unliving thing brought to life. Golems are often sculpted from clay, mud or stone or cast in plaster or bronze. Golems have been created of water and air, though this is very difficult. Golems can be crude or finely detailed, and are usually in the shape of men, although there are notable exceptions, such as the feather bird-golems of Ganifar the Winged.*

My own little gingerbread golem had hitched a ride in my

shirt pocket and spent the first day riding around on my shoulder, observing things.

"What do you think?" I asked him, quite aware that this was ridiculous. The book was very clear that golems were only so intelligent as their creator caused them to be, and I hadn't been trying to make a genius of a cookie.

On the other hand, he had also lasted weeks longer than any cookie I'd ever animated before. Usually I pulled the magic out of them before we sold them, because nobody wants to bite into a *live* cookie. Maybe golems got weird if you left them alive long enough.

The cookie surprised me. He walked down my shoulder and studied the hive of activity in the courtyard. He examined the shields being hammered and nodded approvingly. About the buckets and cauldrons and bathtubs of dough—I think they pulled large chunks of the plumbing out of the palace to provide me with places to store rising dough—he was less approving. He actually pinched some of the dough between his arms and frowned at it, then shook his head at me.

"Too spongy, I know," I said. "And probably horribly bland. But nobody's going to eat it."

The cookie gave me a look. (You wouldn't think icing could *do* that.) Then he waved his arms in the air, as if to say, "Well, fine, if you're *sure*..."

The blacksmiths were the easiest people to work with. You'd think the cooks would be thrilled to have an active role in possibly defending the city from a Carex invasion. And maybe they were, but that didn't extend to being happy about a fourteen-year-old kid taking charge of their kitchen and demanding they do terrible things to dough.

"Let it rise *how long*?" asked the head cook, scandalized. "And you're baking it *where?*"

"I know," I said wearily. "Believe me, I know."

"It'll taste terrible!"

"Nobody's eating it," I said.

"Hmmph. Waste of good flour." The cook sniffed. "Now, if you ask me, young lady—"

Spindle, who had been taking advantage of the cook's distraction to pocket a cold meat pie, part of a ham, and a dozen hard-boiled eggs, turned his head at this. "She din't ask you," he said. "She's *tellin'* you. It's the Duchess's orders!"

The cook turned the color of stolen ham. "Spindle..." I said, torn between being grateful and being mortified.

"It's true," he muttered.

I abandoned all hope of the cook liking me. It didn't matter. If she was furious, so be it. The Carex would be a lot worse. I drew myself up as tall as I could—I came to a little under the cook's collarbone—and said quietly, "Please fill as many buckets as you can with dough. If you run out, the guards will bring you more. Flour is being brought from the warehouses."

"As you say," grated the cook.

"Thank you," I said, and left the kitchen. I dragged Spindle out with me. However mad the cook was now, it was going to get a lot worse when she counted the eggs. My face felt hot. Having a grown-up mad at me... I mean, here I was, trying to save the city from being overrun by cannibal mercenaries, and I felt sick to my stomach because the cook was mad at me. Being fourteen has a lot of drawbacks.

The sun was going down. The cookie and Spindle and I sat on the edge of a low stone wall that separated the courtyard from the stableyard and made a meal of eggs and illicit ham.

"This is pretty horrible," I said.

"S'good ham," said Spindle, with his mouth full. "Dunno what you're on about."

"Not the ham. Everything."

"Oh."

He swallowed. I watched the blacksmith corps swing shields into position. Argonel said that they'd be done tomorrow by noon. The Carex were supposed to reach the big gates of the city tomorrow evening, although they probably would be too busy setting the outlying buildings to the torch to attack the city proper until daybreak.

At the very best estimates, if they'd started marching the minute the message from Gildaen was cut off, the army would still be three days away when the Carex arrived.

"They've told everybody that the Carex are coming," said Spindle, peeling the shell off his third egg. "Criers on every corner."

"How are people taking it?" I asked. Really what I wondered was how Aunt Tabitha and the customers were taking it. Miss McGrammar probably refused to believe it, and Widow Holloway had to have the criers repeat themselves three or four times. Brutus... Brutus might be one of the people who showed up at the gates. We don't have a formal standing militia in the city, but Joshua had said that they were calling on anybody who was able to swing a sword to report to the palace to help man the gates.

Spindle shrugged. "'Bout like you'd expect. Some people sayin' it'll blow over if we pay 'em off. Most people are doin' what they're told." He swallowed. "Even if the Carex take the whole city, they probably won't get very far in the Rat's Nest.

So—uh—you and yours wanna come in, we can probly find a place for you."

"Thanks, Spindle." I dusted my hands off. "Okay. Back to work, I guess."

I got a good few hours of sleep that night. I didn't expect to sleep in a bed again until the siege was over, and I'd expected to be too scared to fall asleep. But I did sleep, and I didn't even worry that much. I think I'd managed to shove all the fear down into the background. Sure, I was scared to death, but it didn't do much good to be scared, so I wasn't going to dwell on it when there was work to do.

Morning brought one really good change, from my point of view. When I went into the kitchen to get a cup of tea and something for breakfast, the angry cook wasn't there. Instead—

"Aunt Tabitha?!"

She was elbow deep in a washtub full of dough. "Well, I wasn't going to let you get killed up here at the palace without me! The orders came down for as much dough as we could make, so once we'd made it, I came up on the wagon alongside. Your Uncle's minding the bakery. He never was much good with the ovens, but he'll keep the place from burning down without us." She freed one arm from the dough and hugged me sideways with it.

"But the cook—"

"Oh, *her*." Aunt Tabitha sniffed. "I don't think much of *her*."

From Aunt Tabitha, this was the equivalent of being consigned to the blackest depths of the abyss. I said, "Yeesh." I wondered where she'd buried the body. The various kitchen attendants were working very quickly, with dazed expressions.

I don't think the cook had been very popular, but lord knows what they made of Aunt Tabitha.

One person, at least, seemed very happy. Jenny the scullery maid grinned at me from the far side of the table.

"I'm sorry," I said to her. "I mean—er—well, I kinda lied to you when I was here before—"

"Lord-love-a-duck!" she said, flapping her apron. "You're a hero! I told everybody it was you who was in here before, but most of 'em didn't believe me." She shot a triumphant look around the kitchen, where various attendants were pretending not to watch us.

"Your aunt's got everything squared away right and tight," she added. "Not like old Sourfingers. And she ain't stingy with the food, neither."

"No," I said. "Aunt Tabitha is never stingy with food." (Frankly, I think Aunt Tabitha feels she was put on this earth to make sure that nobody goes hungry.) "Um. Are you sure you want to be here? Don't you want to be with your family?"

"Ain't got any," she said cheerfully. "I'm a foundling. Somebody left me in a basket on the steps of the Sisters of Unrelenting Virtue. If'n I go back to the convent, I get to spend the next three days on my knees, praying for mercy or divine intervention or whatnot, and those stone floors are *hard*." She narrowed her eyes and looked suddenly, absurdly ferocious. "And if I'm here, I can help. You'll see! I ain't gonna stand around while no Carex rides through my city!"

"Oh," I said faintly. "Well... err... glad to have you?"

Aunt Tabitha swept by, patting Jenny on the back and leaving floury fingerprints on her apron. "That nice blacksmith was in here earlier. Said to tell you that they're on schedule. I don't think he slept at all last night." She waved towards a plate of biscuits. "Here, some dough more or less won't matter, and you need to keep your strength up."

I sat down and had biscuits with honey and butter. It was divine. Aunt Tabitha's biscuits have always been better than mine. She says I work the dough too much and then rely on magic to fix it.

"Brought a friend, too," she said, and dropped a soup tureen down on the floor next to me.

I turned to look at it. It went "blorp."

"Bob!"

"About two-thirds of him, anyway," said Aunt Tabitha. "I put the pot down and told him you needed help. I guess most of him volunteered. Your uncle's supposed to be feeding the rest, but you know how he is, so I left a whole haddock in the old bucket."

"Aw, Bob, I'm glad you're here." I put a hand down in the tureen. Bob belched affectionately and a mushy tentacle of starter rubbed against my fingers. Jenny stared at him, then at me, with her eyes wide.

"Is that your familiar?" she whispered.

"Who, Bob?" I looked down into the tureen. "He's a sourdough starter. I guess... well, yeah, that's the sort of familiar I'd have."

The gingerbread man poked me in the ear and gave me a very severe look. "You too," I said. (Can a person have multiple familiars? I wasn't clear, and *Spiraling Shadows* didn't say.)

"That's amazing!" She grinned. "I wish I was a magicker!"

"Really?"

"Really!" She nodded. "I never b'lieved all that stupid stuff about wizards, and those stupid posters. You're gonna do some amazing magic, I know it!"

Something on one of the spits was burning, and she dashed off to save it. It was nice that someone had confidence in me, even if it was just another girl my own age. I wished I had that much confidence in myself.

I finished my biscuits, rubbing my fingers together thoughtfully. Bob had felt sort of soggy and there was a crust of dried flour forming around the edge of the tureen, and that was all. But the Spring Green Man had accused me of throwing acid on him, and he'd had the scars on his face to prove it. And then there was the matter of the dead rats.

Hmmm.

"Gotta go, Aunt Tabitha," I said. I slid off my stool and gave her a hug. "Thanks for bringing Bob. I think we might have a use for him."

Tracking down Joshua was harder than I expected—apparently he was one of the people in charge of the city's defense now—but when I said, "It's wizard stuff," the guards got very helpful and stopped trying to give me the brush off. I found him on the far side of the stables, where there's a small drill-ground, supervising the newly-formed militia.

He had a gloomy expression. I looked at the men, but since I had no idea what I was looking for, it just looked like a bunch of guys with wooden poles whacking at targets made out of straw.

"Are they any good?" I asked.

Joshua sighed. "No. Some of the ex-military ones are fine, but there aren't enough of them. I've put those with the guard. The rest... well, putting them on the front lines would be murder."

I watched one big man throw himself at a target and reduce it to kindling and hanks of straw. "He looks pretty good."

Joshua shook his head. "Armies aren't made of individual fighters. An army is a group of men who fight together, as a unit. But it takes a lot longer than two days to drill a squad into fighting as a group instead of as a lot of little parts, and we just don't have the time." He ran a hand through his hair and looked tired. "But that's my problem, not yours. What can I do for you, Wizard Mona?"

"This is probably a stupid question, but we're going to be fighting Carex coming through the gate, right? And there are big walls, and you put people on top of the walls, right?"

"Yes. Archers, mostly. And the people in charge, like you and me."

The notion that I was one of the people in charge would ordinarily have reduced me to a gibbering wreck, but like Joshua, I just didn't have that kind of time. "Do you ever, oh, dump boiling oil on them and stuff?"

He laughed. "Boiling oil? More trouble than it's worth. The walls are barely wide enough for two men to pass—there's no place to build a fire to boil anything, and I'm certainly not having men run up the stairs carrying pots of scalding oil. Why do you ask?"

"Well... I have this... thing." Saying *I have a homicidal sourdough starter* sounded much too bizarre. "It's like, um, magic dough. If you get it mad, it'll attack people and try to... err... dissolve them. It burned the Spring Green Man pretty badly, and he was a wizard. I don't know if it'll help, but if there was a way to fling it down onto them..."

"How long will it last?" asked Joshua.

I spread my hands helplessly. "I don't have any idea! I've never done this before. I don't think it could eat a whole person, but I thought maybe if we could throw a whole bunch of little bits..."

To my surprise, Joshua was nodding. "Like burning pitch," he said. "It's used sometimes in sieges, same as your boiling oil. It can kill you if it hits you, but most people only get hit by some of the splash. It hurts, and it slows you down to deal with it. We can't use pitch for the same reason we can't use oil, but if your magic dough doesn't require anything special—"

"Just flour and water."

"—then perhaps we can fill jars with it and put it in slings." He nodded. "Yes. This is a good plan."

"I don't think it'll *stop* them, you understand," I said, worried.

Joshua put a hand on my shoulder. "Mona—nobody expects you to stop them single-handedly."

"The Golden General could do it," I said gloomily.

"No, he couldn't," said Joshua. I stared at him. He sighed. "Mona, did you never wonder why he travels with an army? He throws lightning, certainly, but he could no more face the Carex alone than you could. He just happens to have two thousand trained men at his back at all times. If he were here, he'd tell you so himself."

"...oh," I said. And went back to the kitchens in a speculative frame of mind.

TWENTY-EIGHT

I spent most of the day making a whole lot more of Bob. Dough kept arriving from every bakery in the city: wagons full of barrels oozing with dough, vats full of dough, horse-troughs and pots and buckets of dough. The palace servants stacked it up around the edges of the courtyard.

I stopped in my tracks when I saw a coffin, lid off, dough creeping over the sides. It was a plain pine box, nothing fancy, but it was still unmistakably a coffin. "Where did *that* come from?"

"Church of Sorrowful Angels," said the wagon drover, helping one of the footmen wrestle the coffin off the wagon bed. "They ran out of rain-barrels. They say it ain't never been used, if you're worried."

If we survived this, I was going to have to go find the Church of Sorrowful Angels and talk to their cook. Still, that was a *lot* of dough. I could probably make half a golem out of that much dough.

But I was talking about making more Bob. Generally you have to be careful when you add water and flour to a sourdough starter, to make sure that you've got the right proportions and all, but in Bob's case, it was easy. I stuck both hands into the soup tureen and tried to convince him that what the world needed was a whole lot more Bob.

As this coincided with what Bob himself had always believed, pretty soon I had commandeered a horse trough and had footmen dumping fifty pound sacks of flour into it. I threw in a couple of dead fish when no one was looking.

By mid-afternoon, Bob filled six rain-barrels, and here I found an example of what *Spiraling Shadows* called the magic of sympathy. Despite the fact that they were in separate barrels, they were all still Bob. If I shoved an arm into one barrel and told Bob that he was a good and wonderful sourdough starter, the best starter in the whole world, all six barrels glubbed and belched happily. When I tried to explain about the Carex—that there were mean people in the world who wanted to hurt me and Aunt Tabitha and take away Bob's flour and dead fish, all six barrels hissed and glopped and floury tentacles lashed the air.

"That's not creepy at *all*," said Spindle, turning up at my elbow. "What've you got there?"

"It's only Bob. Well, a lot of Bob. Don't touch him." I rubbed the back of my neck wearily. "Where've you been all day?"

Spindle shrugged. "Out. About. Y'know."

Which meant that he didn't want to talk about it. I gave him a mildly curious look, and he flushed. "Was lookin' for Knackering Molly, if you gotta know."

"Oh." I'd been so busy, I hadn't thought about her. "Is she okay?"

"She's fine. But she won't come help." He folded his arms tight and glared down at his shoes. "Says it's not for little people like her. Says she'll get crushed. I told her that we needed her, that there weren't no more wizards but you, but she wouldn't listen."

I was disappointed, but I tried not to show it. "I think the last war was really hard on her. She went with the army once. They say that's when she went crazy."

"Just 'cos you're crazy don't mean you can't help," said Spindle, scuffing the ground with his foot.

I remembered Uncle Albert saying that if you slap a medal on someone, you don't have to ask questions, or fix what went wrong. Had they given Molly a medal, for making the dead horses walk on the battlefield?

It was too much and I was fourteen years old and if I didn't get back to work, it wouldn't matter how heroes were made and whether that was good or bad or indifferent. I socked Spindle on the arm. "Come and help me get Bob into jars. I'll tell him you're a friend."

It took over a hundred jars to contain Bob. I think we used the entire stock from the palace. We all had pickled beets and pickled eggs and pickled beef and pickled asparagus for lunch and dinner, to free up the jars, and by the end of it, I didn't want to see a pickle ever again. The job was made more difficult because Bob was fighting mad now—I think Spindle dumped a couple of jars of pickled chili peppers into the barrels when I wasn't looking—and was striking out at strangers, so Spindle and Aunt Tabitha and I were the only ones who could get him into the jars.

Jenny the kitchen maid was really helpful. She kept finding jars tucked into corners and bringing them out, which was more than the head cook had done.

"Oh, *her*," said Jenny, sniffing. "She went off with a flea in her ear after your aunt told her off. Don't tell her I brought you the pickled radishes, though. Those are her specialty, y'know. She'd be right mad if she knew that you were stuffing dough into all those jars."

I was latching the very last lid onto the very last jar when Joshua appeared at my elbow. It was early evening. The sky looked old and bloody over the western walls.

"Mona?" he said.

"They're finishing the oven now," I said, not looking at him. "Another hour to get it evenly heated, and we'll start baking."

He nodded. "In that case—"

Something landed on my shoulder.

I let out a squawk and ducked down, and my gingerbread man climbed on top of my head and started waving his arms angrily at my attacker. Joshua, who should have been helping, started laughing instead.

It was a pigeon.

This was a big glossy gray bird, with that subtle oily iridescence along his neck feathers, but still, a pigeon. You get them everywhere in town.

The pigeon puffed out its chest and looked down its beak at me, which is not the sort of behavior you expect from a bird that lives in gutters.

Joshua finally managed to stop laughing and said, "I think that's one of Annalise's. See if it's got a message."

"A message?" I stared at the bird, who was uncomfortably close to my face.

The pigeon lifted one foot. It had a little capsule strapped to its leg. Using its beak, it removed the capsule and held it out toward me.

"Joshua, the bird is giving me something!"

"It's a messenger pigeon," said Joshua. "Annalise—she's a wizard, travels with the army. She does homing pigeons. Unfortunately while she can send them *here*, we can't send them back to her—they're strictly one-way birds. They can find their way home, and that's it. Still, she can usually magick them into finding a specific person."

"Shouldn't it be trying to find *you* then? Or the Duchess?"

"She got one a few hours ago," said Joshua, the laughter fading from his voice. "They got our message. The army is a little more than three days away. They're doing a forced march, and hope to cut it down, but even an army can't run all the way here."

Well. I hadn't had much hope. It felt less like a fist in the gut and more like a confirmation of what I had known all along. The army couldn't save us. The Golden General couldn't save us. It was up to us.

The bird shook the message-capsule at me. I took it gingerly between my fingers, expecting a peck.

There was a note inside. It was written neatly on a sheet of onionskin paper, folded so tightly that an entire sheet could fit into the tiny capsule. I smoothed it out and read,

To Mona, the Wizard of the Bakery, greetings from General Ethan.

Ah. Of course. The Golden General was sending me letters now. Naturally this was the next logical step. After this, Our Lady of Sorrowful Angels would step down off her church spire and roll up her sleeves and begin punching dough alongside Aunt Tabitha.

"From Ethan?" asked Joshua.

I nodded. "How did he know who I was?"

"The Duchess sent a very thorough report with the riders, and you're the only wizard at our disposal. I can't imagine there's too many wizard girls running around the palace right now." Joshua laughed wearily. "Would that there were. A few more like you, and we might not need the army."

"Ha-ha," I said, smoothing the creases out of the letter and reading farther down.

Her Grace the Duchess informs me that in our city's hour of need, you have stepped forward. You have all my gratitude, Wizard Mona. I implore you, leave no stone unturned in your efforts to save our city. Do not be bound by what seems foolish or impossible. In magic, creativity is as important as knowledge. The greatest wizard I have ever known would have been considered a minor talent by our standards, but he was relentless in finding ways to make things work with what he had. I hope that you will be the same.

We will be with you as soon as we can.

Yrs,

General Ethan

Its job done, the pigeon launched itself heavily off my shoulder and circled the courtyard, gaining altitude. It vanished over the top of the palace, presumably to some hidden dovecote where the homing pigeons roosted.

I folded the note and shoved it into my pocket. I hadn't expected a letter from the Golden General in the first place, so it was stupid to feel disappointed that, when one arrived, it didn't include handy advice like, "By the way, I've hidden the magic superweapon in the third broom closet on the left."

Still, a superweapon would have been nice.

You might think that having the Golden General watching over your shoulder—even by homing pigeon—would be daunting. But really, when everybody was going to die if I failed, piling "and the great hero of our army will be very disappointed" on top didn't mean that much.

In a way, the letter was actually encouraging. *In magic, creativity is as important as knowledge.* If anybody knew, it'd be the Golden General. He *was* a wizard, after all, and a very well trained one. If he said that you could do a lot with a little magic... well.

You couldn't argue that my bread golems weren't creative. I just had to think of even more creative things to do.

"We're beginning the heating now," called a blacksmith, as the first load of charcoal went into the oven.

"You can be spared for an hour, then," said Joshua, as I turned away from the ovens "Come with me. The Carex have reached the outlying areas."

TWENTY-NINE

Joshua and the Duchess and I stood on the wall over the great gate of the city and looked out over the army of Carex mercenaries. Oh, it was grim.

They could have reached us by nightfall if they wanted to. All they had to do was keep marching past the outlying farms. But instead they paused at every one and set the fields to the torch. The daylight was fading, but burning wheat made thin bright lines that winked out, one by one, as the farms burned to ash.

I wiped my face. I was so angry I was crying. Spindle stood next to me, his arms on the blocky stones of the battlements, and his face was the same as when he'd found Tibbie's bracelet in the bakery. The gingerbread man hid his face in my hair.

There was no *point* to it. That was the infuriating thing. Sure, the Carex were going to try to kill us because they wanted our city, and that was pretty awful, but at least you could see why they were doing it. Burning the farms was just senseless destruction. We weren't going to get any supplies past their army, so it wasn't like they were burning the crops to keep us from getting them. They were pulling the wings off a fly because they could.

"The people were evacuated this morning," said the Duchess. "The animals, too. Every park in the city is crammed full of pigs and chickens and cows and farmers yelling at each other." She sighed. "At least we won't lose many lives to this. But great good gods, what a *waste*."

The army was close. You could just make out individuals in the ragged lines marching toward us.

There were a lot of them.

Don't ask me how many there were. I can estimate a cup of flour or a tablespoon of baking powder, but armies aren't ingredients. There were a *lot*. Compared to the pitiful number of men I had seen drilling earlier...

So, we're doomed, my gut said conversationally.

Yup, said my brain.

So long as we're clear.

The great gate was closed, of course—all the gates in the walls of the city were closed and barred with iron portcullises—but the city didn't exactly stop there. The problem with having a walled city is that it limits how big you can get. The current walls were actually the third or fourth set of walls around the city, in concentric rings like an onion. Unfortunately previous generations had cannibalized those earlier walls for building materials, so if we didn't hold them at the gate, we didn't have much in the way of a fallback position.

Outside the walls, however, it's not a sharp transition with city on one side and country on the other. There's a whole town of sorts outside the gates. People driving their goods to the city to sell are hot and thirsty by the time they arrive, so somebody sets up a food and drink stand outside to meet them. Over time, the stand becomes a bonafide inn, and then somebody else sets up another food stand, and so on and so forth. Some people can't afford to live in town, and rather than set up in a place like Rat's Elbow, they opt to live just outside the city walls. And there are a whole lot of businesses that you really don't want inside the city, like the knackers and the tanners (the smells associated with leathermaking will make your nose try to crawl off your head) and of course the knackers and the tanners need someplace to live and somebody sets another food stand up to sell to them (although most of them burned out their sinuses long ago and can't taste a thing) and... you get the idea. We have half a mile worth of town along all the major roads into the city, before you get to the walls at all.

I expected the Carex to burn that, too, but they didn't. Joshua shook his head when I asked. "The fire will spread too quickly," he said. "They have to camp there, and there's too much chance that the whole place will go up like a tinderbox. If they're fighting fires, they're not fighting us." He put a hand on his sword-hilt. "They know that there are probably still people in there—there are always people who won't listen to the evacuation order—but even if we had a dozen trained assassins hiding in the knackeryard, they'd still lose fewer people than if they turned the whole place into an inferno."

"*Do* we have a dozen trained assassins?" I asked hopefully. The Spring Green Man had definitely soured me on the notion of assassins, but I was willing to change my opinion.

"No," said Joshua.

Spindle coughed. We all looked at him, and he stared up

into the sky with his hands behind his back and said, "Well... not assassins, 'zactly..."

"Spindle," said the Duchess, with weary amusement, "what do you know that we don't?"

"Coupla the guys," said Spindle. "Outta the Rat's Nest, you know. We ain't like the army, but this is our city too." He scratched his chin. "Heard that a couple of 'em went out the smuggler's tunnels. Slug wouldn't go, but One-Eyed Benji and Leaky Peg did, and most of Crackhand's bully-boys."

"The names of these people amaze me," murmured the Duchess. "Really, the nobles are so unimaginative by comparison. I wonder if Leaky Peg would like a cabinet position?"

"Dunno how much good it'll do, having them out there, but can't hurt," Spindle finished.

"It may help a great deal," said Joshua. "Taking out a few individual fighters won't make much difference, but if they can make the Carex agitated and jumping at shadows—I'd far rather face an army that didn't get a good night's sleep."

"If you get the chance, Spindle," said the Duchess, looking bemused, "please extend the thanks of the crown to One-Eyed Benji and Crackhand and... well, everyone. I doubt they'd like public recognition."

"They're stopping," said Joshua, leaning over the battlements.

He was right. They had halted a few hundred yards from the gate. We could hear them in the distance, a hum of voices and jeers and laughter, not unlike the sounds of the city itself.

"Can't we do something?" I asked. "They're sitting right there!"

Joshua shook his head. "Out of arrow range. They know exactly what they're about. They'll set up camp, and Oberon must have told them that we don't have the resources to lead a charge against them."

We stood on the battlements while the sun went down behind the enemy. Rising smoke from the burning fields made black columns against the sunset.

I turned away. I felt ancient, like I'd aged a lifetime standing there. The Mona who had spent the afternoon putting jar lids onto sourdough starters seemed distant and young and innocent, and the Mona who had found a dead girl on the bakery floor was some other person from somebody else's life entirely.

It's a strange way to feel when you're fourteen.

"I need to get back to the ovens," I said. "I have a few more ideas, but we don't have very much time."

THIRTY

When I got back to the palace kitchens, the blacksmiths weren't ready yet. Argonel was overseeing one of the shields full of hot coals, which hadn't been attached properly and had spilled down over the cookie sheet. "Sorry, Wizard Mona," he said, waving an apprentice into position. "I'd threaten to have the man responsible horse-whipped, but I fear that it was me. We'll have it up in an hour or less."

"It's all right," I said absently, reaching up to pat his arm. He had biceps bigger than my head. "There's something I need to do first."

I'd rather face an army that didn't get a good night's sleep...

I was nearly at the kitchen door when Harold the guard stepped out and pulled me aside. "Wizard Mona—"

I was pretty sure that I was going to get really tired of being called Wizard Mona before this was over. "Yes?"

He shifted his feet and said, "Mona—Wizard Elgar's escaped."

My head was still full of Carex and burning fields and I started to say, "Who?" and then the bottom dropped out of my stomach because he was talking about the Spring Green Man.

"Escaped," I said faintly.

Harold nodded. "He may have had an ally on the inside. We haven't had time to smoke out all of Oberon's people yet. He shouldn't have been able to escape from a wizard prison by himself, but we've been so short-handed that we haven't been checking the cells as regularly as we should, and—well—he's gone."

My stomach seemed to be laying somewhere on the ground several feet away. On the other side of the courtyard, the apprentices yelled, "*Hup!*" and the shield of coals swung clanking on the chains. There was a hiss as coals splashed over the sides and somebody cursed.

"It would be very foolish of him to come after you," said Harold earnestly, putting a hand on my shoulder. "He'll probably go over the walls and try to meet up with Oberon. It would be suicide to try to get to you now."

"He's not right," I said, remembering that voice giggling in the dark in the cellar under the bakery. It wasn't that Elgar was mad. Knackering Molly was mad, and she'd never do anything like that. There was something else wrong with him, some kind of terrible darkness. "I don't know if he'll care that it's suicide."

Harold didn't argue. "I'll be guarding you," he said. "You won't be left unattended for a minute. If he does attack, that should buy you time to do something magical in your own defense."

I nearly laughed or cried or both. Magical in my own defense? What was I going to do, bake an attack scone at him?

Unless Harold managed to buy me two hours in an oven on medium heat, there wasn't a lot I could do without prep work.

I didn't say any of it. It didn't matter if a hundred Spring Green Men were after me, there were still thousands of Carex outside the city intent on coming in. I could do nothing about Elgar right now. I might be able to do something about the Carex.

In magic, creativity is as important as knowledge...

"Fine," I said to Harold. "Come with me."

"Aunt Tabitha?" I said, stepping into the kitchens. "I need to make gingerbread. And I need a bunch of cookie sheets."

These were probably going to be the worst gingerbread men ever. You're supposed to let the dough rest for a couple of hours before you bake it, and I didn't have time. But that was okay, because the worst gingerbread men ever is exactly what I wanted to make.

Aunt Tabitha helped me bash the dough together. It was a big batch, double what we make when we do the cooking in the bakery, and that makes forty or fifty cookies by itself. Spindle hunched up next to the fireplace, watching, and my gingerbread man stood on the mantle and glared suspiciously down at the batch of dough I was making. Jenny ran back and forth, bringing spoons and flour and towels and anything else we needed. Harold stood by the door and looked so tough and professional and guard-y that I wanted to cry.

"Cayenne in gingerbread?" asked Aunt Tabitha mildly. "Mona, are you sure?"

"I'd add broken glass if I didn't think it would hurt my hands," I said, dumping most of the cayenne in and looking around for something worse. "Have we got any rat poison?"

Jenny found it, a big jar full of dusty-looking granules. She brought in the jar, looking proud and worried. Aunt Tabitha ran her hands over her face and said, "*Mona...*"

"Nobody's going to eat them," I said. "I hope. I need them to be *bad.*" I dumped the rat poison into the mixing bowl.

"You know what you're doing, I suppose," said Aunt Tabitha, adding poison to her own batch.

"Not really," I said, and was surprised to find that I was smiling. "But we'll find out."

The dough under my hands was *bad*. I could feel it. There was malice in it. It wanted to hurt people. I fed that as much as I could, pouring all my anger at the sight of the burning fields into it, and all my terror at the news that the Spring Green Man had escaped.

By the time I was done, you wouldn't have had to worry about rat poison. The dough would try to choke you before you even managed to swallow it.

I didn't like doing this. The thing about baking is that you're feeding people and it's nice. You make things that taste good and that make people happy to eat them. The very best thing about being a baker is watching somebody bite into a blueberry muffin or a fresh slice of sourdough dripping with butter and seeing them close their eyes and savor the taste. You're making their lives better, just a little tiny bit. It is nearly impossible to be sad when eating a blueberry muffin. I'm pretty sure that's a scientific fact.

Making cookies that were bad and horrible and that no sane person would eat was... well, it was like being an Anti-Baker. It was the opposite of what I was supposed to do.

I gritted my teeth and remembered the lines of burning wheat.

Aunt Tabitha helped me slap out a big ball of dough on

each cookie sheet, and helped to roll it out flat, but I was the one who cut each gingerbread shape. I didn't have a cookie cutter, so they were kind of irregular, but they had two arms and two legs each, and that was the important thing.

They were also really big, for gingerbread men. It was one to a cookie sheet, about a foot wide and eighteen inches tall. We ended up with twenty-three.

We slid them into the oven. The big palace ovens were perfect for this, because you could fit twenty-three cookie sheets inside without a problem. I took the scraps leftover from cutting the cookies and threw them back into the mixing bowl. If the book was right, that dough should be linked to the cookies, and I was hoping that I could use the magic of sympathy to control the cookies through the dough.

Well. That was half of it down. I turned to Spindle. "Spindle, for this next part, I need your help."

Spindle slid down from the raised brick hearth and fired off a mocking salute. "At yer service, General Mona!"

Aunt Tabitha picked up the mixing and baking equipment and went off to the scullery to make sure that it got cleaned immediately and nobody sampled rat poison by mistake. I leaned against the outside of the fireplace next to Spindle.

"Look, you know people, right? Those people going out to harass the Carex tonight?"

"'Course," said Spindle. "Ran with some of 'em, back in the day. Not Crackhand's boys, but some of the others."

"Do you know anybody who can take out a load of cookies?" I asked, nodding to the ovens. "They're going to be bad. I think I can make them smart enough to start harassing the Carex. They aren't fighters, exactly, but they'll want to make mischief. Some of the ordinary gingerbread men get a little feisty sometimes—they'll tie your shoelaces together and stuff—but these are going to be much worse. I thought they could, oh, spook the horses and cut ropes and put rocks in people's beds—"

"—put pepper in the flour an' set fire to bedrolls—"

"—steal their daggers and their socks—"

"—put out their eyes while they're asleep!"

"Let's not get carried away, Spindle."

"Y'ever try to fight without any eyes?"

"No, and neither have you, so don't start. Anyway, I need somebody to take two sacks of cookies outside the walls and set 'em loose near the Carex camp."

Spindle nodded. "Right. I'll do it."

"No, you won't!" I snapped. "You could get killed! Can't you find somebody going out there—Wiggly Bob or whatever their names are—and have them do it?"

"They've all gone already," said Spindle. "An it'd take hours to find somebody else and convince 'em. I know how to get out. I know the way through the knackeryard. They ain't gonna catch me."

"Spindle, *no!*"

He folded his arms over his chest. "Look, Mona, I can do this. *Let me do this.* I ain't a wizard, like you, and I ain't a fighter. If the Carex get through, I ain't gonna be able to do much. But I'm real good at sneakin' around. I'm not sayin' I could pick the sentry's pockets, 'cos I probably can't and I wouldn't try. But I can get in close enough to set your little things loose."

"But—"

"This is maybe the only thing I'm gonna do that'll be any help, so let me do it."

I probably should have said no. It was crazy to let him go sneaking around outside the walls. But he was also right, and this wasn't that much more dangerous than sneaking into the castle, was it? He'd done that ten times as well as I had. I'd gotten stuck in a toilet.

Besides, if he was outside the walls, at least Spindle wouldn't be in the crossfire if the Spring Green Man came for me. "All right," I said heavily. "You can take them. But be careful. If they kill you, I will never never *never* forgive you."

"Yeah, yeah..."

It took me ten minutes to make up a big batch of icing, and by the time I was done, the cookies were coming out of the oven. Aunt Tabitha emerged from the scullery and Spindle acquired two burlap potato sacks by the simple expedient of dumping potatoes all over the pantry.

"You know, we *had* leftover flour sacks..."

"So now we've got potato sacks too."

Jenny put her hands to her mouth and giggled. "Oh, Cook'll be mad as fire when she sees that!"

We yanked cookie sheets from the oven and dropped them on the big wooden table. I hurriedly iced eyes and mouths onto each one. I gave them little fangs. They wouldn't be able to bite with them, but they seemed appropriate.

When they were all treated with icing and had cooled a bit, I grabbed the ball of leftover dough and took a deep breath.

"Okay, cookies, listen up!" I said. "We've got a job to do. You're going to go out there and make a whole bunch of people miserable. Now get up!" And I pushed magic and will into the ball of dough and through it into the cookies.

There was a long, long moment when nothing happened, and I pushed the magic even harder, screwing my face up and

—I can't explain it, sort of *shoving* with the inside of my head—and then one of the gingerbread men sat up. The kitchen filled with soft ripping sounds as the cookies pulled themselves free of the cookie sheets, sitting up and stretching and looking around.

"Okay," I said. "Here's what we're going to—"

One of the cookies picked up a mixing spoon and bashed the cookie next to it over the head. The cookie recoiled with a spray of crumbs and threw itself at its attacker, leaving one of its legs behind on the cookie sheet. (Apparently the grease hadn't gone on quite evenly on that one.)

"Stop!" I yelled, rushing forward, as the one-legged cookie hopped furiously after the spoon-wielding cookie. "Stop, stop!"

Other cookies charged into the fray. Some of them went for their neighbors, while others started arming themselves with kitchen utensils. Two formed a temporary alliance and flipped up a cookie sheet as a makeshift barricade.

"Everybody *stop!*"

They weren't listening. There was a jar of walnuts at one end of the table, and the two cookies behind the barricade broke into it and began pelting everyone indiscriminately with the contents.

Spindle dove under the table. Harold drew his sword and waved it vaguely, apparently not sure on whether he should be defending me or running a rogue cookie through. Aunt Tabitha whipped a frying pan around and connected with a cookie that had a whisk in each hand and a homicidal expression on its icing face.

This is horrible, I thought, sinking my fingers into the ball of gingerbread scraps. *I've completely blown it. What was I thinking? You make evil bread, and it's not going to listen just because you ask nicely. I'll have to pull the magic out of all of them. What a waste of time and energy—*

Suddenly, there was a loud banging. I looked up. Everybody looked up. My faithful gingerbread man was standing in the center of the table, clanging a spoon against a cookie sheet like a gong.

I expected the bad cookies to pelt him with walnuts and was about to dive to his rescue—he was a quarter of their size, and he was so stale, the walnuts might just bounce off, but what if he shattered?—when I realized that all the other cookies were staring at him.

When he was sure he had everyone's attention, he set the spoon down and waved his arms, stomping back and forth and glaring.

It's completely ridiculous and I still don't quite believe it, but somehow he communicated with the other cookies. Don't get me wrong, dough's not smart. It's not like they talked philosophy and spoke a language called Cookiese.

Nevertheless, my gingerbread man somehow managed to convey something to the bad cookies. It was mostly mime and arm waving and glaring. It went on for a minute or two, while the bad cookies looked—insomuch as cookies can—a bit embarrassed. The spoon-wielder set down its spoon and helped the one-legged cookie pry its missing limb off the cookie sheet, and the walnut-throwers put the lid back on the jar and tried to pretend they hadn't done anything.

"Well, I'll be..." said Aunt Tabitha under her breath.

My gingerbread man finished his arm waving, turned, bowed, and extended an arm in my direction. The bad cookies looked to me expectantly.

I figured that was my cue. I cleared my throat. "Right. Um.

Well, if you are all willing to climb into these sacks here, my friend Spindle is going to take you someplace where you can be as bad as you possibly can. There'll be a whole lot of people trying to sleep, and I want you to make sure they get as little sleep as possible. Cut all the ropes and knot every lace and... and..."

I trailed off. The cookies were grinning like wolves, if wolves were flat and golden brown and smelled vaguely of cayenne. It occurred to me that something made of rat poison and mischief was probably going to have better ideas about how to harass a sleeping army than a mere human baker.

"Err. Do your worst, then. But not until you're released from the sack and Spindle gives you the go-ahead. That's an order."

The cookies shifted their feet and looked, not at me, but at the stale gingerbread man, who shook a fist (or as much a fist as a gingerbread man can make) at them. Spindle climbed out from under the table, and with remarkably little fuss, the cookies climbed into the sacks. I had been afraid that they would make an untenably large pile, but they all laid down flat and stacked together, so when Spindle slung the sacks over his shoulder, he looked like a tinker with a pack rather than St. Nicholas doing his rounds at Yule.

"You're sure you can do this?" I asked him worriedly.

Spindle looked at the sacks suspiciously. "'Long as they don't get any ideas..."

Without any prompting, my gingerbread man hopped onto the sack and climbed to Spindle's shoulder. "He'll go with you," I said. "If they get out of line, he'll take care of them." I hoped that was true. I hoped the cookie would keep Spindle safe, or Spindle would keep the cookie safe, or...

"Both of you stay safe," I said helplessly. "Come back as soon as you've dropped them off." It was full dark out now, and Argonel was at the door of the kitchen. I could see the red glow of our outdoor oven reflected against the side of his face. It was time to make the golems.

"I'll be fine," said Spindle. "Won't get anywhere near 'em." He switched the sacks to the other shoulder then gave me a quick, awkward hug with one arm. "See you in a few hours. Knock 'em dead!" and went out through the pantry. Aunt Tabitha gave me a suspicious look, as if she knew what Spindle was planning, then very obviously decided not to ask about it, and looked away.

I took a deep breath. I didn't have time to worry. There was too much else to be done.

"Your oven awaits, Wizard Mona," said Argonel.

"Don't call me that," I said tiredly, and went to go build the city's defenders out of bread.

THIRTY-ONE

The dough golems were going to be lumpy. There was really no getting around it. They were made out of a couple hundred pounds of dough apiece, and what we wound up doing was throwing head-sized lumps of dough onto the big cookie sheets, creating bigger and bigger piles until we'd built a roughly man-shaped form. The end result was going to be completely flat on the backside, and I was already worried about how we were going to pry it off the cookie sheet—Aunt Tabitha had dumped an entire bucket of warm oil down on the surface, but it was burning off fast.

We'd be lucky if oil was all that burned.

You generally bake bread for about half an hour in the oven, maybe more or less, depending on the size of the loaf. A hotter oven cooks things faster, but there's a limit on it—you can't shove dough into a blazing inferno and expect to have baked bread in five minutes. You'll get a lump of raw dough with a burnt black shell.

I had no idea how hot the outdoor oven was. Hotter than I'm used to, anyway. The blacksmiths were heating it like a forge. Argonel apologized to me twice about the fact that it wasn't hotter. "Couldn't work good iron in this," he rumbled, holding a hand out over the coals.

"Bread's a little easier than iron," I said, hoping it was true. I was going to get charred black golems with raw hearts at this rate. Maybe that wouldn't matter, but...

I gritted my teeth, stuck my left hand into the raging heat, and touched a fingertip to the golem's head. *Don't burn. You don't want to burn. There's a lot of heat there, but just pass it through to the center, you don't have to burn...*

There was a lot of dough to convince. When I pulled my hand out, my index finger was angry red. I stared at it vaguely, and Aunt Tabitha swung me around and jammed my hand into a bucket of water.

"God's teeth, Mona, are you trying to burn your fingers off?"

The water was so shockingly cold that I yelped. I pulled my hand out, and most of it was fine, except the fingertip. A big watery blister was already forming, and I noticed vaguely that all the little tiny hairs of my arm had burned off.

"I had to touch it," I said grimly, cradling my hand. "This isn't all one batch of dough, I can't talk to it at a distance like I did the gingerbread. It's not all one thing. I have to *make* it all one thing."

She gave me a look of incomprehension, but Argonel nodded. "Not a wizard," he said. "Worked with a wizard-smith once, though, and he said the same thing. He was always burning himself on alloys."

"You're not telling me that you're going to have to reach

into the oven and burn yourself on *every one* of these things?" said Aunt Tabitha, horrified.

I could feel a hysterical laugh somewhere under my ribcage and shoved it down. I needed Aunt Tabitha to trust me, or at least to not stop me. "It's nothing compared to what the Carex will do," I said, staring down at the blister. "If they get through the walls..."

There was a long silence, broken by the hiss of coals and the steaming of too much dough baking too fast over too much heat.

"Honey's good for burns," said Aunt Tabitha grimly. "I'll get the crock and some gauze. And try to remember that you're the only wizard they've got, and it won't do anyone any good if you hurt yourself too badly to work before the battle even starts."

"Yes, Aunt Tabitha," I said meekly.

It turned out that I had to touch the golems twice. The first time I had to convince them not to burn, and the second time I had to get them to stand up.

"Hands heal quick," said Argonel, putting one of his on my shoulder. He had such ugly hands. Mine were going to be ugly too, after much more of this. It didn't matter. If I was alive to have scarred hands, I didn't care.

The shields over the top of the cookie sheet were swung away. Under them, the bread had turned a lovely golden brown and risen a bit more. The resulting golem was about twelve feet long and maybe two feet thick. He was going to be an awfully skinny warrior.

"Up!" I told the golem, fighting the urge to snatch my finger away from the heat. "Get up! We need you to fight!"

Spiraling Shadows was right. It wasn't any harder to animate something that size than it was to animate the bad cookies. The problem wasn't getting it to *live*, the problem was keeping it together.

It tore itself off the cookie sheet. The bottom had burned as black as char, despite the magic, and it left large rags of dough behind it. The holes made raw white wounds in its back. "Scrapers!" I gasped to Argonel, my hands deep in the bucket of water. My burnt finger throbbed furiously. "We need to scrape it down—somehow—"

He nodded. "We'll take care of it. You take care of *him*."

The golem was swaying unsteadily on the far end of the cookie sheet. It was huge, taller than a one-story house, and it looked ridiculously thin and wobbly. Could it hit the enemy? Would it break apart if it tried? How stupid were we to think of fighting the Carex with something made out of bread dough?

It took a step forward and tottered.

Oh, gods, I didn't think about the feet, they're gingerbread men feet, how is he going to stay upright?

I dropped the bucket and lunged for the golem. It didn't have expressions, but I could feel bewilderment through the magic between us.

The feet were indeed the problem, or rather the lack of them. Our gingerbread man can balance on the ends of their legs because they're so small and nimble. The bread golem was about as far from nimble as you can get. Its legs were uneven lumps, same as the rest of it, and if it tried to walk on them, it was going to fall forward on its face.

"Hold still!" I told it. "Don't fall! Err—lean against the wall, there, we'll figure something out!"

The cookie slumped against the wall. It was gigantic. It had arms like flattened tree-trunks. It was completely useless if I couldn't get it walking and on the way to the gate.

Argonel and Aunt Tabitha came up behind me. We were joined by a skinny apprentice with no eyebrows. All of us stared at the gingerbread man.

I thought I might cry. My brilliant idea, and all these people working so hard on it, and the stupid thing couldn't even walk. What kind of wizard was I, anyway? And I couldn't just bake him with more dough at the feet, because dough doesn't work like that. If you pile up cookie dough, you get wider cookies, not taller ones. Gingerbread men are all kind of flat when you look at them.

"The base," said the eyebrow-less apprentice suddenly. "If he had a broader base to walk on, it wouldn't matter. We could strap some kind of plates to his legs, maybe."

"Of course! He needs shoes, the poor thing," said Tabitha. "Argonel?"

The blacksmith nodded. "I think... barrels. If he can step into a barrel for each foot, we'll pack it with straw and lash it onto his legs with harness leather."

"Do you think it'll work?" I asked, looking at the strange, thin, gangly golem. "I thought it'd be more... more... warlike..."

Argonel paused in between waving apprentices towards the barrels. "Wiz—Mona—I think if I was the enemy and a giant man made of bread came at me, even one as strange as that, I would think twice."

Harold, who had been standing a little ways back and scanning the scene with wary eyes, stepped forward. "A soldier's strength is limited, Mona. If they have to hack their way through your bread dough army, that's strength they won't have to use on our men."

I sighed. They were right, but it wasn't enough. I'd hoped deep down that my bread dough men would completely turn the tide, that maybe if I raised enough golems they'd stomp the enemy flat and none of our troops would get so much as a hangnail.

Instead I had one golem who could barely stand up. How many more would I be able to bake before dawn?

There was only one way to find out.

When the next golem was baking, I went back to the first. I suppose I had some notion that he might be panicking—he was blind and couldn't stand upright on his own—but I really shouldn't have worried. Bread doesn't panic. You can throw bread off a cliff and it will fall without a care in the world. It doesn't have nerves.

The golem had been told to lean against the wall, and it was prepared to lean against the wall forever if necessary. It wasn't worried.

The apprentices, who were wrestling barrels onto the ends of its legs, were a bit more worried. I darted forward and put a hand as high up the golem's leg as I could reach.

Lift your foot so they can slide your new shoe on.

It lifted a large foot.

"Whoa!" Aunt Tabitha stood on top of a ladder with a mixing bowl full of buttercream frosting. I grabbed for the bottom of the ladder, which had shuddered when the foot it was leaning against moved.

"Aunt Tabitha!"

"Just a minute, Mona, dear—I have to give the poor fellow eyes."

I held the ladder while the apprentices packed straw furiously into barrels and my aunt leaned out across the expanse of baked face. When she finally stopped slathering, the bread golem had small frosting eyes and a vague, goofy smile.

"Did you have to make him smile, Aunt Tabitha?" I asked.

"I thought it might make him look more friendly."

"He's supposed to be trampling Carex mercenaries!"

"Fine..." She sighed, took another handful of icing and drew slanted, angry eyebrows. "Happy?"

"Not even a little."

The eyebrowless apprentice took the ladder. He had a blister on the side of his face, probably from an encounter with the oven. I glanced down at my burned finger and couldn't resist rubbing another fingertip over it and making the fluid in the blister squish from side to side. (Oh, like *you've* never done that.) It hurt. I suspected it was going to hurt a lot more before the night was through.

By midnight, two more golems were leaning against the wall and I had a blister on my middle finger to match the first.

The barrel shoes worked. When I asked the first golem to march up and down the courtyard, it did. It had a ten-foot stride and splintered a horse trough without even noticing. I started to feel a bit more optimistic about its chances.

The strain of keeping the golems going wasn't too bad. I've animated dozens of gingerbread men at a time, and three golems wasn't much. What was really wearing on me were my bad cookie saboteurs out there in the dark. Twenty-three smart cookies was a lot to keep going. It wasn't exactly that I had to *do* anything, but I could feel my energy draining away, a little at a time. My muscles were a little more tired than they should have been, and when I stood up, my knees were a little bit wobbly. It felt like I was doing everything while carrying a twenty-pound pack on my back—it hadn't seemed all that heavy at first, but after a few hours it was really starting to wear on me.

With the fourth golem baking and the second and third being fitted for barrels, Aunt Tabitha dragged me into the kitchen. "Eat," she said, shoving ham and pickles in front of me.

I was glad it wasn't a sandwich. I don't think I could have eaten bread right then.

Unexpectedly, the magical weight on me lessened a fraction. It took me a minute to realize that one of the bad cookies must have been destroyed. I frowned into my pickle.

I'd been planning on pulling the magic out of them when all this was done—those things were way too dangerous to be allowed to run around loose—but I still didn't like the thought that some Carex had wrecked one of my cookies. I hope he hadn't tried to eat it. They were the enemy and all, but there were limits. I felt like having people eat rat poison cookies went against everything being a baker stood for.

I'd gotten halfway through the ham when another cookie went, then two.

The bowl of bad gingerbread scraps was still on the mantelpiece. I took it down and stuck my fingers in it. *What's going on out there?*

I didn't get anything clear. There was a spatter of images inside my head—*flick flick flick*. It was like the experiment where I tried to listen through the scone, except that there were pictures this time, because I'd given the gingerbread men eyes. They went stuttering by too fast to make anything out. I smelled fire and heard men shouting and felt the malicious satisfaction of a rat-poison cookie who had just done something wicked. I think one of them was running through grass, and another one was dumping gravel into a shoe. One of them was surrounded by legs and was running between boxes, and then somebody was roaring and there was a frying pan the size of a wagon wheel coming at me–

I dropped the gingerbread ball. A few seconds later, I lost another cookie, probably the one smacked with a frying pan. I hoped it had managed to do some damage in the kitchen tent beforehand.

"Mona?" Aunt Tabitha looked at me. "You're white as a sheet, girl. What's the matter?"

My head was throbbing, too. Using gingerbread men as spies was never going to catch on. If I tried to do that for very long, I'd have to lie down with a cold rag over my eyes. Seeing the world through frosting is *hard*.

"Nothing," I said hoarsely. I washed my hands before finishing off my pickles. "Nothing I can do about it, anyway. Time to go raise the next golem."

Through the rest of that long, long night, I can only remember two coherent thoughts.

The first was that I was so tired that if the Carex breached the walls and killed us all, there was an excellent chance I'd sleep through it.

The second wasn't so much a thought as a question, and it repeated itself every time I had a breath to spare.

Where the heck is Spindle?

THIRTY-TWO

An hour before dawn, Joshua came out to the courtyard.

We'd raised the last golem. There were seven of them, and I knew from one look at Joshua's face that we wouldn't have time for an eighth.

"Time to go to the gate," he said. "The Duchess is already there, arranging the troops. Mona—"

He stopped there, because if he kept talking, he had to ask a fourteen-year-old girl to come to the front lines of a battle, and he hated it and he knew he had to do it, and I knew I had to come because somebody had to tell the golems what to do.

This is a lot to not actually say. I hunched my shoulders and said, "Yes. Let's go."

We loaded the wagons with leftover dough. There was still a lot of it, maybe two wagons full, although Our Lady of Sorrowful Angels only knew what I was going to do with it at the front lines, without an oven. Still, we brought it.

Between the wagons, bringing their barrel-shod feet down with a sound like gigantic hoofbeats, walked the golems.

They were staying upright. That gave me hope. Each one of them carried a fence post in one hand to use as a club. (Argonel had offered to commandeer the huge ceremonial axe that the Duchess's very remote ancestors had used to chop the heads off bulls. I declined. On the one hand, an axe takes a lot more brains to work than a club, and on the other, I still felt kind of bad for all those ancestral bulls.) Aunt Tabitha had put an icing face on each one, although the later golems did not have angry eyebrows, and the last three didn't even have mouths.

There was no one else in the streets. We reached the gate just as that odd grayish-brown light that precedes dawn was starting to seep over the walls.

On our side of the big gate was one of the largest squares in the city. It had to be, to accommodate all the wagons and carts coming in, and to give them space to turn so they can get to their particular roads. Four roads led into it, not including the one through the gate—two running parallel to the walls, and two coming in at angles on the far side from the gate.

All but one of these roads had been blockaded with overturned wagons and wooden barricades. They weren't pretty. They looked like a cross between a furniture shop and a hedgehog. There were chairs and beds and big wooden planks nailed haphazardly to fill in the gaps, and some of them had sandbags piled up at the bottom or wedged in between the chairs. Spears bristled out of them.

The golems could look down on them, but the enemy was going to have to climb.

"We have recruits manning the spears on the other side of

each barricade," said Joshua quietly. "And every archer in the city is either on the wall or on top of the buildings circling this square. We have to hold them here, or they'll get into the city, and it'll be house to house."

He didn't have to say any more. I could imagine what it would be like, huddling in your basement, hearing the doors being forced, and then men with swords bursting in, and...

"We'll put the golems in the square, then," I said briskly, rubbing my palms together. The fingers of my left hand had been slathered in honey, which is good for burns, and wrapped in gauze. They throbbed in time to my heartbeat.

Joshua nodded. "They'll be waiting when the Carex break through the gate." (Not *if*, I noted. *When.*) "If they are able to drive them back through the gate, do so."

I nodded. I had, in a large bowl, seven lumps of half-cooked dough, which I had pulled from each golem. Argonel had found some paint, and each golem had a drippy armband in a different color, which was also splashed on the bread, so theoretically, I would be able to control each golem individually with the magic of sympathy.

It had worked getting them to march. We hadn't had more than a few minutes to test it. I had no idea how well it was going to work with complicated orders. The golems were dumb, even for bread, and I was incredibly tired.

I'd lost more than half of the bad cookies by now. I had managed to grab ten and twenty minute cat-naps while the golems cooked, but every time a bad cookie went, I had jerked awake again. Nothing like that had happened with the other baked goods, probably because I always pulled the magic out of them before they got eaten or destroyed or whatever. It was a nasty feeling. Exhaustion was starting to creep around the edges of my vision like gray mold.

When the golems were settled, the last road was barricaded up. The wagons that had brought us here were unloaded and turned on their sides. Soldiers dragged out big wooden barriers —I recognized barn doors from the paint—and braced them between buildings.

"Argonel..." I said, as the barricade went up, leaving him on the other side with the dough and a dozen replacement barrels.

"It's been an honor, Wizard Mona," he said, smiling down at me. "Don't worry."

"Thanks, Argonel," I said. "For, you know, all of it."

He nodded. We didn't say anything more, because I was pretty sure if I said too much more, I was going to start crying, and maybe he would have too, I don't know. Wooden planks filled up the space between us.

"How do we get out?" I asked Joshua.

He nodded to ladders laid against the wall. "We'll pull them up once the fighting starts. Shall we go up now?" Harold came up the ladder behind me, and Aunt Tabitha came up behind him. I could hear the archers shifting and talking quietly on the roof. Somebody told a joke and somebody else laughed, one sharp bark.

The view from the top of the wall was of darkness, broken by the red glow of Carex campfires. I could see shadows of men moving, but nothing more.

The Duchess was waiting at the top of the wall. She was wearing armor. When she saw me, she smiled.

"Mona, my dear..." Her smile faded. "Can we not find armor for her?"

"Mona's not trained to fight in armor," said Joshua. "Even if she was, we don't have much for young girls." He nodded to an aide, a tall man standing just within earshot. "Krin, run over to the armory and see what you can find for the wizard and her aunt."

Aunt Tabitha laughed. "I suspect you'd have an easier time fitting Mona!"

The Duchess reached out and took Aunt Tabitha's arm and said, "Madam, we will not lose you or your niece, who have done so much for us, to a stray arrow or a misplaced blow."

Aunt Tabitha, who had lost much of her fear of the monarchy in the last day, actually patted the Duchess's hand and said, "Don't worry, your grace. It will take a great deal to get rid of me. Someone must make sure that all you wizards and warriors remember to eat."

Another of the bad cookies winked out. I was down to ten. I wondered if they'd done anything, beyond leaving me tired enough to curl up right here on the stone wall and take a nap.

Where is Spindle? Is he out there in the dark? Did he make it back inside the walls? Did he do something stupid?

My little gingerbread cookie was still out there somewhere too. I didn't know where. I didn't have anything to track him with, like the bad cookies, but I was sure I'd feel it if he vanished.

"Should the Duchess be up here?" I asked Joshua in an undertone. "I mean, if they get into the city..."

The Duchess had very sharp ears. She came and leaned on the battlements next to me. "I could hide in the palace," she said. "There are very thick doors. I could spend the next two days cowering in a dark room, while my people die, waiting for the doors to finally be broken down, and the Carex to come for me. But I have cowered enough these last few months. I find that I fear that dark room more than I fear dying out here, in the open air." She shrugged.

"What will happen if we lose?" I asked.

The Duchess sighed. "If he has control over the Carex, then Oberon will take me prisoner, and most likely have me executed immediately after a trial designed to convince the nobles that we are still under the rule of law and they can continue pretty much as they always have. You... well, it is hard to say, my dear, but you have been a threat and a nuisance to him, and I suspect that he will have you executed if he can catch you." She tilted her head. "If he does not have control over the Carex, then we will mostly die once they break through our defenses."

I nodded. It was what I had expected.

That my knees went weak and wobbly and I could feel my stomach churning... well, I didn't say anything about it. The Duchess had put on that royal mask again, being strong and competent and inspiring, and I didn't want to whimper in front of her.

"He'll have to go through me," growled Aunt Tabitha.

"And us as well," said Joshua dryly, "but I doubt that will be a problem once the city is breached. There are simply not enough of us."

The runner arrived with his arms full of leather and chain. As Joshua had predicted, there was very little that fit me. I had to settle for a leather cap and a heavy vest made out of leather with metal bits sewn to it that Joshua said was usually worn by the drummer boy. It wasn't too bad. The vest was a bit like the apron I wore at work, just heavier, and at least my arms were still free.

Aunt Tabitha, on the other hand, had a full suit of chainmail. A lot of guards are big. They generally weren't big in quite the same places as Aunt Tabitha, but she made it work.

It was frighteningly appropriate. If she hadn't been a baker, Aunt Tabitha would probably have been one of those northern warrior women with the big breastplates that sing opera and carry off the souls of the valiant dead.

While they were outfitting her, I went back to staring out at the Carex camp. "When is something going to happen?" I asked Joshua.

"Things have been happening all night," he said. "One of the big cook tents went up in flames a few hours ago, and they've had some trouble with the horses. I assume it's the men that Spindle told us about, harassing them."

I grinned. Spindle's friends, or maybe a pack of really bad cookies.

"They should attack at dawn," said Joshua, as my grin faded. "Or as soon as it's light enough to see."

The attack came twenty minutes after sunrise.

Aunt Tabitha said it had been twenty minutes, anyway. She's got a pretty good internal clock, always knows when the muffins are ready to pull out of the oven. It didn't feel like twenty minutes. It felt more like twenty *years*.

The sky looked like a raw egg, runny with streaks of red in it.

"They're forming up," said Harold, standing with us on the battlements. Joshua had gone to address the archers off on the left side of the wall.

I couldn't really tell what was going on, except that the

milling Carex were milling more or less in our direction and forming into a large crowd aimed our way. It looked more like the crowd you get when the circus comes to town than anything military.

Then they started to move towards the wall.

"Archers!" cried a voice, and "Archers!" "Archers!" "Archers!" ran along the top of the wall, as the officers picked up the cry and passed it down.

On either side of our little knot, men with bows stepped forward and set arrows onto the strings.

"Hoooold!" cried the voice. ("Hold... hold... hold..." echoed past us.)

The Carex broke into a run.

"Steady..." murmured Harold, to no one in particular. "Steady, steady, wait until they're in range..."

It seemed to take forever. I wanted them to fire and get it over with, shoot the people coming at us waving swords and axes and—I didn't even know what *that* was, looked like a ball with spikes on it, who carries around a ball with spikes on it?—but the archers held and held and held and then:

"FIRE!"

("Fire! Fire! Fire!")

Arrows rained down, with a hiss like butter on the griddle, magnified a hundred times.

It didn't do anything.

Well, I'm sure it did something, I heard some Carex scream and a few fell down, but if there were any gaps in the crowd, they filled in immediately. It was extremely discouraging.

There was another volley. The Carex army continued to run towards us. There were so many of them that the ones in back hadn't even left their camp yet. They could afford to throw *waves* at us, while the rest sat around the campfire and toasted marshmallows. This struck me as desperately unfair. They could at least pretend we were dangerous. You know, out of common courtesy.

"Slings!" shouted the voice down the wall. ("Slings!... Slings!")

The archers stepped back and drew more arrows. Fifty fighters (none of them guards—I saw women and a few kids barely older than I was) carrying leather slings stepped forward, fitting jars full of angry Bob into their weapons, and began to twirl them over their heads.

This is it, Bob, I thought hard at my favorite sourdough starter. *This is your big moment. I hope you're good and mad!*

It was an awkward fit. Sling stones are usually a lot smaller than jars. A couple of them fell out and smashed on the wall, and a few more failed to get more than a few feet beyond the wall, but the majority sailed into the ranks of the Carex with the crisp sounds of shattering glass.

That they noticed. Part of it was the simple fact that if you get clocked over the head with a jar, you tend to pay attention. But Bob was angry this morning, and he'd had all night to stew in his own juices, both literally and metaphorically. The Carex who got hit by jars found themselves with a furious slimy mass that burned like acid and which was trying to crawl under their armor.

There was a lot more yelling. Gaps opened up in the line as individual Carex stopped running and started trying to yank their armor off to get at the Bobs. Other men slowed down to see why their comrades were yelling and stripping on the middle of a battlefield, and some of them got hit by stray bits of Bob, which immediately tried to go up their noses.

"Get 'em, Bob!" cheered Aunt Tabitha next to me. "Show those filthy mercenaries what for!"

"Slings!" ("Slings... slings...")

The second wave of Bob hit the enemy. Given how much chaos he was causing, I was starting to wish I'd spent less time on golems and more on making wheelbarrows full of Bob. I still had a jar with me, and a half-bucket or so back at the palace, so if we held them for a full day and they retreated at night, I might be able to whip up some more.

The slingers stepped back, and the archers, who had picked up fresh quivers, stepped forward. The gaps in the enemy line that Bob had opened got bigger as the archers fired, and the crowd that finally surged against the gate was ragged in places.

I expected the crowd to fill in, but it didn't. Some of the mercenaries that had gotten a face full of Bob were down, and nobody wanted to get too close to them. Bob was fully capable of jumping if he was angry enough. He'd almost pounced on one of the guards moving barrels earlier.

The downed mercenaries were twitching a bit, but that was all. I felt sick. On the one hand, I hated them for burning the fields, for attacking my city, for working for Oberon... but still. Death by sourdough starter. Not a good way to go. You had to feel sorry for them, and I was the one who'd brought it about.

If you'd just leave, I thought. *If you'd just turn around and leave, we wouldn't have to do this.*

The ranks of Carex opened. A man on a horse rode down the aisle they formed. Behind him were two more men, also on horses. One was carrying a white flag.

"Now for the farce..." muttered the Duchess.

"I suppose it's too much to hope they're surrendering," I said.

"Far too much. I believe that's Oberon."

It was. The former Inquisitor rode until he stood perhaps twenty feet from the wall and looked up. The horseman who wasn't carrying a flag rode even closer.

"Some kind of herald," murmured Harold. "And definitely Oberon."

"Shoot him!" I hissed, practically hopping up and down. "We've got archers! Shoot him!"

"He's under a white flag," said the Duchess wearily. "You don't shoot people with white flags."

"But it's *Oberon!*"

"Believe me, Mona, I am entirely sympathetic to your feelings, but we don't shoot people with white flags, in hopes that someday, if we're under a white flag, they'll return the favor. Rules of warfare."

"His Lordship Oberon, Inquisitor of the City, would address the Traitor Duchess!" shouted the herald. His voice was loud and carried across the walls.

Men along the wall booed.

The Duchess rolled her eyes and stepped up to the battlement. She cupped her hands around her mouth and shouted "If Oberon wants a traitor, he should look in his own mirror! I am the Duchess, rightful ruler of this city!"

The men cheered. The herald's horse sidled and stamped its feet.

"His Lordship makes you the following offer: That you now, at once, open the city and lay down your arms, that all aggression against our Carex allies ceases, that the Duchess be handed over—"

"I can save you the trouble!" called Joshua, from farther down the wall. "His Lordship can stuff it in his arse!"

"We will never surrender!" shouted the Duchess. "We will never submit to the rule of a traitor, backed by hired killers! We will fight for our city to the last man!"

Great waves of cheering broke over the walls. Men waved their swords and bows in the air. Under the chorus, the Duchess muttered, "At least not until sometime this afternoon, when it's that or have the city burned down around our ears."

Aunt Tabitha snorted.

The herald turned and rode away.

THIRTY-THREE

The Duchess caught my eye and her lips twisted in something that vaguely resembled a smile. "It wouldn't help if we surrendered, Mona. The Carex would pillage the city anyway. Oberon may *think* he can keep them on a leash and use them as his army, but once they're inside the walls, they'll tear the city apart looking for food and gold, then squat in the ruins. And when the army gets back, they'll be the ones laying siege to the walls. The best we can do is reduce their numbers and make them pay for every inch of ground they take." She sighed. "The Golden General will make a good ruler. Probably a better one than I've been. I only pray that there will be enough left for him to rule."

Oberon rode away down the aisle, with the herald and flag-bearer. The crowd of Carex closed around them.

I peered over the edge of the battlements. "Err... now what do they do?" None of the surrounding buildings were tall enough for them to reach the top of the wall, or anything like it.

The city laws were very strict about that. And there wasn't much point in attacking a stone wall with a sword, although some of the Carex were pounding on the wall with their sword hilts anyway.

"They try to break down the gate," said Harold. "They're bringing up the battering ram now." He pointed to a thick line of men with shields over their heads to ward off arrows. They were carrying a very large log. The end of the log was a big ball of steel, molded into the shape of a fist.

"It's a Knocker," said the Duchess. "Dear me. I knew they probably had one, but I'd hoped I was wrong."

I didn't ask why it was called a Knocker. It was pretty obvious. The Carex were going to knock on the gates, and then knock them down.

"There's an iron portcullis, isn't there?" I asked. "Shouldn't that hold up?"

Harold shook his head. "Oh, it might hold up. The mortar likely won't. Something like that can knock the portcullis right out of the wall holding it or bend it so far out of shape that they can wiggle past."

Thunk! The Knocker hit the gate.

"Doesn't look like it did much..." I craned my neck, trying to see. Aunt Tabitha grabbed my collar and hauled me back.

"Just wait," said Harold.

Thunk! A faint shudder went through the stones of the wall.

Thunk!

Thunk!

Thunk!

"I really don't like this," I said to no one in particular, as dust sifted down from the top of the wall. It felt like the

Knocker was going to bring down the whole wall, not just the gate.

"Me neither," said the Duchess.

Thunk!

Thunk!

CRUNCH!

"That was a bad sound."

"Oh, yes."

Skreeeee-crunch!

"Almost through the portcullis," said Harold.

I had expected the gates to last a lot longer. Until mid-morning at least. We had to hold them off for two days minimum if the army was going to show up and save us all, and in half an hour, they were most of the way to breaching the walls.

This was bad.

"At least they're not coming over the walls," said Harold, answering my thoughts. "Knockers are heavy equipment to lug around. They can't afford to drag any more siege equipment with them."

The archers kept firing. The slingers flung stones. The air hissed with arrows, punctuated by the crunching thud as the Knocker chewed away at the gates.

Crunch!

Crunch!

Every time one of the men holding the Knocker fell, another ran up under a shield to take his place. I wished I had an ocean of Bob to drop on their heads.

Joshua ran up, jogging with his head down to stay below the nocked bowstrings of the archers. "Mona? They're almost through. It will be time for the golems in a moment."

I moved to the other side of the wall, looking down into the courtyard. My ears buzzed and my feet seemed a long way away.

"Yes," I said distantly. "Yes, of course." I picked up the bowl full of dough.

Crunch!

Crunch!

CRACK!

The wood splintered. The next blow went right through the gates and I looked down and saw the metal fist of the Knocker emerge into the square.

Joshua had suggested the arrangement of golems—three in front in a semi-circle around the gate, four in the back in a larger circle. I grabbed the three balls of dough in front—red, blue, and black—and thought *Forward. Stop those men!*

The golems stepped forward. Their barrel feet clopped loudly on the stones, audible even over the shouts of the Carex. The enemy poured through the splintered gate, past the men holding the Knocker, into the square... and stopped.

Well, they'd probably never seen a twelve foot tall man made out of bread before. Let alone seven of them.

The golem with the red band on its arm lifted its club and smacked the warrior in the lead on the head. He fell down.

The mercenaries looked at their leader and at the golem. They did not look up the wall, thankfully, where they might have seen a fourteen-year-old girl scowling ferociously into a bowl full of bread dough.

To give credit where it is due, the Carex did not stay surprised for long. There was a reason that they were the most feared mercenaries in the land. They might not use magic themselves, but they understood when they were facing it, and while they were afraid of it, they didn't back down.

Neither did the golems.

Red, Black, and Blue swung their clubs, knocking warriors into each other, into the walls, and sending them rolling across the cobblestones. I was absurdly proud—there was *weight* behind those blows. I'd always been impressed at the strength of the gingerbread men in relation to their size, and my golems were just as strong. They might only be made of bread, but the way they moved, they might as well have been made of stone.

The first group of Carex through the door didn't even make it past the first three golems. The second group, rather than engage, tried to charge past them—and found themselves running into the arms of Green, White, Orange and Purple.

Well... not *arms* so much as *knees*...

The third group of Carex paused at the gate and seemed to be having a heated discussion with one another about the best way to proceed. The archers picked off a few more.

I grabbed the ball of dough belonging to Red.

Down in the square, Red dropped its club, took two heavy strides forward, and grabbed the end of the Knocker.

It couldn't quite pick the battering ram up—even magic bread has limits—but it hauled the Knocker into the square. The men on the other end yelled and squawked and hung on, until they realized that they were being dragged inside the walls. Having seen what had just happened to the other Carex, they prudently let go. Red dragged the Knocker inside and dumped it against one of the walls.

"You know, I always wanted one of those," said the Duchess.

Red picked up its club in time to meet the next wave of Carex.

This time they'd gotten smart. They went for the golems' knees, just above the barrel. I imagine that they were thinking (and probably rightly so) that if they could hack through the bread there, the golems would be down and helpless.

It was a pretty good plan. However, as you probably know if you've ever tried to cut a loaf of bread, you can't just stab it with a sharp knife. Stabbing it doesn't do a whole lot, except get your knife stuck in the crust. You need a serrated blade and you need to saw back and forth with it to slice the loaf off. It takes a little time.

I sank my fingers into the dough. Generally when I had the cookies do this, it was a dance number to amuse the customers, but...

"Are they doing the *can-can?*" asked Harold in disbelief.

"Battle can-can," said the Duchess wisely. "Very old tactical maneuver. Used to defeat the waltzing berserkers of West Quillmark, as I recall."

"You just made that up."

"Well, *obviously*."

The golems could do a pretty good high kick. It got their legs out of range of the Carex and generally took the swords along with them. Red had a sword stuck through its left knee, and Blue had two swords in the right, and Black took the prize with three swords and one axe buried partway up the thigh. Since bread really doesn't care if there's a knife stuck in it, this didn't slow them down at all.

The kicks also meant that the owners of those weapons had all just taken a high-velocity barrel to the torso and were mostly out of commission.

There was a brief pause while the Carex tried to figure out what to do next, while staying out of the way of our archers. A semi-circle of clear ground formed in front of the gate.

I took the opportunity to slump against the battlements. The magical weight that I seemed to be carrying around got a lot heavier when the fighting started. Even the loss of a couple more bad cookies sometime during the battle couldn't balance it out. I felt like I was trying to jog uphill carrying a backpack full of rocks.

Aunt Tabitha felt my forehead. "You're flushed," she said accusingly. "And you feel hot."

"Aunt Tabitha, we're having a war. I don't think I can go have a lie-down."

She frowned. "Just don't hurt yourself, girl. You're the only niece I've got."

"I'm the only wizard the city's got, too." I pushed myself upright.

The only wizard, aside from Knackering Molly. I wish she were here. I don't know if it would help, but... it would be nice not to be the only one.

And more than anything, I wish Spindle was here. I hope he's okay.

A group of Carex carrying bows came through the crowd of their fellows, which was now largely standing around, holding shields over their heads.

"This is where you see the advantages of military discipline," said Harold. "Our troops would keep attacking until they brought them down through sheer force of numbers. But none of the mercenaries want to be the first one through the gate."

Their archers reached the front lines, knelt, and began shooting at the golems.

I started laughing. I couldn't help it. Stab a bunch of toothpicks into a loaf of bread, and you've got... I don't know, an appetizer or something. Not a dead golem, anyhow. Clearly the Carex still had no idea what they were dealing with.

Our archers had to lean over the edge of the battlements to shoot, but there was a minute where the Carex shot at the golems and our men shot at the Carex and by the end of it there were a lot fewer Carex archers and Red and Black looked like hedgehogs. Blue, who had been mostly shielded by the broken gate, just stood there until a foolish Carex came around the edge of the wall and got a face full of fence-post.

The archers retreated. There was more hurried discussion on the ground.

This time when they attacked, they sent twice as many men in. The four golems in back had to do the can-can as well, but after about ten frantic minutes, I had a pounding headache and the Carex hadn't gotten anywhere. Two or three had managed to get past the golems to the barricades, where they were promptly picked off by archers on the roof.

I was feeling a grim sort of hope. Even looking over the other side of the wall and seeing just how many Carex remained couldn't quite squelch it.

"Blue's barrel is getting pretty beaten up," said the Duchess.

I nodded. "Argonel is supposed to have some spares at the wagons." I had Blue fall back—White took his place—and walked Blue over to the barricade on the palace road. It was the lowest of the bunch, and Blue was able to step over it somewhat awkwardly.

Seeing the number of golems diminish, the Carex attacked again. They were beaten back, but more made it through to the barricades, and Black was limping now. A suicidally brave Carex with an axe had actually climbed onto Black's leg and gotten a couple of solid hacks into his knee before the golem managed to detach him.

"Can you heal them?" asked the Duchess.

I chewed on my lower lip. "He needs patching. It's not a wound, exactly, his leg just won't hold him up all the way. I've got dough, I can fix it, but I need to be down there to make it work."

Blue stepped back over the barricade and back into the fray. The Carex retreated again.

Harold and the Duchess held a brief conference. "Quick," said the Duchess. "Before there's another wave. Down onto that roof there, and around the back—Harold knows the way. Hurry!"

I followed Harold. Aunt Tabitha came down the ladder after us. It took us down to a roof, and then we went down the fire-escape and into the streets.

It was much scarier down on the ground. You couldn't see what was going on, you could just hear the dull roar of the army outside the walls. I fretted. If the Carex attacked before we got back, the golems could fight on their own, but if anything unexpected happened—well, bread's not good at independent thought.

If the Carex broke through the barricades while we were on the ground, then we were going to get overrun by angry people with swords. That would be exciting, for about thirty seconds, but not in a good way.

It seemed to take a lot longer to go around the square than it had to cross it, even though we ran. The cobblestones were the rounded ones that look like sweet buns, and we had to be careful, because those always get a bit slippery underfoot.

When we finally rounded the corner and saw Argonel and the barrels, I let out a cheer.

Argonel whipped around and very nearly cracked Harold over the head with his smith's hammer before he realized who it was. "Oh, it's you! Wiz–Mona, the golems are doing much better than we hoped." He grinned. "But what are you doing down from the walls?"

"It's Black," I said, grabbing the black-marked dough ball and ordering him to come back over the barricades. "He's going to lose a leg in a minute if I don't fix him."

Argonel nodded. We all scattered to the walls as Black's foot came down. He wavered for a moment–that knee was definitely going–then caught his balance.

I grabbed a glob of dough out of one of the barrels and crammed it into the wedge the axe had cut in Black's leg. (I had to climb up the barrel to do it. The Carex axe-man had been a lot taller than I was.) Aunt Tabitha came up behind me and handed me several more handfuls, until we'd managed to fill in the gap.

"All right," I said. "Let's see if this works." I put my hands on either side of the raw dough and thought hard about how it wanted to fuse with the bread around it, seal up the gap, become part of the golem.

It was hard. The magic of sympathy was working against me here–this dough wasn't part of the same batch and hadn't been baked together. I was already feeling magically exhausted, and for a minute or two, nothing seemed to be happening.

C'mon... c'mon... you can do it...

There was a yell from the barricade. I jerked my head up and saw that the Carex had taken advantage of the gap in the line to charge again, and this time they kept coming. And climbing. Men on the barricades were stabbing with spears to try and fend them off, but as I watched, two helmeted heads popped up over the top.

Argonel and Harold rushed to help.

The first two Carex were knocked back down, but now three more were coming up on the sides, and one was—

Oh sweet Lady of Sorrowful Angels, one was actually *over* the barricade and coming this way—

Aunt Tabitha yanked a hammer from the fingers of an apprentice, who had turned sort of green, and charged the enemy, whooping.

I grabbed the dough in front of me and thought, *You play nice and be a patch on this golem RIGHT NOW!*

Black grunted. The patch of dough oozed into position and hardened into a floury crust. I scrambled down, just in time to see Aunt Tabitha reach the Carex.

The enemy warrior clearly had no idea what to make of the berserk woman charging at him, with her housedress flapping madly over her jingling armor. He gaped at her. Aunt Tabitha whacked him with the hammer so hard that his helmet got knocked halfway around his head, and he fell down. She kicked him a few times. Aunt Tabitha had very definite opinions about people who tried to invade her city.

Standing up made my head spin, and for a minute I very nearly fell down myself. The magic was draining out of me in a steady drip-drip-drip like an untreated wound.

But if Aunt Tabitha was fighting the Carex, I didn't have time to faint. I bit my lip hard and thought *You stop that!* and the world stabilized and stopped going fuzzy and gray around the edges.

I exhaled. Time to get Black back into the fray... I turned to pat him on the leg. "Back you go, there's a good golem—"

That pat saved my life.

The Spring Green Man's knife hit my shoulder at an angle, instead of the back of my neck, and the point skittered off the armored jerkin.

I yelped. I wanted to scream, but a thin little yell was all that came out. Harold and Argonel and Aunt Tabitha were busy on the barricades and there were Carex coming up over the sides and Black was knocking them down but some had still gotten over and the Spring Green Man was lifting his knife for another blow and that familiar, heavy sweet smell was all around us and he bared his teeth at me like an animal.

"Third time pays for all, little bread wizard," he hissed, and I knew that my luck had finally run out.

THIRTY-FOUR

There was something stuck in his teeth. Here I was about to die, stabbed to death by a deranged wizard, and that was what I noticed—there was something green stuck in his teeth.

Fortunately, the rest of my body knew what was important. My knees decided to throw me sideways without bothering to consult my brain.

I caught myself and took off at a run, sliding on the cobbles. If I could get back to the wall, surely Joshua and the Duchess could defend me, or we could knock him off the ladder or something. He couldn't climb the ladder with a knife in his hand, could he?

Right away, I realized that I was in trouble. The weight of magic was still with me, even if I was running for my life. It was like trying to run with concrete blocks strapped to my ankles. I dropped the rest of the bad cookies ruthlessly, and got a little bit back, but I didn't dare cut off the golems. The golems were the only thing standing between the Carex and the city.

Oh god oh god I'm going to die...

I could hear Elgar's footsteps pounding behind me. Where were the archers? Couldn't one look this way and see what was happening and shoot him? And the jerkin, which had saved my life before, might kill me now. It was so hot and so heavy and I couldn't seem to breathe right with it pressing down on me and that horrible spicy smell was filling my lungs and making it even harder to breathe.

Is this the street that goes back to the wall? I think this is the street. There's the building at the end, the red brick one, with the fire-escape—

The Spring Green Man grabbed my shoulder, wrenched me around, and slammed me into the wall of the nearby alley.

Guess it doesn't matter now.

Elgar grabbed my wrists in one hand. (It is completely and utterly unfair that when you are a fourteen-year-old girl, even if you have amazing forearms, your wrists are still small enough for somebody else to hold with one hand.) I flailed, and I think he was surprised at how strong I was, but I didn't go anywhere except back against the brick wall, hard. Blood thudded in my ears.

He lifted the knife. The blade gleamed. The sun was shining down into the alley, and that meant that it was nearly noon. We'd held out until noon. That was pretty good, wasn't it?

"You're not getting away from me again," Elgar said. "I wasn't leaving this city until I saw you dead." I could hardly hear him over the pounding of blood in my ears and the shouting of the battle a few yards away, but I got the gist.

"Would have—thought—you'd be with Oberon—" I panted.

Elgar spat. "That idiot. Once he took the city, I was going to kill him anyway. A wizard-emperor! Just think of it!"

I guess really bad people all think they're using each other and being really clever about it. And they all want to be in charge. You never see them stabbing each other over who gets to be the baker.

And because I was really going to die, right this minute, and it didn't much matter anymore, I said, "You've got something stuck in your teeth."

He blinked. I guess this is not the sort of thing that people say when you're about to stab them. "What?"

"In your teeth. Um. Sort of green—"

"What is *wrong* with you?"

This was an excellent question. I was sort of wondering that myself.

The Spring Green Man lifted the knife higher, and then something happened very fast and something made of rag and bone sang past my face and Elgar was flung halfway down the alley because Nag had just kicked his head in.

Apparently, that thudding noise had not been my heart pounding in my ears after all.

"Oh yeah!" yelled Spindle, scrambling down from behind Molly, as Nag's hooves landed back on the cobbles. "Oh yeah! That's for Tibbie, you green monster! I 'ope you *rot!*"

Nag, being dead himself, did not object to Spindle jumping off his back, nor did he seem to notice when I threw my arms around one of his back legs and hugged him furiously. Knackering Molly snorted.

"Seems like I keep finding you in trouble, baker girl."

"I'm alive!" I moaned into Nag's hipbone. "Molly—Nag —*Spindle*—"

Spindle looked up from Elgar's limp body. "What?"

"You're alive! I'm alive!" I started giggling hysterically, because otherwise I was going to sit down and sob right there in the alley. "We're all alive! Except Nag! We're all—urrgh—"

My stomach clenched. I went down to my knees and last night's dinner came back up.

"Ewww," said Spindle, who had left off kicking the late Elgar and was going through his pockets.

"It happens," said Knackering Molly firmly. "Takes everybody differently, so don't you go making fun, Spindle."

Spindle rolled his eyes.

I wiped at my mouth and felt somebody pull my hair back. When I looked, my gingerbread man was standing on my shoulder. He waved.

You can't really hug a cookie, but I leaned my cheek against him, feeling deep relief.

"What *happened* to you?" I asked. "I've been worried sick! I thought the Carex got you!"

Spindle rolled his eyes. "They may be good with their swords an' all, but they ain't got the least idea how to catch a sneak. I got in and got out, and last I saw, those nasty little gingerbread mites were cuttin' up the ropes on one of the supply tents. No, the problem was getting back in." He spat on the cobbles. "That stupid thief Slug caught me and started tellin' people I was a spy and not to let me back in the city. Thought it was funny as anything, the great lump."

"Lucky for him, I came along and convinced Slug otherwise," said Molly mildly. She slapped at Nag's shoulder. "Figured I should bring him up here on my own, though. City's lost its mind now there's a battle on."

I exhaled. My stomach stayed quiet. My cookie was fine. Spindle was fine. Everybody was—

A golem winked out like a dying star.

"The golems!" I shot upright. There wasn't anything left in my stomach anyway, but even if there had been, I didn't have time to be sick. I had to get back to the golems, *now*.

I ran back down the alley. Spindle cursed and ran after me. I could hear Nag's irregular hoofbeats following.

I shot out of the mouth of the alley and practically into the arms of Aunt Tabitha.

"Mona! We thought something happened—"

"Something did happen! Elgar tried to stab me and Nag saved me and—oh, it doesn't matter now! We've lost a golem!"

"Two," said Aunt Tabitha grimly, and before she'd finished speaking, I felt another one fail. "They've figured out to knock them over, and then they can't get back up again."

We rushed back to the barricade. I grabbed for my bowl of dough, but it was too late. A third golem teetered and fell down like a great tree, and Carex jumped on it, hacking and sawing with sword, like blind men trying to slice bread.

There were mercenaries coming up the barricades now. Ours was the lowest and least built-up of the walls, and they clearly knew it. If they could get over our barricade and tear it down, they wouldn't have to scale any of the others—they'd have a straight shot into the city and could come up *behind* the defenders on the other streets.

I ordered the four remaining golems into a wedge defending our barricade. That would buy us time, but time for what?

There was still dough left. When they unloaded the wagon, they'd left a half dozen barrels in neat lines on either side of the street, and that ridiculous coffin from the Church of Sorrowful Angels was laid on top of them.

Argonel and Harold stepped back from the barricades. The golems were keeping enough of the Carex back that the regular guards could handle it.

Harold said, "Mona, we have to get you away from here, they're going to break through—"

"No," I said. My plan was crystalizing inside my head. It wasn't a good plan, but what else was new? "No, help me empty these barrels. I need as much dough as we can get."

"But—"

Argonel shoved him aside, grabbed a barrel and shoved it on its side. Dough glorped stickily into the street. It wasn't right for bread dough. There was more sugar and dark brown lumps floated on the surface.

"Chocolate-chip cookie dough?" asked Aunt Tabitha blankly. "Who went to all the trouble of making cookie dough?"

The name on the side of the barrel was one of the most exclusive pastry shops in the city. We dumped out four more barrels, and three of them were chocolate chip.

Well. Okay. Chocolate-chip cookie dough. I can do this. It shouldn't be any different than bread, just... raw.

Another golem went down. The roar of triumph from the Carex crashed over the barrier.

I shoved both my hands up to the elbow in the pile of dough and tried to think. Aunt Tabitha and Argonel continued dumping dough around me. It made a pile on the street as high as my knees. Not a gingerbread man. Standing upright wasn't going to be much help, and anyway, I would have needed a rolling pin as big as a tree trunk. Something lower and legless and oozy...

Wake up, I told the dough frantically. *Wake up. Get up. We need you.*

The dough didn't want to. It didn't like the shape I had chosen. It wasn't a real shape. It wasn't baked yet. It was cold and stiff from sitting overnight in the barrels and it was feeling obstinate.

We don't have time for this! Get up!

There were too many different doughs all muddled together. They weren't combining. I jumped onto the pile and began stomping around, kneading with my boots. *You are one. You are the same. Get up!*

My gingerbread cookie yanked on my ear. I looked up and saw one of our guards—nobody I knew, but one of ours—fall down from the top of the barricade. A Carex stood up there, with a bloody sword in his hand, *and nobody was stopping him.*

Argonel and Harold leapt up and placed themselves between me and the barricade, but I knew that we were out of time. Even if we stopped this one, there would be more.

GET UP! I screamed at the dough. I had so little magic left, I couldn't see straight, but I had plenty of rage and horror to go around, and I poured it all down my hands and into the pile of dough. *GET UP, YOU STUPID THING, GET UP AND FIGHT!*

It got up.

It was... well, I suppose it was a slug, as much as it was anything. I tried to think of it as a slug, because the magic works so much better when things are shaped like animals or people. So, a slug. A slug with fists. It was only about waist high, but the front pulled itself off the ground and two flailing arms came out, and it slithered across the cobbles towards the barricade and two startled Carex standing on top of it.

"Gods and devils," said Knackering Molly. "What've you done, baker girl?"

"The best I could," I said, and tried to stand up. My knees buckled. I realized, with mild surprise, that the energy that normally went into making my legs work was now going into animating the chocolate-chip slug-monster.

The slug reached the barricade. Our guards scrambled out of its way. It slimed over the top easily. The dough was sticky enough that it didn't have any problems with the footing, and anyway, it didn't exactly have feet.

One of the Carex hacked at it with his sword. The sword sank into the dough with a *gloop!* noise and didn't come back out again. The slug lashed out with a tentacle and knocked them both backwards into the square.

It wasn't very fast, but it was *scary*.

Still, what could it do against thousands of Carex?

Aunt Tabitha grabbed my shoulder. I swayed under her hand.

I'd given too much magic to the dough bird, and it had exploded. If I gave the slug too much magic, it would also explode. If I could just get it out into the main body of Carex, I could pour magic into it and it would turn into a giant mobile bomb.

I knew, even as I hung limply in Aunt Tabitha's grasp, that this would be the end of me. I had pushed the magic much farther than I thought I could, but it was done. If I tried to pour that much of myself into the slug, it would be with the energy that kept my heart beating and my lungs moving. I could send it oozing across the battlefield and blow it up, but that would be the last thing I did.

I thought it likely the golems would keep going for a little while after my death. A few minutes at least, maybe even an hour. Probably not long enough to save the city, but maybe long enough to make a difference. Maybe Aunt Tabitha and Spindle and Argonel would have time to get away.

"Get me over to the dough," I choked out. My tongue felt thick and strange in my mouth.

Aunt Tabitha shook her head. "You're done," she said. "I've seen corpses that looked better than you right now, Mona."

I wanted to laugh. In another minute, that wouldn't be a problem. "I have to," I said, forcing the words out. "There's no other wizards left!"

I tried to crawl forward. The gingerbread man grabbed my ear and tried to pull me back. I needed that dough for the magic of sympathy. Why were the barrels so far away? If I couldn't get to the barrels, I couldn't blow up the slug.

There was a long pause, while Aunt Tabitha wrung her hands, and then Knackering Molly slid down off her horse and said, "There's one more, anyway."

THIRTY-FIVE

Raising my head was a greater effort than anything I'd ever felt. If we hadn't lost another golem, I'm not sure I could have done even that. But the little thread of energy came back to me, and I looked up.

Molly held my eyes for a long moment. Hers were dark and deep. I don't know what she read in mine.

She turned away and went to Nag. He lowered his bony head and they stood with their foreheads pressed together, the living woman and the dead horse.

"We have to get away—" Harold started to say again, and then the world jumped about six inches sideways and I fell over.

"Mona!" said Aunt Tabitha. "'Ere, what's wrong?" asked Spindle. They both grabbed for me, and I realized that neither of them had felt it.

I looked up. Molly was swaying. Nag's bones rattled a strange rhythm—*tha-thump, tha-thump, tha-thump*—

I would bet everything I will ever own that it was the sound of Knackering Molly's heartbeat.

She walked stiffly around Nag's side and climbed onto his back. He continued to rattle a bone heartbeat.

"Do you hear something?" asked Spindle.

In the square, the Carex fought the slug and arrows hissed and the army roared and steel clashed—but on our side of the barricade, everything seemed strangely silent, except for Nag's bones.

Then I heard it. It sounded almost like running water, far in the distance, coming from within the city.

Knackering Molly bent low over Nag's neck. She was shaking like a woman sobbing, but she made no noise at all.

The sound was getting nearer and louder and deeper. If it was running water, it was a flash flood, not a stream.

"Molly—" I said. She'd done something magical. Something that made the world jump, something *huge*—

Knackering Molly looked over at me and smiled, just a little. Her fingers flicked out in a small, ironic salute.

The road began to shake. Buildings rattled as if the Knocker were thumping into them. Aunt Tabitha yelled, "*Earthquake!*" but Spindle let out a whoop and pointed down the street.

Knackering Molly had called the dead horses of the city to its defense, and the horses had come.

They were made of bone, like Nag, and flashed ivory in the sun.

Many of them must have broken from the ground or from underground crypts, and bits of dust and dirt still clung to them. Some were so old that there were hardly any bones, just clouds of dust formed into the shape of running horses. The magic that held them together was so much stronger than anything I could do—than anything I'd ever *seen*—

It was no wonder the army had tried to recruit Molly. The amazing thing was that they'd ever let her go.

Aunt Tabitha picked up Spindle with one arm and me with the other and shoved us back against the wall. Out of the corner of my eye, I saw Argonel throwing his apprentice into a doorway. The men on the barricades stood and gaped at the horses —first the slug, now this—and then some of the smarter ones realized that anyone standing in the way of that charge was going to be trampled. They scattered.

The horses hit the barricade and it fell apart under their hooves. Bone dust manes whipped behind them. Watching them leap over the remains of the wall was like watching a great waterfall of bone. I have never seen anything else like it, and if I live to be a hundred years old, I imagine I never will.

"How many *are* there?" asked Aunt Tabitha, almost to herself.

I tried to think of how many there *could* be. Our city is hundreds of years old and many generations of horses have lived and died within its walls.

Knackering Molly had called them *all*.

They charged into the square and through the gate, into the Carex army, with Nag at their head and Molly on his back.

When the bone army had finally passed us by—a matter of minutes, I suppose, although it seemed to go on for hours—it took a bit before any of us were willing to leave the walls. When you have seen a thing like that, a thing impossible and glorious and horrible all at once, it takes a minute before you can really think again.

"Oh," said Aunt Tabitha finally. "Oh my."

It broke the spell. Spindle jumped up and down and punched the air and shouted "Hooyah! You show 'em, Molly! Give 'em one for Tibbie!"

"Is it over?" asked Argonel. "Wizard Mona, do you know?"

"I haven't a clue," I admitted, testing my feet cautiously. They seemed to be working, mostly. "Should we, um, go look?"

As a little knot, Harold and Argonel and Aunt Tabitha and Spindle and I, plus an apprentice and three or four guards, crept to the edge of the street. The barricade had been pounded into splinters, and we peered out cautiously.

There was nothing living in the square. The slug monster oozed a slow circuit around the walls. The broken gates had been torn completely off their hinges.

We inched forward. I leaned heavily on Spindle, partly to keep from falling down, partly to keep him from running off.

At the gate, we peered out over the battlefield.

It was a sea of bucking bones.

Hundreds of dead horses, from nearly full skeletons to roiling dust, were trampling across the Carex. The greatest concentration of horses, after all, was not inside the city but in the bonepits of the knacker yards and slaughterhouses, which are all outside the walls. Hundreds of horses came from inside the city, but thousands rose from outside it, and they hit the Carex army like a hammer.

The mercenaries were backing away from the city, trying to fight, but bones are worse than bread—if you stab a skeleton with a sword, it doesn't stop the skeleton, and the odds are good your sword will get wrenched out of your hand in the process.

"They're retreating," breathed Harold. "Sweet mother of us all, they're actually *retreating*."

Nobody was shooting from the battlements anymore. I

suspect that the archers, like the rest of us, were simply staring down with slack-jawed awe.

We picked our way a little farther out from the wall. The road dipped a little, and we could see the skeletal army's charge laid out in front of us, an arrowhead of bone driving deeper and deeper into the enemy ranks.

"They're nearly through," said Argonel. "Are they going to turn around?"

Harold shook his head. "I don't think we're dealing with normal tactics here anymore."

The arrowhead pierced through the other side. The mercenary army was cut in half. And apparently that was the final straw, because as we watched, the men stopped even trying to fight back. The retreat became a rout and the rout became a desperate, scrambling flight.

The Carex army broke and ran.

When we found Knackering Molly at last, she was dead.

I had expected it. I think I had known since the first moment when she pressed her forehead against Nag's. She had done what I had thought to do with the last golem—poured herself into the magic and driven it forward with her death.

I had still hoped that I was wrong.

She was lying in a little clearing in the middle of the battlefield, with five hundred bone horses facing inward around her, watching. There wasn't a mark on her. She was curled up on her side as if she had slipped off Nag's back and collapsed from exhaustion, and I imagine that was pretty much what had happened after all.

"It was the magic that killed her," I said hoarsely.

"She allus said that getting mixed up with armies and generals would get you killed," said Spindle, wiping at his eyes. I could tell he felt guilty for persuading her to come at all... and yet, she'd saved us. If he hadn't, the Carex would be running through the streets even now.

The Duchess and Joshua had come down from the walls, and we all walked through that silent army together. Empty eye sockets turned to follow us as we strode past. It would have been unbelievably creepy, but I was so very tired, and the Carex army was routed and there was nothing left to feel but relief.

And grief. There was still room for grief.

"She saved us all," said the Duchess. Joshua leaned down and closed Molly's eyes.

A great sigh filled the air, and the bone horses folded up and dropped to the ground. Clouds of white dust roiled up and settled slowly around us.

Nag was the only one left standing, and as we watched, he went down to his knees and stretched out his head along the ground by Knackering Molly, and then he was only old bones and rags of tattered cloth. That made me cry even harder, because that was when I knew it was really over.

The Duchess looked at me helplessly. "Mona—you knew her. She saved us. Without the two of you... What should we do? What would she want?"

Spindle and I looked at each other, but it was Spindle who spoke up. "She an' Nag should be buried together," he said, dragging a sleeve across his face. "An' not in one of those big fancy tombs. She'd think that was stupid. Maybe a park. She would've liked a park."

"With a statue, perhaps?" asked the Duchess. "We have to do *something*."

Spindle and I looked at each other again. I choked down the lump in my throat and tried to talk. "A statue of Nag would be okay," I said. "But not a stupid one. It has to have Nag in it like he really was. Not... you know... heroic. She shouldn't have had to be a hero."

"No," said the Duchess. "No. No one should."

Joshua picked Molly up, very carefully, and carried her back to the city.

Our city.

And we all went home.

THIRTY-SIX

The army arrived two days later—a day late, as it turned out—but that was okay. Most of the Carex didn't stop running until they hit the mountains. The army got home in time to mop up some of the stragglers and most of the wounded, all of whom wanted to surrender. They got put to work rebuilding the outlying farms. The Duchess had a certain sense of poetic justice.

All told, apart from Knackering Molly we lost seven people. Five of those were on the barricades, one was an old veteran who had volunteered to help fight and whose heart gave out in the middle of the battle, and one guard was found in an alley with his throat cut. We're pretty sure that was the work of the late Spring Green Man. There were a few more on the outlying farms who'd refused to evacuate, but there wasn't anything I could have done about them, and I tried hard not to feel guilty.

Joshua says that we took so few casualties (what a stupid word, there's nothing *casual* about it) because the golems held them off until Knackering Molly did her part. I'd like to think he's right. The Golden General offered me a post in the army, but I told them I didn't want to even think about making golems for at least a year, and Aunt Tabitha pointed out that I was *fourteen* and not nearly old enough to go traipsing about with the military. Which was sort of embarrassing, but also a relief. It's hard to say no to someone like the General.

And I was going to say no. I still liked Lord Ethan, but I wasn't going to be responsible for turning other people into heroes.

Oberon's personal possessions—a ring and some papers—turned up on the battlefield, but they couldn't identify a body. Spindle has a theory about this, which involves the phrase "mangled beyond recognition." He is quite gleeful about it. I have a different theory—I think it's possible that he got away, and left a false trail behind him. As long as he stays far, far away from my city, that's fine. I'd like to see him punished, but even more than that, I just want him *gone.*

Spindle lives with us now. We repainted the room so it's not pink and doesn't have a sampler in it. I'm not sure if he really wanted to live with us, but the Duchess threatened to knight him, and if you're going to be a knight, you have to be a squire first. When he found out that you spend all your time taking care of some guy's armor and his horse and taking lessons in chivalry, he couldn't get out fast enough.

There was still the matter of the ceremony, mind you...

"Stop fidgeting," said Aunt Tabitha, straightening the folds of my dress. "Don't wring your skirt in your hands. You'll get it all crumpled."

"It was very kind of the Duchess to do this all at once," I said faintly, trying not to grab handfuls of cloth and twist them frantically. "If I had to go through this for every single medal, I'd die."

"You won't die," said Aunt Tabitha. "You'll do fine." She fussed with my hair, which was hopeless.

Everybody will be looking at the Duchess, I thought. *Or at Spindle.* Compared to Spindle, I was positively presentable. The Duchess would happily have given him a dozen suits of formal clothing, but he was having none of it. We compromised on the page's uniform he'd worn that long-ago night in the palace. (Two weeks ago. It had been two weeks ago. I felt like I had aged so much in the last two weeks that I half-expected my hair to come in white.)

Spindle tugged at the collar of his tunic and muttered something in Thieves' Cant. The gingerbread man stood on my shoulder. He had new icing buttons for the occasion.

Joshua opened the door and said, "We're ready for you."

"I'm scared," I whispered.

"So am I," Joshua whispered back. "I hate these things. You're up first, so you get to leave early. I think I'm getting made a Marshal, and I have to stay until the end."

This made me feel a little better. At least they weren't making me a Marshal.

We stepped out of the room into a narrow corridor with a door at the end. Joshua opened the door, which led onto a courtyard. We were having an outdoor ceremony. Two guards on either side clicked the butts of their halberds against the floor. I gulped.

"Straight ahead," murmured Joshua. "Stop on the third step of the dais, next to the General. Spindle, go right behind her, and stop on the second step."

We walked in. I went up three steps, staring at my feet to

make sure that I didn't trip and fall. When I reached the Golden General, I looked up.

He looked just as tall as he had the first time I had seen him, but a lot more tired. His shoulders were a little stooped, and he had lines around his eyes.

He winked at me.

The Duchess stood in the middle of the dais, on the highest step. "My people..." she began, waving to the crowd, and then I couldn't hear her anymore, over the cheering.

"Cor," muttered Spindle, at my right hand. "Lookit all those swells!"

The "swells" were the entire assembled court. There were a lot of nobles. I guess those were the council. Most of them looked old and richly dressed and somewhat disgruntled, but there was one plump woman who grinned at me. I think she was the representative of the various Guilds. Aunt Tabitha was a Guild baker, so technically I was one of her people. I wondered if having a baker save the city would have any political repercussions.

Uncle Albert was in the front row, off to one side, and Aunt Tabitha came out and joined him. Argonel was there too. I'd asked if Jenny could join them, and she was wedged in behind Aunt Tabitha. All of them were grinning hugely, except for Uncle Albert. He met my eyes and nodded just slightly, and I wondered what sort of ceremony they'd had when they gave *him* a medal for a siege that shouldn't have happened.

Past all the brightly colored nobles were several ranks of guards in shiny armor and a huge crowd of plain ordinary citizens. My people. They were packed to the walls of the courtyard and out past the carriage drive, standing on each other's shoulders to try and get a better view. I actually saw Widow Holloway on the shoulders of Brutus the chandler.

That was a lot of people. I wondered if I was going to faint or scream or wet myself or otherwise disgrace myself. It seemed likely.

Blueberry muffins. Think about blueberry muffins. What's the recipe? Step one, get some fresh blueberries...

"Don't usually get a crowd like this unless there's a hanging."

"Don't *help*, Spindle."

The Golden General chuckled.

"The first time is the worst," he murmured to me. "The first time I won a great victory and had to get medals, I almost wished I'd lost instead. They get easier after this. You'll see."

"I don't intend to do this again!" I whispered.

"No?" He arched an eyebrow at me. "I expect this won't be your last set of medals, my dear. Heroism is an unfortunate habit."

It would not have occurred to me two weeks ago to argue with the Golden General, but I opened my mouth to do just that and then I heard the Duchess say, "Mona, the Wizard of the Bakery, step forward!" and the crowd went completely wild and Lord Ethan put a hand on my shoulder and steered me forward.

I looked up at the Duchess. She smiled down at me, wearing the mask of royalty, and then *she* winked too, which was rather less royal of her.

She put something over my head. It was a round disk with sheaves of wheat stamped on it. That's the Silver Sheaf, the highest honor our city gives out, "for exceptional valor." Then there was another one, which she pinned to my chest, which had a golden lion on it, "for extraordinary service to the crown," and then there was another one on a pin, which looked like an extremely ugly bronze cow folded into a little square, "for courage under fire." The crowd roared for each one. I closed my eyes and thought very firmly about muffins.

"It pleases us to recognize the service and exceptional courage of one of our youngest citizens. Henceforth, let it be known that Mona, Wizard of the Bakery, is appointed a Royal Wizard, with all the rank and privileges thereof!"

A Royal Wizard? Like Master Giladaen, and Lord Ethan? I gulped.

"And for you, little friend—" said the Duchess.

For a second I didn't know who she was talking to, and then, on a very small ribbon, she pulled out a medal that looked like the Silver Sheaf, only about the size of a penny. She placed it around the neck of my gingerbread man.

You haven't lived until you've seen a cookie look smug.

"Turn around," murmured the Duchess. "Count to five and then step to your left. We'll get Spindle up here and then you can both leave. Lucky you!"

It occurred to me that the Duchess probably hated these ceremonies almost as much as I did. At least I only had to do it once, no matter what the Golden General said.

I turned around. The crowd cheered so loudly that it no longer sounded like voices.

And I'll tell you, for just one minute there, I bought into it a little. My city. Right there. I almost forgot to count.

One... Two... Three... Four... Five...

Spindle came up. He got the lion and the folded-up cow, and a Bronze Sheaf for slightly less extraordinary service to the crown. (He didn't seem to mind.) The crowd cheered for him, too, and Jenny blew kisses from behind Argonel.

And then the cheering faded and Harold, who was standing on the far side of the stage, beckoned, and we went walked down the dais and through the door and were finally allowed to go home for good.

THIRTY-SEVEN

Things do go back to normal eventually. Joshua comes in sometimes for muffins. Once or twice I've been up to the palace to have tea with the Duchess. It's awkward. Not so much because she's the Duchess, but because after everything was over, I realized that I was still angry at her for not being braver or smarter or more... more *something*. When you're in charge of the whole city, you're responsible. It shouldn't be up to a couple of kids and a madwoman on a bone horse to fix the mess you allowed to happen.

But then I go have tea and I look at her and I don't know if she really could have fixed it. She's only in charge because she inherited the city, the same way I'll inherit the bakery. I think maybe she's not as good at ruling as I am baking. And then I don't know what to think or who to be mad at any more.

I did hear from Jenny that something's gone a bit odd in the palace kitchens. Something keeps knocking over the pepper shakers and putting salt in the sugar bowl. One night it tied all the aprons in the place together and hung them on the roasting spit.

I think it might be one of the bad cookies. I *thought* I pulled all the magic out, but you know, it was a frantic time and maybe one squeaked by. One of these days I'll go to the kitchens and get to the bottom of things... if the cook asks me nicely.

As for me, I work at the bakery, and I'm glad to do it. Sometimes people come in to see the medals and talk to one of the heroes of the Dead Horse War, but more often they come in for muffins and scones and gingerbread cookies. We still have the best sourdough in the city, even though Bob's experience in battle has made him extra rambunctious, and we have to feed him on the end of a pole. Sometimes he dissolves the pole. Uncle Albert won't even go in the cellar now.

My own special gingerbread cookie is with me still. He stands guard on a shelf over the bakery counter and keeps a careful eye on the customers. Oberon and the Spring Green Man may be gone, but still, you never know.

The Golden General took me aside, a few days after the battle. I told him what Master Gildaen had said about him, and he laughed.

"It's all true," he said. He didn't look nearly as much like a young sun god in his office with his boots up on the desk. "I really couldn't hold off an army by myself. You, though..." His eyes were fixed on my face. "You did, for quite a long time."

"An hour or two!"

"An hour in a battle is an eternity," said Lord Ethan. He took his feet off the desk and leaned forward. "You need to be trained. Magic like that is too powerful to waste."

"I don't want to end up like Molly," I said. *A gov'mint*

wizard, she'd called Lord Ethan. *No good for the likes of you and me.*

And yet... and yet... the Golden General. Hero of the realm.

Ethan sighed and ran a hand through his hair. "Poor woman. Power like that... well. I wasn't even a raw recruit when she went into battle, and I shudder to think how they mishandled her. We failed her. I want to make sure we don't fail you."

I stared down at my hands.

"I meant what I said at the ceremony, you know," he said. When I looked up, he had a rueful smile—the smile you give to a friend or a colleague, not to a little kid. "Heroism *is* a bad habit. Once you've done it, other people start to expect it. If the city's in danger again, everybody will remember that you saved them last time, and they'll forget all the nasty exhausting bits where you nearly died and had to sleep for a week and your headache didn't go away for three days."

"It was only two days," I mumbled. The headache in question had hit me like a ton of bricks on the walk off the battlefield. Joshua actually carried me to bed. Apparently that's normal with magic when you really, really overdo it.

"Well, you're young. If I tried magic like that now, I'd have to hope it killed me, because recuperating from it would be worse."

I snorted.

"Come up to the palace when you can," he said kindly. "We'll give you some training. You might find it useful. We're not going to drag you off. If we tried, your Aunt would have something to say, and lord, I'd much rather face the Carex!" He shuddered theatrically, and I had to laugh, but it didn't last for long.

"The Duchess..." I began, without knowing how I even wanted to finish the sentence.

"Yes?"

"If she'd just stopped Oberon," I cried. I felt like something had building in my chest since Knackering Molly died. I wanted to scream or weep or rage or... something. Something to make sense of it all. "Why didn't she *stop* it? Why didn't *anyone* stop it?"

His eyes flicked to the door. I think he was making sure that it was closed and no one was listening. It occurred to me that what I had just said might be treason and of course I had said it to the man in charge of the army. Maybe his next words were going to be to tell me to shut up or be thrown in the dungeon.

Instead he said, "I know."

I put my head in my hands and stared at the floor. The carpet had a pattern of interlocking lightning bolts.

The Golden General sighed. "I've been exactly where you are," he said. "But what can we do? You can't put the military in charge of the city. We're useful servants but terrible masters. And if I took it in my head to declare myself a wizard-emperor, like Elgar dreamed of doing... well, I hope like hell someone would stop me."

We met each other's eyes, and then we both looked away.

After a minute, I said, "I never wanted to be a hero."

His face was solemn. "Nobody ever does."

Probably I will go up to the palace to learn, a least a few things. There's a lot of concepts in *Spiraling Shadows* I still don't understand. And the General was right about one thing. Nobody was going to forget who saved them. You never know when somebody's going to need you to defend the city. But learning is as far as I'm willing to go. Molly was right too. People in power can crush you like a bug. I don't want to be crushed and I also don't want to be in the position to crush anyone else.

At the moment, though, all I want to do is make muffins and bread and learn to be the best baker in the city. Magic is exhausting.

So if you ever happen to be passing down Market Street, before you get into the Rat's Elbow, take the turn onto Wallfish Street, and go down about half a block. You'll find yourself at the very best bakery in the city.

And if I'm in a good mood, and you ask nicely, I might even make the gingerbread men get up and dance.

ACKNOWLEDGMENTS

Mona's story took longer to get into book form than almost any other project I've ever worked on. I began it at the tail-end of 2007. I didn't know how to bake (and still don't) but I bought a Kitchenaid mixer and began grimly following recipes, not so much because I wanted to become a baker as because I needed to understand how dough felt and what it did when you shoved your fingers into it.

The route "that bread wizard book" took to publication went from pillar to post and back again. It was bought, edited, re-edited, dropped, abandoned, handed off to other editors, sold back to me, pitched again by my unfailingly optimistic agent, and editor after editor could not figure it out. Many of them liked it, but what would they do with it? It needed to be darker. No, darker. No, wait, too dark! Mona was too old. Mona was too young. Mona was the correct age, but now sounded too old, and need to be made sweeter. Did I really need to start with the dead body? Could we maybe ease into the dead body situation?

Ultimately the problem was that it was a fairly dark children's book and I, under the name Ursula Vernon, was a writer of whimsical upbeat books. If a publisher bought it, they would need me to write about four other books first before they could slip it into the line-up, or else my brand would be in limbo. (Mind you, I have always felt that kids like much darker books than adults are comfortable handing them, but I also understand that parents and librarians are the ones who control the book buying, and a weird little anti-establishment book with carnivorous sourdough and armies of dead horses was too hard a sell.)

Eventually it just became easier to publish it myself, as T. Kingfisher, whose brand is mostly "things I felt like writing." *Minor Mage*, my first kid's book that was also too dark to really be a kid's book, found an enthusiastic audience. I hope that *A Wizard's Guide To Defensive Baking* does as well.

Ironically I am publishing this in the midst of COVID-19, when we all started making sourdough at home and then started protesting police brutality. Suddenly a twelve year old book was actually relevant. Go figure.

Thanks go as always to the lovely guys at Argyll for putting out the print volume, to my awesome proofreaders Jes and Cassie, and my long suffering editor, KB. To Shepherd for insisting that it was "good, really" even if they did try to change "monarch" into "parasite on the working class" in the edits. And, as always, to my beloved Kevin, who reads things when I am panicking and convinced everything is awful. You are all wonderful and I love you like gingerbread loves spice.

T. Kingfisher,
North Carolina
June 2020

ABOUT THE AUTHOR

T. Kingfisher is the vaguely absurd pen-name of Ursula Vernon, an author from North Carolina. In another life, she writes children's books and weird comics. She has been nominated for the World Fantasy and the Eisner, and has won the Hugo, Sequoyah, Nebula, Alfie, WSFA, Cóyotl and Ursa Major awards, as well as a half-dozen Junior Library Guild selections.

This is the name she uses when writing things for grown-ups. Her work includes horror, epic fantasy, fairy-tale retellings and odd little stories about elves and goblins.

When she is not writing, she is probably out in the garden, trying to make eye contact with butterflies.

ALSO BY T. KINGFISHER

As T. Kingfisher

Paladin's Grace

Swordheart

Clockwork Boys

The Wonder Engine

Minor Mage

Nine Goblins

Toad Words & Other Stories

The Seventh Bride

The Raven & The Reindeer

Bryony & Roses

Jackalope Wives & Other Stories

Summer in Orcus

From Saga:

The Twisted Ones

The Hollow Places

As Ursula Vernon

From Sofawolf Press:

Black Dogs Duology

House of Diamond

Mountain of Iron

Digger

It Made Sense At The Time

For kids:

Dragonbreath Series

Hamster Princess Series

Castle Hangnail

Printed in the USA
CPSIA information can be obtained
at www.ICGtesting.com
LVHW030314200923
758648LV00064B/915